ROBERT ALLEN

A SLEEPWALKER'S NIGHTMARE

First edition

ISBN: 979-8-9859619-1-1

This book was professionally typeset on Reedsy.
Find out more at reedsy.com

Contents

Foreword

From the Author.

A note to the readers.

Thank you. Thank you for taking a chance on this book, I am truly grateful and hope that you are entertained by this work of fiction straight from my imagination. The town in this story is fictional, it doesn't have a name in the story just to keep everyone guessing, it may have some resemblance to many small towns in Oregon but you won't be able to find it on a map. Feel free to make comparisons to towns that you have seen in Oregon, they are all quite beautiful. I needed a setting to place this book and this is what I chose. I hope that you find it entertaining. Enjoy.

own. "Why so far away?" his mother asked. "There aren't any mountains here mom," John replied. He wanted to see what it was like to live where there were mountains and trees. He wanted to take business classes to start out, then maybe decide on a more prestigious degree. College didn't last long and John gave it up in the middle of his second year. He found it was too difficult to work part time to pay for school and keep up with his studies. The alternative to going home was to find a job and go to work full time to make a living of his own. He didn't want to go back to Nebraska, to him, that was a sign of failure.

1

Monday

John walks to work every day, rain or shine. Not that he can't drive, he can, and does have a car, but that is an expense that is more than he needs right now. It just seems like walking is the better use of his time rather than spending the money on gas. He walks from his apartment in rural Oregon, just off the main Route 18 that runs through his small town. It's a smaller suburb of the metropolis of Portland, there are lots of them in this area. It takes just 90 minutes from downtown Portland to get out into what feels like the country, where people have nice sized lots of land to spread out, while being surrounded by trees and wildlife. Small communities like this are backed up to mountains all around, rivers and creeks flow year-round. In the summer everything is lush green and beautiful. In the fall the leaves burn bright orange and yellow in the sun. John found it a wonderful place to live, he feels at home and happy with his choice to move to Oregon.

The little town John lives in, isn't much on the map, just two stop lights, a couple of gas stations, a pub, some locally owned restaurants and shops, antiques, hardware, and a tiny grocery store. The town was built around the railroad years ago, where they transfer loads into a warehouse and move them onto trucks to be delivered around the area. The biggest store in town is Ted's Grocery, where John stops frequently on his way home. A person would have to go closer to Portland to find a chain store or a chain fast food restaurant.

However, John has been feeling that things are not as good as they used to be. He has never been one to care that much about what's happening in the community. He isn't a community minded person or political in any way, it's not his personality to be that way, but he has been noticing the increase in graffiti, how many protests happen downtown, and all the people living on the streets. Seeing these things weighs on his mind and eats at his subconscious. He can see it moving out of the city, creeping out to small towns at an alarming rate. It used to be that those things were confined to the big city, downtown areas. If you didn't want to see that kind of thing or be around it, *'Just don't go downtown, simple as that.'* John feels like it's everywhere, closing in around him, all the cities surrounding Portland have homeless problems and drug problems. All these things swirl in John's brain, that doesn't mean it's really that way, that's just how John sees it. It's on the news every day. *'Is it all because of the homeless people?'* The question rings in his head. He feels that when the homeless move into an area, crime and drug problems follow them. That's the way the reporters make it sound too.

It's surprising to John how many homeless have moved out into the smaller towns. *'They must think they won't be bothered since there are smaller populations and smaller police forces, but they don't just come in and lay low.'* John's mind runs through a

2

checklist, *'They cause problems digging through people's trash, they trespass and make huge messes, spread graffiti, break into homes and businesses, not to mention the drug use. All of this with no recourse for their actions. Seemingly, no one notices.'* He's noticed, and it's on his mind, right or wrong, it's bothering him more and more every day. He can't let it go easily and as he walks to work his brain churns on it, turning it over and over. The same thoughts repeat as he hangs his head, walking to work.

John skirted the edge of the road, it's narrow, only inches from the white line to the gravel of the ditch. There is no spring in his step, no sense of urgency even when he's late, which happened often, just like today. No feeling that what he is doing is worthwhile. It's just a regular pay-the-bills job after all. Pumping gas wasn't something he aspired to do when he was young and now in his late 20's, he is paying the price for not taking school seriously. His lack of education on paper hadn't helped him get ahead in the work-a-day world. John has had plenty of jobs and some that could have led to better opportunities, better pay, maybe an easier life, but his personality has held him back. He has worked construction, retail and food service. The only one that he sort of liked was construction, even though he was really just a laborer. It suited him, he is built for it. At 6 foot 1" with a stocky build, not fat but naturally muscular, it allowed him to move materials easily, lift and shove, and seemingly work hard without putting much effort into it. The job really fit him because he was left alone by everyone as long as he did the work. He just had a hard time getting to work on time and when he was there, he didn't move very quickly. One speed, that's all he has. John is the type of

3

person that is hard to read, to say the least. He has a very blank look on his face most of the time, no smiles, no frowns, not a wince in pain or surprise, no expressions what-so-ever. He is smart enough to do more with his life, but he isn't sure he wants to do more. So, for now, pumping gas to pay the bills will have to do.

Monday when John showed up late, the first time that week, his manager Steve, just gave him a glare and stated the obvious, "I don't pay you to show up late." That was fine with John, one of the less dramatic interactions he's had about being late. As he put on his reflective vest and checked the pump readings of the islands he would be working, his co-worker Clint drug himself around the corner to say hello. Clint, with his medium toned voice, almost with a drawl, "Hey big man, how's it goin' today?" Clint literally looks up to John as he stands about 5'7" to John's 6'1" height. "See anything worth talking about on your way in this morning?" John flatly replied, "No, not so much. Some roadkill a mile or so back, looked pretty fresh." John thought that that would be the end of the conversation, *'No one needs to talk about roadkill.'* Clint got rather excited, "What was it, dog or cat?" John, not enthused by this conversation, and somewhat surprised that Clint actually wanted to continue it, "No, looked like a raccoon with a bushy tail." Clint couldn't help himself but to dive into a story about how he swerved to hit a possum in his pickup truck and how the sound of it going under the tires was really gross, thud thud. "I swear I could feel it squish under the tires when I ran it over." Knowing that he just killed a living thing made Clint a little giddy. He also described how he hit it again the next day just to see if he could make a bigger splat on the

4

road. John, still with no expression on his face but curious now, "Why? Do you get some kind of thrill from hitting an animal?" "Well, yeah," says Clint, "Just a big rodent anyway, the way I see it, I'm helping keep the rodent population down." John just went back to checking the pumps and helping the next customer that pulled in. He was thinking about what Clint said though, keeping the rodent population down, population control by way of killing. *'I suppose that's a thing. I think it happens in more rural areas when the coyotes and cougars get overcrowded and start coming after the farmers' animals.'*

Several hours went by without much talk between the two of them, John was still thinking about the dead animal on the road. "Hey Clint, have you ever hit any other animals?" Clint got a ponderous look on his face and smiled a little when he started to reply. "Yeah, I've smashed a few. Some big ones too, those are the ones that cause damage to the truck though. I decided it was too expensive to try and hit them on purpose too often." John had to ask, "Like what?" Clint got comfortable leaning against a gas pump. "Well, the last big one I hit was a deer, but it was more like, it hit me. Thing come running over the edge of the road super fast like something was chasing it, ran right into the front right side of my truck. Killed it quick. Knocked the headlight out of my truck and dented it some, broke the grill a little bit. Not so bad I couldn't drive it though." Clint's old C-10 was showing a lot of dents and rust, it was to be expected from a 40-year-old pickup. Clint rarely fixed any of the dents unless it was hindering the doors from opening or the wheels from spinning. John just nodded, "What did you do with it?" Clint gave him a sideways look. "What? The deer? Just left it at the side of the road, let the coyotes take it." John gave a half nod, "Oh sure, that would make sense.

But have you hit anything bigger on purpose? Like you saw it coming and aimed for it?" Clint looked at John kind of hard this time and it took a minute for him to come out with it. "Yeah. I aimed for our neighbors' dog, big ole German Shepherd. Damn thing was always making a racket and chasin' cars and kids on bikes, things like that. I seen him wandering out in the road after he had been chasing another car and I aimed for him and gunned it, really didn't think I would hit him cause he's pretty fast. Turns out I hit him alright, made a mess of him, killed him right there in front of their house. That one made me feel pretty bad 'cause even though they treated that dog badly, he was still a dog and he just needed better owners. So now I just aim for the rodents." John almost smiled at Clint feeling bad about hitting a dog on the road. He did smile inside but not out where anyone could see it. "Should've aimed for the owners" John said, "They are the ones that deserved it." Clint chuckled at that but didn't take it seriously.

After John's shift he started walking home by way of Ted's Grocery for dinner supplies. He picked up a few items, just enough for a meal or two. He didn't want to carry too many things on the 4 mile walk back to his shanty of an apartment. It was a rundown place on the outside, built in the 70's and looked like it had never been maintained. Cheap rent doesn't get you much, however, John's apartment was kept perfectly clean, everything in it had a place. It's part of John's make up, his personality. He always puts things in the same spot when he's done with it, always keeps his clothes picked up and the kitchen clean. He was grateful for his apartment, at least he wasn't sleeping in a tent off the side of the freeway like so many are these days. There are several homeless encampments that John passes every day on his way to and from work. Some of them pushed back into the trees, some right near the road, but one thing they all have in common, they are a mess. John's thoughts wandered to this often as he passed the camps. *'For some reason the homeless can't seem to be bothered to clean up after themselves. Where do they even get all the crap that they drag to their camp? Why drag all this crap to a camp on the side of the road to just throw it into the weeds and leave it there? Are they like rodents? Constantly digging through the trash looking for the next meal or something to drag to their nest and sleep with until it gets wet, then on to the next piece of trash?'* His frustration and disgust made him angry with the people in the homeless camps. He's heard that other cities give homeless people bus fare to another place just to get them out of their city. *'It's a cheap solution, moving rodents from one place to another. Why would anyone go from a warm climate to a place where it rains two hundred days a year? That's ridiculous, move south, go where it's warm.'* John looked intently at the camps as he walked by, rarely did he see anyone there but judging by the mess, you would think they have a raging party there 7 days a week. He kept strolling at his single speed. It took a little over an hour for John to walk home with his groceries in tow. He was ready for some mac-n-cheese and to put the homeless camps out of his mind again until tomorrow. It was starting to get dark by the time he got home, only 6PM now but the fall days were getting shorter and cooler. He couldn't imagine having to live in a tent during the wettest parts of the year.

Jesse Kohl has been known to be quite full of himself, he has calmed down a bit in recent years since he met his girlfriend Katy, but he still likes to tell a grand story now and then. If someone has a story to tell, Jesse will tell one better, even if it means exaggerating to make it more interesting. Even though Jesse exaggerates a little he is a good natured guy and almost always in a good mood. Aside from being a bit of a one upper, most people find Jesse to be a good person. He treats his girlfriend like a princess and wouldn't let anything happen to her. Jesse has lived in the Oregon area all his life, as has his good friend Clint. Jesse is in his mid 20's, about 5'9" and slender, sandy brown hair, hazel eyes, and considers himself a redneck. He likes to fish and hunt, he doesn't mind hard work to earn his days pay. Jesse graduated high school but never attended college, he figures he'll do just fine without it. Jesse's passion in life is hunting game animals. He loves the thrill of the hunt as much as the kill. He likes everything it takes to get ready for it, from planning his hunting area, preparing his gear, right down to selecting what ammunition he will use when he hunts. Something about the whole process allows Jesse's brain to focus in on the single tasks like nothing else he has done. He has told his best friend Clint that some day he would like to be a hunting guide and lead expeditions for big game hunters.

Jesse and his girlfriend, Katy Robinson, live in the same apartment complex as John Dell. Not neighbors, not even aware that each other exist. Jesse has seen John at the gas station while John was working, but hadn't noticed him near their respective apartments.

Jesse and Clint have known each other since 7th grade. Clint is aware that Jesse has an issue keeping his stories straight but really doesn't care because often the stories are good to listen to and mostly, they don't affect anyone one way or another. No harm done in his eyes. Clint and Jesse get together to have a beer every so often, maybe once a week, sometimes more if nothing else is happening that would otherwise keep them occupied.

While John was walking home, mulling over the homeless problem that seemed to be out of control, Jesse and Clint decided to drive to the lake to have a few beers and see if the geese or ducks were migrating for hunting season, even though they were about a month early. Clint was telling a story about the "cuntasaurus" that came into the station complaining that they didn't fill up her car all the way but charged her for a full tank, and how she was going to call the cops and report that they were stealing from the customers if she didn't get a full tank a gas for free. "She was out of her mind yelling and screaming about how we robbed her. My manager, Steve, even came out and tried to calm her down, but she just kept at it." Clint was getting worked up just telling the story, "Damned if Steve didn't just give in and fill her car up just to get her out the way. It's not even possible to charge someone for gas they didn't get. Stupid bitch! I wanted her to go ahead and call the cops so they could come and lock her ass up for lying and trying to get free gas." Jesse started laughing and handed Clint another beer. They sat on the tailgate of Jesse's truck, dangling their swinging legs off the end of the gate, looking across the grassy glades in front of the lake and out over the water. After a couple of minutes of silence Jesse spoke up, "I stopped a guy from robbing a truck yesterday." Clint perked up a little, "Oh really? What happened?" Jesse adjusted himself on the tailgate trying to get a little more comfortable. "Yesterday afternoon I was getting lunch at the burger joint next to the hardware store, there was a delivery truck sitting there with the back all opened up. Guess the driver was taking a load of whatever into the store and didn't close it when he left. I glanced into the truck as I walked by to go and get me a burger, and saw it was loaded up with all those battery power tools, that stuff is expensive. I didn't really think much of it, I was focused on food. I only had about 45 minutes left for lunch break. When I came back by, 15 to 20 minutes later, there was a fella in there breaking open boxes and making a pile of stuff. He was all ragged, wearing some nasty clothes and I knew he wasn't the driver, no way. I yelled at the guy, 'Hey, what are you doing in there?' The guy looked at me kind of sideways and just went back at the boxes. So, I yelled at him again, told him to get himself out of there and that ain't your stuff. Well, he told me to mind my own business kind of, cause I could barely make out what he said, all mumbling and such. So then I had to reach in there and I could just barely reach his ankle cause he was sitting on the floor and I grabbed him and drug his ass out of the truck and proceeded to punch the dumbass a few times. He was trying to cover himself from being hit and all, yelling and acting like he wasn't doing anything wrong. About then, the driver came running out from the store and he got all excited and started yelling at me till he realized what was happening. I stopped swinging at the guy long enough, he got to his knees and scrambled away, then got up and ran. I was going to chase after him then I saw I dropped my burger on the ground and was kind of mad about that. Turns out the driver was pretty happy I saved his truck load of tools, so he bought me another burger."

"Damn!" Clint said, looking over at Jesse, holding his beer up in a cheers motion, they tapped bottles and took another swig, "Look at you, being a good citizen, stopping that guy, nice goin'! That driver should have given you some tools or something for saving his ass. He probably would have lost his job if you hadn't done that." Jesse smiled, knowing it was mostly a big story. In reality Jesse had seen the homeless guy rummaging through the box truck attempting to steal tools but as soon as Jesse yelled at him the guy stopped what he was doing and fled the scene, no other interactions were had. Both of them sitting on the tailgate of the truck, still swinging their legs about to finish off another beer each. "Aw he couldn't do that then he would have lost his job anyway, that's okay though, he bought me another burger and a shake to go with it."

"Man, that guy was pretty gutsy just getting up in that truck like it's his own." Clint said, shaking his head. "I can't imagine just goin' in there and opening up boxes and takin' stuff like that. What do you think they would do with the stuff? Not like they are building anything with it out there at their camps. Probably trying to sell it or pawn it off." Jesse took another long swig of his beer before he replied. "Yeah, I would bet they would try to pawn it off and make a quick buck." Both Jesse and Clint paused for a few minutes and looked out over the lake, watching geese congregate a few hundred yards north of them. Jesse pointed toward them "Over there in those reeds would be a good spot for the blind." Clint nodded agreement and reached for another beer, handing one to Jesse. "Let's walk up that way and find a good spot before it gets too dark." They followed the trail around the lake as close as they could get to the reed covered area, making plans to put the floating blind at the edge of the reeds where the boat could still get in and out easily.

2

Tuesday

Early the next morning, as John was walking to work, the sun was coming up, but not breaking through the low clouds and fog of the fall morning. It was brisk out, a sweatshirt and light jacket were enough for John to be comfortable on his walk. For some reason, he had struggled with the thought of the rodents/homeless people that kept coming into his mind. The comparison seemed to fit to him. This morning, while making breakfast he thought of them, *'Do they have breakfast, do they have food, are they warm at night?'* All these questions but not in a compassionate way, more of a comparison to actual rodents. When these thoughts came to him, his stomach churned and he felt an anger that he couldn't explain. *'Why are they like this, why are they everywhere?'* As he came upon the first of many camps alongside the road, he stared at the mess. His teeth clenched in anger and his expressionless face seemed to take on a stern look. *'Rodents, rodents, rodents.'* He thought to himself, *'How do you get rid of rodents? Chase them out? Put a cat in the field and let them be eaten? A feral cat, a really big*

feral cat.' This made him laugh inside, t̶
chasing the human rodents from their te̶
them and tossing them about with a sin̶
'Messy but effective. Traps? Perhaps, the st̶
move when they walk on it, but then how ̶
sticky mess? Or perhaps the snapping traps with a peanut butter
sandwich for bait?' Again, he laughed inside at the thought.
'Not sure a peanut butter sandwich would do it but if the rodent
was hungry enough it might. Oh well, not like I can do anything
like that.'

John was walking past the next camp with its shopping carts
strewn about and broken bicycles, mostly with no wheels or
with wheels but no tires. He wondered, *'What do they do with*
the tires? Burn them for heat? Always bicycles with no tires.' John
couldn't help but think, *'Everything they have here is stolen, the*
bicycles, the tents, the sleeping bags, pop up tents, all of it. Pop
up tents mostly with broken legs. Propane bottles, but nothing
to use them with. I feel bad for the people that all this stuff was
stolen from. Sure, some of it may come from the shelters in the next
town over or donations from churches, but they are just feeding
the infestation of rodents.' The laughter inside had died down
as quickly as it had come up, fantasizing of ways to take care
of the rodent problem. *'Burn them out.'* John's chest heated
up with the thought. *'Just start a nice fire at the up-wind edge*
of their camps and let it go. Watch them scatter as the flames get
higher, just like rodents they will run from the heat and try to
take cover to avoid being burned. Hmm.' He smirked slightly
as he walked past the last camp before coming to the edge
of town. *'I could never do that though.'* He would be at work
soon and continue to entertain himself by pondering ways to
evict the rodents from their camps. John's mind was getting

⌐ with every moment spent contemplating how to reduce
⌐ rodent population. His face never showed emotion, just a
serious blank look.

As he walked into the break area to check in for work, Steve and
Clint were getting coffee. Steve looked toward John. "Nice you
made it on time today, what happened? Couldn't sleep?" John
glanced over at Steve with his very hollow look. "Good morning
to you too. No, I really couldn't, got a lot on my mind." Steve
was surprised at the response, he didn't usually get that much
from John. He thought about pressing for more just because
he really doesn't know John that well but decided better of it,
something about John made him feel uneasy. Besides, there
were customers waiting and the shift transition hadn't been
smooth this morning. Clint was on his way out the door. "Good
morning John, coffee is hot and sort of fresh," Then headed
out with his coffee and started fueling rigs. John got a hot cup
and followed suit.

The morning seemed to drag, the fog and low clouds had
hung on longer than usual, making the morning cold and
dreary. Customers seemed to be a bit snippy this morning as
well. It was midweek but no one seemed so happy about going
to work, or being alive really. Clint was less talkative than
usual but that was about to change. During a lull in customers
they were standing between the islands, John with a broom
in his hand and Clint with some rags and polish cleaning the
pump glass. "I went out to the lake last night scouting some
hunting spots, saw a ton of geese. We found a great area to set
up a blind. Have you ever hunted?" John was facing Clint but
moved to the side to fill a car. "No, I never got into it. Never
even tried actually." John replied. "Seems sort of weird to

14

go out and hide in the bushes so you can shoot some birds." Clint smiled. "Yeah, when you put it that way it's a little weird, but I think we like it just as much for getting out and doing something as we do for the challenge of shooting a bird out of the air. We don't have dogs though so retrieving the birds can be a bit of work. We got a little boat that we go out in the water and get them with." The pump clicked off, John returned the handle to the pump and gave the customer a receipt. "That sounds cold, I don't care to get cold like that. To each his own though. You keep saying 'we', who's 'we'?" Clint rubbed his hands together to get some warmth and took a drink of almost cold coffee. "Oh, it's my buddy Jesse, we've known each other since we were in 7th grade. He has a boat he keeps at his parents' place. We've been going out hunting and fishing and stuff like that together for as long as we've been friends." Clint moved toward the break room to get more coffee. "You want a reheat while I'm getting some?" John looked around for his paper cup and didn't see it. Clint knew what he was looking for. "I'll get you a new one." "Thanks Clint, it's still cold out today. I wish it would warm up a bit, I didn't wear warm enough clothes." Clint disappeared into the break room to retrieve the hot coffee. John sauntered over to a truck that had just pulled up for a fill. As Clint came back out of the break room, he recalled the story Jesse told him the day before. "Hey John, I gotta tell you about what happened to my buddy Jesse a couple days ago. He told me he was taking his lunch break and going to get a burger at The Burger Joint by the hardware store. He said he was walking by and there was a truck backed up there delivering some tools or some such thing, and the driver had left the back of the truck open when he went in. Nothing strange there but when he came back out a while later there was a homeless guy in the truck going through the boxes of power tools that were back there. Jesse said he yelled at the guy but he didn't pay any attention to him and just kept going through the boxes, so Jesse knew he wasn't supposed to be there, he could tell because of the tattered-up clothes he was wearing and he looked kind of a mess." John was listening intently but getting uncomfortable, feeling very irritated with the direction this story was going. His dislike for the rodents made his stomach churn uncomfortably on the fresh coffee. The pump clicked off and John hung it in the cradle. Clint wasn't slowing down. "So, Jesse reached in there and grabbed the guy by the leg and started dragging him out of the truck, but the guy started yelling at him and kicking him, putting up a big ole fuss. Even though he knows he ain't supposed to be there. Jesse was getting madder at the guy cause he was kicking at him so he got a good hold and yanked him off the end of the truck. It was one of those delivery trucks you know? They stand about 5 feet off the ground, so the guy falls off there and smacks the ground hard!" Clint knew this was not part of the original story but was taking some creative liberties to make it more interesting. "After the guy hit the ground Jesse gave him a swift boot to the legs and started yelling at the guy to get a move on, calling him a thief and such like that. Well, the guy didn't like that, so he got up and started taking swings at Jesse. I don't think he connected with much, but Jesse swung back and landed a few punches on the guy and they ended up in a full-on brawl. Then he said that the truck driver finally came out of the store all excited, not sure what was happening, and he started shouting at the both of them. Well, I guess that distracted Jesse enough that the homeless dude ran off." Clint started to slow the story down at this point, he had gotten pretty excited and worked up in the telling of the tale. "Jesse said he had dropped his burger in the scuffle and the driver was so thankful that he stopped the guy from stealing out of his truck that he bought Jesse a new one and a shake to go with it." John didn't have much reaction outwardly but inside he was fuming. "I can't believe how aggressive that rode- homeless guy was. Man, that kind of thing has gotten out of hand around here, way too many homeless hanging around." John wasn't moving, just looking at the ground considering what he just heard, thinking that this just shouldn't happen here. "Where do you think that guy came from? The homeless guy?" Clint looked around as if he would actually see where the guy was living from where he was standing at the gas station. "I don't know for sure, maybe one of those camps down Route 18, there's a few of 'em down that way. Don't you live out that direction?" John almost made a face at that, a grimace of sorts. "Yeah, I see those places every day when I'm coming and going." John shuffled his feet around and took a deep breath, trying to let go of his clenched anger. Clint had moved to another fuel island to help a customer but raised his voice enough that John could hear him. "I thought I'd seen you walking out that way, my buddy Jesse lives out that way too, he's always griping about the homeless camps, says he wants to drive his truck through there and watch them all scatter like rats." In John's mind he was in total agreement. "Can't say that I blame him, I'm pretty sick of the mess they all make all the time and they don't have any reason to clean up after themselves." Most of the day John was in a funk, he didn't want to talk to Clint anymore and just kept to himself as much as possible. Clint really didn't seem to notice the difference since John was standoffish anyway and unreadable with his expressionless face. John was feeling pretty dark inside, violent, not sure how to let it out. On his walk home that evening he went extra slow passing the camps, he found it hard to walk the thin margin between the white line and the ditch. He was watching the camp very closely for movement, they always seemed deserted. *'Where are they? When do they build these pop-up campsites and bring all the trash in here?'* As he was thinking this, he spotted some movement from a tent toward the back of the camp near the tree line. The gray tent was half obscured by scrubby little bushes and stood out against the green backdrop of the trees behind it. The tent was shaking and the faint sound of a zipper floated past him. John came to a stop and seemed entranced as he glared toward the tent. Waiting without breathing, several cars blew past whipping cold wind over John but he barely noticed as his stare continued to be intent on the camp. It seemed to be taking forever for someone to emerge, *'Are they coming out or not?'* He thought of throwing a stone just to get some attention, to see if he could stir something up. He glanced quickly at the ground for the proper rock, then back at the tent. He didn't want to miss seeing someone come out. He decided to go for it, thinking, *'I can't wait any longer, I need to see who is camping in this shit hole.'* He grabbed a rock and had to wait for several more cars to fly by, then threw it, on target but short. The rock bounced a few times but didn't touch the tent. A quick glance at the ground and he found another stone that would work, he grabbed it and without hesitation, let it fly. This time hitting the tent just to the side, glancing off, but it was enough to get some attention. He realized what he had done and that someone would be coming out and looking for the thrower of the rock. He panicked and started walking faster than his normal speed, looking over his shoulder to see if someone really would reveal themselves. Sure enough, there was some scrambling around and up popped the head of a scruffy man with unkempt hair and a rough looking beard. He didn't say anything but caught sight of John and watched him until the sight line was broken up by trees. John's thoughts were amused as he walked away, *'At least I've seen one of them now, so I know they do exist in those camps. I'm not completely crazy.'* The rest of John's commute home was uneventful until he arrived at his apartment complex.

He noticed a car that had a passenger door left open just slightly, parked on the street. *'That isn't something you see here every day.'* He detoured to the other side of the street to take a closer look. On the inside, the car was sacked, everything had been tossed around and gone through, looked like a typical break in but who knew what would be missing. There was just random paperwork strewn about and personal belongings not worth anything. The radio was still intact so whoever did it either wasn't interested in that kind of thing, or didn't have the tools to remove it. He left it as it was, nothing he could do for whomever the car belonged to. This struck John as unfortunate though since it was right in front of the complex he resides in. He could feel the heat of anger rise up the back of his neck, *'The crime is getting closer.'*

John went up to his apartment feeling worn down, not just physically tired, but worn down mentally. He couldn't put a finger on the reason though, the homeless problem had been bothering him quite a bit, as well as the crime that had risen in the community. In his mind, things were spiraling out of control. He knew even though most people wouldn't think twice about these things, that they crept up on a community, before anyone knew it, there would be more crime, more homelessness, more drug use, but it was largely overlooked. People knew it was a problem but didn't know what to do about it. As he entered his apartment, feeling the weight of his life on him, he hung his jacket by the door and collapsed on the couch. *'Just a couple minutes here and I'll make some food.'* The moment he laid his head back he fell into a deep trance of sleep. John was struggling with the rodent problem even more than he realized. He had become fixated on it, his brain not willing to let it go, it was deep in his subconscious, it had gotten into his dreams.

When John was young, he would get this way, fixated on something, he would keep working at it until he either found a solution or the problem just went away on its own. It would sneak up on him, mostly not realizing that he was obsessing over something. His fixations never seemed to be harmful to himself or anyone else, but they were never meaningful either. He wouldn't fixate on homework for instance or a school assignment. He was more apt to fixate on other students missing the trash bin with a piece of garbage. John never thought of being fixated on something as a problem, but he never got fixated on things that could help himself or others, they were always trivial things that anyone else would just let go of. His tendencies to be fixated seemed to ease up by the time he was 15, at least that was when his parents stopped noticing. John would also sleepwalk as a child, but that had gotten better by the time he was in the 4th grade. He never went too far, usually to find a stuffed animal or to find the family pet, then he would go back to bed. His parents had taken him to counseling off and on as they could afford it, mostly for the fixations. They had told the doctors about the sleepwalking but it was never thought to be a problem. John forgot about the sleepwalking, he was very young. His parents had told him about it on several occasions, reciting funny or cute stories about him sleepwalking as a little boy, but he never experienced it knowingly for himself.

3

Wednesday

When John woke Wednesday morning, he didn't remember moving to his room, getting undressed and going to bed. He just thought he must have been so tired that he did it automatically to be more comfortable. *'I'm still tired,'* he thought. *'I slept for 11 hours and still feel tired, I must be catching something.'* As he got up, he stepped over his pile of clothes that he was wearing when he got home the night before. Picking them up he noticed his sweatshirt was a little damp. *'Hmm, strange, was it damp last night when I got home?'* Not putting too much thought to it he threw the clothes into the laundry basket and moved on with getting ready for work.

While he was getting ready, he realized he hadn't eaten last night and was very hungry. *'I'm running late already.'* He threw some bread in the toaster to grab on the way out the door, then returned to his room to finish getting ready. As John was leaving his apartment, he noticed that the little red car from the previous day was still in the same spot. The door appeared to be closed now, but something wasn't right. "What's going on?" John actually said out loud. He couldn't place it at first but then realized the windows were completely fogged over on the inside, almost to the point where water droplets had started forming and running down the windows. The sun hadn't come up yet, the streetlights were still on, but the closest one was a hundred feet from the little red car casting a gray, flat light from behind the car. John walked slowly over to the car and stood right at the front looking in, he bent down at the waist trying to peer into the front window. There were shapes in the car that looked like there could be people sleeping in it. "Huh," again out loud. Thinking to himself, *'I know I've seen this car in the lot before. Maybe someone had a fight with their significant other and had nowhere else to go.'* He caught himself thinking, *'That would suck. Still though, after it got broken into yesterday, to then sleep in it that night? Kind of weird. Someone was not having a good night.'* He stood up and walked past the car feeling a strange sensation of deja vu, he looked in the side windows, just seeing heavy shadows, then continued his w alk to work trying to figure out why he felt like he had seen that image before.

It was cool again in the morning and seemed to have rained a little overnight. As John passed the homeless camps, he could see that the tents were sagging with the weight of the rain, cardboard used as shelters and everything that they had left out was now soggy. Blankets and clothes that had been left out lay in wet piles here and there. His thoughts again turned to confusion and disgust, *'Why do they just leave shit laying around? Now it's useless, wet, and muddy.'* John was on the verge of being late to work, had taken too much time getting out of the apartment that morning and then even more time looking at the car with the sleeping people in it. Then the realization came, '*I forgot my toast! Damn I'm going to be hungry.*' John doesn't like to buy lunches, it's far too expensive on such a tight budget. He trudged on toward town to his meaningless job as cars passed, spraying the wet roads on him. He pulled the collar of his jacket up around his neck and put his hood up, he would be a little damp by the time he got to work. It was almost time to break out the rain gear for his walks to and from work. If John had a hustle speed, now would be the time to use it, but he doesn't, so he just kept walking at his single speed.

Later in the afternoon Jesse stopped in at the GasNGo where John and Clint work. Clint was the first to Jesse's truck to chat and fuel his truck up. "Hey bud! How's things for you today?" Jesse took a deep breath, "Not so bad I guess. I just stopped by my apartment to grab some lunch and there are cops all over the place." Clint's eyes got wide, "Really!? What's goin' on over there?" Jesse was slumped down in the seat of his truck. "Man I don't know for sure, I didn't have time to check it out, but they are all over one of the cars in front of the complex, they've got crime scene tape up and must be six cop cars out there." Clint looked over the pumps to see if he could spot John. He saw him coming out of the break room and gave him a shout. "John! Come here a minute." John strolled over with a Coke in his hand, "Yeah, what's up?" Clint gave a head nod toward Jesse, "This is my bud, Jesse, he's the one that beat down that homeless dude the other day." John remembered the story and looked Jesse over. From what he could see of him in the truck, he didn't seem like the type to beat anyone down, pretty lanky, not much meat on the bones. He couldn't really tell how tall Jesse was but thought he couldn't be over 5'8" or

9". John reached his hand out to shake with Jesse "Hi, nice to meet you. I recognize this truck, you live off 18 and Fir at the apartments?" Jesse with a little surprise. "Yeah, me and my girl Katy have been there for a while. Where have you seen the truck?" John seemed a little reluctant at first but decided talking to Jesse was okay. "I live at those apartments too." "Oh damn, small world." Jesse replied. About that time the pump clicked off and Clint hung it back in the cradle. "Well guys I need to go, have to get back to work for a little OT today. See ya later, nice to meet you John." John nodded, "Nice to meet you too, I suppose I'll see you around." Jesse cranked his F150 to life and was off with a wave out the window. Clint looked at John, "Did you hear him say there was some police activity at the apartments?" John slowly looked toward Clint, "No, what happened?" Clint shrugged, "He didn't know, he just said there were cops all over the place and they had some crime tape set up." John nodded, "Wonder if it will still be there when I get home." "I guess you'll find out pretty soon, almost time to go." Clint said with a smile, "Nothing better than getting off work. Well, there's better things but right now it seems pretty good." John was thinking about meeting Jesse, "What does Jesse do for work?" Clint raised a hand and pointed to the eastern edge of town. "Oh, he works the early shift out at that trucking warehouse out at the edge of town by the railroad crossing. He drives a forklift, loading and unloading trucks and train cars." Clint started moving to take care of another customer. John thought that over for a moment, "That seems like it would be good work. Probably be a better place to work in the winter than out here in the rain." Clint smiled at that, "Yeah, I'll bet it would be, wonder if they're hiring." John was thinking the same thing. The rest of the shift went fairly quickly, a steady flow of customers helped the time pass.

John made a stop at Ted's Grocery to pick up supplies for a few meals. He was hungry shopping since he hadn't eaten since the day before. As he left the store with his plastic bags bouncing along at his side, he passed a well-used trail that cut across an open field. He doesn't take it any longer because he gets uneasy passing that close to all the homeless camps that now reminded him all to much of rodent infestations. Instead he took the long way out of the parking lot, then down the narrow edge of the road. A few minutes into his walk John noticed a pair of officers talking to the scruffy man he had roused out of his tent the day before, when he threw the rock. His pulse quickened and he couldn't take his eyes off the encounter. The scruffy man was looking past the officers and straight at John, it felt like his eyes were boring into his brain. He felt panic, his chest got tight and his breathing was short, it was shutting down his ability to think. Their eyes locked even at 25 yards for what felt like 5 minutes in slow motion, but in reality was just a few seconds. His brain was going blank, *'Why is he staring at me? He must have gotten a better look at me than I thought.'* One of the officers noticed that Scruffy wasn't looking at them and turned to see John passing on the road. John wasn't watching where he was going and veered into the lane of traffic as a car went whizzing past. It startled him and he corrected back to the white line. Now looking down, he followed the line for another 15 minutes before he started feeling somewhat normal, but he had gotten tired mentally and wondered if he had just had an anxiety attack. *'I never knew that was a real thing, always thought it was a bullshit cop-out for people that couldn't cope with life.'* Feeling his brain clear, he took a deep breath to help regain his composure, he resumed his slow pace with the shopping bags bouncing at his leg.

It was another 20 minutes before John made it to Fir Street, as he turned the corner into the complex there were several police cars and yellow "DO NOT CROSS CRIME SCENE" tape stretched around the entire area in front of the apartments. John's heart jumped and then pounded heavily in his chest even though he was expecting to see police activity. His mind started racing, *'What is happening around here!'* He had stopped in his tracks, rather startled at the sight, and just stood still, gaping at the scene. Aside from the police cars and officers, it all looked exactly as it had when he'd left for work that morning. All these cops here and the crime tape were more than he had expected. *'What happened?'* About the time he had finished his thought a police officer started walking his way. John isn't against police or afraid of them, but some gut reaction made him want to turn and walk the other way. He started to in his mind, but his body didn't react soon enough. The officer started talking before he could turn around. "Excuse me sir, do you live here in the area?" John, expressing no emotion, replied flatly, "Yeah, I do. The building right over there." Nodding to the back and left of the scene. "Great," replied the officer. "I'm Officer Roak. We had a report of this car being stolen and people possibly sleeping in it, turns out they are no longer with us. Wonder if I could ask you a couple questions?" John nearly flinched and the officer caught a hint of it in John's face. "First off, can I get your name?" John hesitated and wanted to give him a false name but realized he had already told him that he lived here in the complex, it would be too easy to come find him again. Especially if he figured out that he had given him a different name. "John Dell." John replied in a

PM when he walked in. His girlfriend Katy was watching TV and waiting for him before they got dinner. Katy and Jesse had been together for 5 years. High school sweethearts, she moved to town as a sophomore and they started dating senior year. She stands about 5'8", long brown hair, with a slender build. Katy is usually a very happy person, pleasant to talk to and enjoys talking with other people. She works at a local diner that's open until midnight, daily. "Hello love, I thought we could order in tonight if that's okay." Katy got up to give him a hug. "Yeah, sounds great. What are you craving?" Katy pressed a finger to her lips and made a thinking face, "I would like either Thai, or pizza." Jesse's eyes lit up, "Good choices! Tell you what, I am going to take a shower and clean up, why don't you order a pizza and when I get out, we'll go pick it up?" Katy whirled around and grabbed her phone, "Sounds great! I'm on it!"

It took about 15 minutes for them to get out the door, they took Jesse's pickup. The pizza place is just a few miles away, so it didn't take long to get there. On the way back, Jesse spotted someone on the edge of the road, just to get a rise out of Katy he swerved toward him and made Katy scream. He started laughing as he swerved back the other way and missed the person. Katy gasped and put her hand on her chest, as if it would help her catch her breath, "Why did you do that!?" With a grinchy smile on his face Jesse replied, "Just to make you jump." "Well it worked! You scared me, that would be so awful, I can't even imagine." Katy was sitting rather rigid after that as if he was going to find another person to swerve at just to get another rise out of her.

Jesse got an eerie grin on his face, "What did you think of the police activity today at the apartments?" Katy turned quickly and looked at Jesse with a surprised look on her face. "What activity? I didn't see anything. I got home about 30 minutes before you did. What happened?" Jesse now looked surprised, thinking that she would have seen the police when she came home. "I came home to grab some food before going back for overtime tonight and there were police all over the place. It was about 3:30. I didn't have time to poke around and see what happened. There was a car there, that little dark red hatchback that's usually in the lot next to the mailboxes. They had it all surrounded by police tape and the cops were taking pictures of stuff. Not a lot of other action that I could see but there were about six cop cars there." Katy looked astonished. "I'm going to have to ask one of the neighbors if they saw anything or if they know what happened." Jesse was looking straight ahead, negotiating some light traffic, "Yeah, for sure, I would like to know what was going on. Maybe you should ask around tomorrow since you're off work." "Oh, I will," Katy said with an air of gossip, "I'll ask Berta down in the end of the unit, she always knows what's going on. I think her son or nephew is a cop. Maybe she will know what happened."

Pulling into the complex on Fir Street, Jesse pointed out where the car had been and where all the police tape was strung up around the area. Before they got out of the truck Jesse told Katy about his plans for tomorrow, "I get off work at 2 tomorrow and Clint and I are going out to the lake to fish for a while, so I won't be back until after dark." "Okay, fine." Katy said with a playful smile, "I guess I won't tell you what I find out till late then. If it's really juicy I'll call you." Jesse looked over at her "I can't answer the phone if I'm working." Katy, with a duh look on her face, "I know, I was joking, I probably won't know anything new anyway."

4

Thursday

When John woke up Thursday morning, he could see bright light streaming through the bedroom window of his little apartment, the smell of bacon that someone had cooked for breakfast smacked him in the face, 'Damn that smells good.' He glanced outside into the bright, sun lit courtyard of the apartment complex, it was a very nice day, some small puffy clouds, but mostly sunny skies. A welcome sight going into fall, as most northwestern residents know, this time of year the weather could change in five minutes and they want to hold onto the sun as long as possible. He swung his legs out of bed, his body felt heavy, but he got up anyway and went to the kitchenette to get the coffee started before jumping in the shower. After getting ready for the day and pouring his first cup of coffee, he made some eggs and toast. While John was eating, he decided to get out of the apartment for a while and take a drive out to the lake, recalling Clint telling him he had gone out there to scout hunting areas. John wasn't interested in hunting, but taking a hike around the lake sounded refreshing.

He made a sandwich, grabbed a bag of chips, a granola bar and a couple bottles of water for lunch, dropped them into a backpack and headed out the door. As he was about to go, he decided to change his shoes. He found some hiking boots that were stuffed in the back of the closet. *'I haven't seen these in quite a while.'* Slipping off his everyday sneakers, he put on the stiffer hiking boots, grabbed his keys from the side table and went out the door. John's little Ranger pickup was tucked at the end of the lot near the dumpsters. He didn't drive it much, so he tried to park it out of the way of everyone that commutes daily in and out of the lot.

At the empty trail head parking area there are signs for different trail routes around the lake, some picnic benches, a few outdoor fire pits in the park, and a boat ramp with docks. John decided to walk the trail all the way around the lake. It's about a six-mile loop that winds its way up to the top of a cliff overlooking the lake that has some beautiful views. It's about 75 feet above the water at its highest point, but that offers a somewhat challenging hike for John, even though he walks to work every day, he doesn't get out and do much of anything else. The trails were damp, but not muddy, from the moisture over the last few days and walking in the fresh air felt good. John was feeling happy, content being outside. The fresh air and sun on his face felt good and it was helping clear his head. It was early fall, late September, but some of the leaves were turning yellows and oranges which made the views spectacular, with the backdrop of the lake and the blue sky with white puffy clouds floating lazily above. John almost smiled, he was feeling so good. Walking past the north end of the lake it was very flat and the trail skirted just outside the boggy area where Clint and Jesse had scoped out the area to set up their blind for the coming hunting season. There was another trail head parking lot not far from this spot, but with no boat ramp. At the highest point of his hike, at the overlook about a mile and a half from the bogs, on the north of the lake, John decided to stop and have his lunch. His legs were feeling a bit loose from climbing up the steep grade. The trail was good, not too slippery and only a few large rocks and tree roots to climb over. He found a nice outcropping of rocks that weren't too wet to sit on, and dug into his pack. As he sat there, enjoying the view and having a bite to eat, John realized that he hadn't seen anyone else in the park.. *'I guess that's the perk to having a Thursday off, not so many other people out and about.'* Just after taking the last bite of his sandwich he caught a hint of something in the air, *'Is that smoke?'* He looked around from where he was seated, not seeing anything, he stood and walked closer to the edge of the drop. Still nothing visible, but he could definitely smell it. He hadn't seen another person out today, but smoke can drift in from a great distance. It smelled close though, it had a strong burnt pine odor. He didn't give it much more thought and packed up his lunch, then continued his hike. Going down the other side of the hill was a little more treacherous than coming up, he slipped a few times on some loose rocks, but managed not to fall. Near the bottom, where it started to level out, John was able to slow his pace down and look around a bit more, taking in the scenery, enjoying his surroundings. He had been hiking almost three hours and was nearing the trail head where he had parked the truck. Clouds had moved over and it had cooled off considerably with the wind. The smoke smell had gotten stronger as he got closer to the parking lot. John came around a bend over a slight rise in the trail when he spotted a camp with a smoldering fire, a blue haze covering a small area in the trees. The sight of the tent made John a bit curious at first. *'I don't think camping is allowed in this park. Especially with a fire.'* As he got closer, he started to see garbage laying scattered around the site, then blankets and clothes, a bicycle and bags of things that appeared to be trash, an old mattress that was now wet and useless. His astonishment couldn't be read on his face. *'Why? Why here? It's bad enough to have the rodents in town on every corner, on every open lot. Now in the parks as well? My god, I can't get away from it.'* John was disgusted and disgruntled at the situation. He moved slowly along the path, watching the camp to see if anyone was around. Taking note of the piles of trash everywhere. *'It's so sad to end the day like this. It's such a beautiful area, slowly it will be turned into a rodent infested dump.'* There was a trail that led right into the middle of the camp, but John kept to the trail that stayed close to the lake, it took about 20 more minutes before he was back at his truck. He had spent several hours out hiking and had not seen even a hint of another person until the very end. He was extremely disappointed to see evidence that the rodents had moved in. As John opened his truck and threw his backpack on the passenger seat, the skies opened up and it started to hail. He got in and just sat there for a few minutes and listened to the hail tap on the top of the truck, slow at first, then increasing in speed, louder, louder, and louder still. The ground was turning white, pellets bounced when they hit the ground or the hood of the truck. The sound drowned out his thoughts, it felt good, it was so loud there was not room for thoughts in his head. After sitting in his truck watching the hail bounce off the ground for several minutes, John started the truck, flicked the wipers on and rolled slowly out of the parking lot, the hail still coming down hard enough that he couldn't hear the motor running. Driving out of the lot, he left his tracks behind in the white of the hail. Those tracks would soon disappear as the hail turned to a downpour of rain, and the white turned brown with mud.

He drove carefully at first, not wanting to slide on the hail covering the road. Then it turned to rain and the roads were running rivers of rainwater, pushing ice pellets off the sides of the road. Soon, it wasn't slippery, but visibility was tough due to the downpour. It took about 30 minutes to get home and the rain had slowed considerably by the time he pulled into the apartment lot. The spot that he had been parked in when he left was still open, so he put his Ranger back in the same place. *'That's nice, they saved my spot.'* John felt lucky to have stayed dry on his outing, he hurried up the steps to his door and stepped inside quickly, dropping his keys on the table and kicking off his shoes. The rest of the day he spent cat napping on the couch and watching TV, trying not to think about the homeless camp in the park.

Jesse works the early shift Monday to Friday at the railroad transfer yard on the end of town. He's on the clock by 5 AM and usually done by 2. The job isn't for the railroad, but the trucking company that moves the materials for distribution all over the metro area. It's good work, not too strenuous, and Jesse likes the hours. Plus, the pay is pretty good. He and Katy are planning to get married next summer, and he is saving for his first house.

Thursday was no different, clocked in by 5 AM and driving his forklift shortly after that, Jesse and 3 other fork lift drivers kept pretty busy all-day, unloading train cars and separating materials, then loading them onto trucks to be delivered elsewhere. There was a point in the day that they had some trouble around 11:30 when a hailstorm moved through the area and some of the loading ramps got too slick to drive the forklifts on. The hail only lasted about 20 minutes, then turned to rain, allowing them to drive the lifts again, up and down the ramps, across the loading dock, in and out of the trucks and train cars.

After work, Jesse stopped by his parents' house and hooked up his little boat that he and Clint use often for fishing and hunting, then went out to the lake where he met up with Clint a few days before, this time at the trail head with the dock. Jesse put the boat in the water at the same trail head that John had been at earlier in the day, tied it to the dock, then got everything ready so when Clint got there after work, they would be ready to go. The rain had subsided a couple hours ago, now there were just some darker clouds hanging overhead. As Jesse was getting everything situated, he noticed a little smoke coming through the treed area just past the trail head. He was ahead of schedule and Clint should be along any minute, but he decided to take a quick walk over toward the smoke and see what was happening. The trails were quite muddy from the rain earlier in the day, but Jesse had his mud boots on, so he just tromped down the middle of the path. As he got closer to the area the smoke was coming from, he noticed a tent, tarps, and trash. Not looking where he was going, he slipped on wet roots and almost took a tumble. Jesse stopped there and looked at the area for a moment, then turned and headed back to the boat ramp.

Clint got off work at 3, so the timing worked out well. Clint showed up right on time, ready to go. He had brought a cooler with some food and beer because according to Clint, "You can never have enough beer, and what is fishing without beer?" Not to mention, there might not be that much catching happening. After greeting Clint with a smile and a high five, "I saw some other boats out a ways, so we might get some action." "Well, that's promising, I brought snacks and beer just in case." Clint said with a smile. "Excellent," replied Jesse as they climbed into the little aluminum boat. Jesse fired up the little 10 hp motor, cast off his lines and they headed out into the lake. Jesse piloted them toward the smoke he saw coming through the trees. "Where are we goin' bud?" Clint asked with a baffled look on his face. "I saw something over this way, I just wanted to take a look at it from the water before we go out." Clint turned toward the front of the boat and watched as they got near the rising smoke. "Oh, we got ourselves a camper." "Yeah, we do," Jesse said with a curious tone. "It's kind of a mess, I just wanted to see if anyone was around." They trolled past at a fairly slow pace, "I don't see anyone moving around, got a fire going but no one watching it." Jesse then turned the boat toward the southern end of the lake and increased the speed to get over to their desired fishing spot. It took a good 10 minutes to get out to the clearing where they wanted to be, floating near the reeds, then parked themselves. They settled in a little bit as they waited for the water to calm down. Both of them reached for their gear at the same time to make sure they were ready for action. They nearly simultaneously cast out lines, then Clint broke out the snacks and beer. He handed one to Jesse, "And now we wait."

Mid-morning Thursday, Katy decided to go over to Berta Jones' apartment and have a chat about what happened the night before. Berta was elderly, had retired long ago, and lives alone on the bottom floor of the apartment complex. Her daughter comes to see her on a not so regular time frame, as does her son. Her nephew, Jamie, comes to see her routinely, they have diner together and chat about this that and the other thing. Berta is a happy, outgoing woman, speaks her mind and talks to everyone. She loves a good bit of gossip and doesn't mind spreading it around. She says, '*Gossip makes the world interesting.*' Usually, just about that time, she will tell you something juicy with a big smile on her face. Katy will often go sit with Berta on her porch in the summer and have iced tea and talk about all the comings and goings of everyone they see. She stops in to check on Berta from time to time outside of the summer months as well, it is always a welcome visit. Katy gave a rapid knock on the door, it took nearly a minute before Berta answered, "Katy, young lady, how are you!? So good to see you, come on in and chat for a bit." Katy stepped in and gave Berta a hug, "Good to see you too, how're things on the bottom floor?" Berta smiled and started to lead Katy into her living room "Well I'll tell ya, I would probably have a better view up a floor or two, but I don't want to walk up them stairs. I was just about to make some hot tea, would you like some?" "That sounds wonderful, can I help put that on?" Katy responded and started to go to the kitchenette. Berta laughs, "Yes please, I love it when someone comes over and waits on me." As Katy put on the kettle for the tea, "So Berta, tell me what happened here yesterday, I missed everything, and I hear there was some excitement." "Oh my goodness, yes there was." Berta jumped right in. "Have you seen that couple that drive that little red car, Perkins is their name? I think you have, we've talked about them before. Well, they are a nice couple, they've got a cute little boy about 7 years old." Katy agrees, nodding her head, stopping what she was doing, "Oh sure, I've seen them before, that little boy is cute as can be. Oh I hope nothing happened to them." Berta shook her head. "No, no, nothing happened to them. Their car was broken into though, and I don't think they even know it yet. They went on vacation to go see Mr. Perkins' parents somewhere out east. Supposed to be back Sunday night I think she said." Katy shuffled about in the kitchen getting the mugs out and finding some tea bags. Berta sat on a stool at the counter and took another big breath. "So, from what I saw, someone took that car from the lot, it was gone since Monday. Now, I didn't think anything of it cause I thought the Perkins' had the car. Then it showed back up late Tuesday night, or early Wednesday morning, it could have been even earlier than that. I don't remember seeing it, I'm not really sure what time, 'cause I got up to use the bathroom early in the morning, still dark out, then I came out to get a glass of water. Just so happens, I stood here and looked out the window for a while and saw it parked along the side street out there. I can just see the street down there from my window and usually nobody parks out that way. Well, it was pretty dark, and I couldn't tell what car it was till later in the morning, that's when I could tell it was that little red car." Katy could hear the water starting to simmer and got up to pour it into the mugs. "So you think someone stole their car?" Berta with a big nod, "I sure do, maybe just some kids taking it for a joy ride. But that's not where it ends!" Katy poured the hot water and slid a mug to Berta with the bag on the side. "Oh no? Tell me more!" Berta was nodding again, "I got up about 8 and that car was still sitting there, and I could tell it was Perkins' little red car and I knew that it wasn't right sitting over there, 'cause they're out of town, so I called my nephew Jamie and told him what I saw." Katy stopped her. "Why would you call Jamie?" Berta smiled, "You haven't met Jamie have you?" Katy shook her head as she lifted her tea up to blow across the hot surface. Berta continued with an explanation. "Jamie's a police officer here in town, he's a good kid so I knew he would check it out. I'll try to remember to introduce you to him one of these days." Katy finally got a sip of hot tea without scalding her mouth, "I seem to remember you talking about a police officer before but for some reason I thought it was your son." Berta nodded her head, "Jamie is like a son to me, we spent many of his adolescent years together, I would take care of him right along side of my own kids while his mother was working, that boy makes me smile, he is such a wonderful person." Katy had a big smile on her face listening to Berta talk about Jamie, she could tell Berta cared for him a lot just by the tone in her voice. "What happened after you called Jamie and told him about the car?" Berta snapped right back into the story she was telling. "It wasn't too long after I called him, sure enough the police showed up, Jamie and his police friends, to check on that car. He came over and told me what happened later, after they had been there an hour or so. He told me that I shouldn't spread it around, but he said there were a couple of people that they suspected of being homeless in that car and that they had died." Berta's eyes got wide with a look of astonishment on her face as if to say, 'Can you believe it?' "WHAT?!" Katy exclaimed, "They were dead?! Oh my gosh, do you know what happened to them?" Berta reached over and put her hand on Katy's, just for a moment. "Oh Katy, I don't know for sure, he wouldn't tell me what happened, he said it was official police stuff that he couldn't share." Katy still felt shocked. "Has it been on the news or anything?" Berta shook her head. "No, not that I have seen yet. Now, Jamie usually comes over and tells me all kinds of things that he's been seeing, I don't know if it's just a way for him to let it out or if he just likes talking about it, but I have a feeling he will tell me what happened sooner than later." Katy turned and stared into her mug with a sigh. "Wow, I can't believe that. That's so crazy, and too close to home." Berta sipped her tea. "It really is surprising to have something like that happen right in front of where you live."

Katy and Berta talked and sipped tea for another hour and a half before Katy excused herself to go run some errands. "Berta, I'm going to check back with you on this one, let me know if you hear anything else please?" "Oh I will, this one's a big one." And with a hug, Katy left.

Clint and Jesse didn't have much luck fishing, besides catching a buzz and a chill, they caught some bottom feeders, not exactly what they wanted. They called it quits just before dusk. The snacks were gone and Clint had gotten a bit cold since he hadn't brought a coat. They trolled for fish all the way back to the dock, just in case they might still catch something before they were done, but no luck. Clint helped get the little boat loaded on the trailer. "I'm gonna head out, I'm super cold. Need to go get warmed up." Jesse gave him a thumbs up. "Okay man, I'll see you later. I just have a couple things to put away then I'm out of here too." Clint was gone in a flash, leaving Jesse in the near dark of the boat ramp, alone. Jesse turned toward the trail head that led toward the homeless camp, wondering if there was anyone at the camp now. There hadn't appeared to be anyone there when he and Clint went out to fish, but that was several hours ago. *'Hmm, it's almost dark, I would think they wouldn't want to be wandering around after dark. Maybe a quick peak.'*

Jesse returned home around 8 after dropping the boat off at his parent's place. When he came into the apartment, he found Katy napping on the couch with the TV on. He sat down next to her and gently woke her up. "Hey babe, how was your day?" Katy looked up and smiled. "It was pretty good, work went fast today." Katy wrinkled her nose a bit, "You smell smokey." Jesse pulled his shirt up to his nose and sniffed it. "I don't smell it, must have been the fire pit out at the boat ramp." Katy nodded, "Did you guys catch anything?" Jesse got up to go change his clothes while talking over his shoulder. "No, I thought it would be better out there today. There were a lot of other people out on the water too, but I don't think they were catching anything either. I guess we all thought it would be better. Anything exciting happen around here?" Katy had sat up on the couch. "Oh yeah, I had a chat with Berta down at the end of the complex. She had some very interesting information." Jesse's head turned quickly toward Katy with his eyebrows raised, "She's always got the inside scoop, do tell." Katy went into the story about the Perkins car and how Berta knew they were gone, then she saw it show up in the middle of the night and called her nephew the police officer the next day to report it. Katy held the fact that the people in the car were dead till last. Jesse gave her a blank stare, "There were dead people in the car? Wow, that's crazy." Then his face broke into a smile. "Do you know anything about them? Who was it?" Katy looked at him like he was crazy, "Why are you smiling? That's weird." Jesse stopped smiling, "It's kind of exciting, it's like a mystery right in our own neighborhood."

Katy gave him a half smirk, "I don't really like this kind of mystery, it's too close to home. And no, I don't know anything else. I asked Berta to keep me posted if she hears anything else." Jesse gave her a more understanding look, "Okay, I understand that feeling, it will be okay once it all blows over. If you hear anything else let me know too, I think it's interesting." With that, the subject was dropped. Katy continued to struggle with the fact that she liked a little mystery, but this just felt too close to home. Katy and Jesse wouldn't see each other until Saturday. Katy works odd shifts at the local diner, never seems to be the same days or hours from week to week. She was working late and Jesse would have to go to bed early since he worked such an early shift on the weekdays.

5

Friday

Friday morning John was back to his workday routine, making coffee, getting ready for work, making lunch and heading out the door.

Just before John went to leave the apartment, as he was putting his sneakers on, he found that they were damp on top with slimy dark mud on the soles. He was very bewildered by this, he looked at his hiking shoes confused, they were fairly clean on the bottom. He sat there for several minutes trying to figure out where he went that he would get mud on his sneakers. Finally, since he couldn't seem to figure it out, he grabbed a paper towel and wiped the edges off before putting them on. He threw on his jacket, grabbed his keys, then went off to work. He was going to be running late again if he kept getting distracted. John walked across the parking lot toward Fir Street. Halfway to the street he stopped cold. Standing there frozen, a tingle went up his spine that made him stand straight up. He slowly turned around to see that his Ranger was no longer parked near the dumpsters where he liked to park if he could. He knew he parked it there yesterday. Instead, it was parked four spots over. Slowly he walked over to the truck and noticed mud on the tires and sides of the wheel wells, the same dark slimy mud that he just found on his sneakers. He pulled his keys from his pocket and looked at them puzzled. *'The truck key is right here. I only have one key.'* He opened the door and saw that there was mud on the floor mats as well, the footprints were all smeared but he picked up one foot and looked at the bottom of his shoe to see if he could make out the pattern. *'Wow, I am losing my mind. Where did I go that there was mud? There wasn't any mud at the park yesterday. Not where I parked, it's a gravel lot. AND this is not where I parked when I got home!'* He stood there confused for several moments, wracking his brain to figure out what had happened. Finally, he gave up, closed and locked the door of the truck, slowly turning to continue walking to work.

John walked to work with his head hung down most of the way, following the white line. Another cloudy morning, with temps below 50, it was cool, but he didn't notice, his mind was working hard on what had happened last night. *'Was it even possible that I went somewhere and didn't know it? I think I need more sleep. Where did I go? Where did I go?'* Kept repeating over and over in his head. With the same answer every time, *'I don't know, I can't remember.'*

John walked into the break room to check in five minutes late. Steve was just getting his second cup of coffee, "John, why can't you show up on time?" "I don't know, I just get distracted sometimes and lose track of time." John replied in a defeated tone as he sat down at the table. Steve looked at him with as stern of a face as he could muster, stirring sugar into his coffee and walking over to the small break room table, "Well, maybe if you weren't out all hours of the night you could manage to get up early enough to make it here." That made John look up and into Steve's eyes, "What are you talking about? I was home all afternoon. I went out to the lake for a hike in the morning then stayed in for the rest of the day." Steve smirked at him. "I saw you driving your little Ranger last night at about 11:30 out on Bridge Street, that intersection by the river, you were going pretty slow, I'm sure it was you." John felt his heart start beating heavily in his chest, now he had confirmation that he really was out last night, *'I don't remember any of it.'* He wanted to ask, *'Which way was I headed?'* but thought better of it, deciding he didn't want to let on that he had no idea he was even out last night. Instead, he just shook his head, "Yeah, you're right, I should get to bed sooner." With that, John got some coffee and went out to the pumps to start his shift, trying his best not to let on that he had no idea what Steve was talking about. Once outside,a memory came to John that this isn't the first time he had done something in the middle of the night and not remembered. When he was a kid he used to sleepwalk, he didn't have clear memories of it, mostly just stories from his parents telling him how he would get up and wander through the house in the middle of the night, pick up a toy or stuffed animal then return to bed. There was an instance that he went out into the back yard on a cold night, his dad heard the door close startling him awake. His father George, found him on the swings humming a tune, pumping his legs to get higher and higher on his swing, George had to coax him back inside carefully so John wouldn't wake up and be traumatized. John was sure over the years that there were other instances of sleepwalking that he wasn't aware of, just because he would find things out of place in the mornings and be confused by it, often followed with a sense of deja vu, usually not strong enough to pin it to a sleepwalking event but he kind of figured that was what was happening. It seemed extreme now, he had never left home that he was aware of and been able to put clues together to figure out where he had been.

Clint and John work mostly the same days unless one of them asks for a shift change. They work well together. "Good morning Clint." "Hey good morning, how are you today?" John wanted to say, *'I'M FREAKED OUT! I DON'T KNOW WHERE I WAS LAST NIGHT!'* but he didn't. "I'm okay, how was your fishing outing yesterday?" Clint threw his hands up, "It wasn't great, we didn't catch anything worth keeping. There were other boats out, lots of people fishing, but nothing biting." John nodded in agreement, "Yeah, that'll happen I guess." Clint went over to help a customer, John followed along since there was nothing else to do. "Where did you go last night?" Clint said, looking over at him. John almost rolled his eyes, Steve had talked about seeing him already. "Honestly, I don't even know. Whatever I did, I blacked out. I don't remember a thing. I have watery memories like I was dreaming but nothing is clear enough for me to put it together." Clint started laughing. John looked at him with a blank look. "What? I don't get it. What are you laughing at?" Clint was still laughing. "You must have had a great time if you don't even remember it!"

That got John to thinking, *'What if that's what happened? I was already out...no, I didn't go anywhere.'* "Yeah man, I don't know. Last I remembered I had just eaten and was watching TV, sitting on the couch. Next thing you know my alarm is going off in the morning and I'm in my bed." Clint started laughing more and just shook his head as John walked away to help other customers. The rest of the day was just another

49

typical workday. John and Clint chatted more throughout the day, but not about John not knowing where he was the night before. Clint brought it up just as they were getting off shift. "Hey John, don't wander off in the middle of the night and forget where you are." Then he laughed and gave him a wave, "See you tomorrow." John laughed a little bit too, "Okay, see you tomorrow." John didn't make any stops on his way home from work, but he did cut through the grocery parking lot and he decided to take the cut trail through the vacant lot, even though that meant he would have to pass very close to the rodent camps. Half way through the field, John decided that this was a mistake. He saw that there was a man and a woman standing near the trail engaged in what appeared to be an argument. He wanted to go the long way around them but that would mean walking through other camps. Now John felt very out of place and a bit of panic was rising inside. 'Should I turn around?' He made a quick decision to just put his head down and walk past them like he belonged there even though he couldn't have felt more out of place. The man and woman stopped their argument and stared at John as he approached, making this whole thing feel even more awkward. They both looked rather like cave dwellers, his face was heavily bearded and his eyes were sunk back in his head, his skin was very weathered, wrinkled from the sun and harsh elements, not to mention years of abusing his body with drugs and alcohol. She wore long black hair pulled into a knot between her shoulders and her face was leathery and dark, her eye sockets weren't as deep as his but still sunken, her upper teeth protruding in a mild beaver bite looking situation. The man spoke up looking directly at John, his voice was rough and matched his appearance. "Hey pal, would you have any change? A buck or two would be great." That struck John wrong, his out of place panic feeling changed to anger and he stopped walking right in front of the man. "NO!" It came out as a shout, surprising himself. "I don't work everyday to give it away to people that don't even try to support themselves!" The man had a surprised look on his face, "Whoa, okay man, just asking. I've seen you walking past here all the time. Figured maybe you could help." John started walking again, nearly shoulder checking the man as he passed. His mind racing and anger swelling inside. John was mad at himself for taking the trail, he knew better, then he got angry at himself as he thought of other things he could have said in the exchange, *'Clean up after yourselves, why are you here, why do you have to make such a mess, this is disgraceful, it's a dump.'* Also realizing none of it would have done any good. John passed several other camps on the way home but barely looked farther than 15 feet in front of himself until finally reaching the parking lot. John looked up from the pavement to see his truck in the fourth spot over from the dumpsters, tires muddy from who knows where, mud under the wheel wells, splattered up the fenders. He forgot about the cave dweller looking couple and the exchange he'd just had completely. He stood in the parking lot for a minute considering what he should do about the mud on his truck. *'Should I try to wash it off?'* John looked back down at the pavement, then closed his eyes with his head still down, standing in the parking lot. Another minute passed when finally John drew in a deep breath, raised his head and walked toward the stairs leading to his apartment. *'I'm exhausted.'* The walk home after running into the cave dwellers did little good to clear his head, but now that he was home John would try to relax and leave the exchange behind. He didn't have the energy to clean his truck today, it would have to wait for another time.

6

Saturday

Saturday afternoon Berta's nephew, Jamie, came by for lunch and to catch up with his favorite aunt. Jamie is a good guy, does his job well and believes that he does what is right by his position and his community. He comes by to see Berta for a couple of reasons, one, she is alone and enjoys the company, and two, because she listens intently when he talks. They have great conversations about world events down to local events. Sometimes veering off, reliving family times, good and bad in the past for both of them. Jamie does tell Berta a lot about work, it's a release for him. It's somewhat therapeutic to be able to tell someone all about what goes on without worrying about it getting back to the wrong people. He knows a lot of what he tells her, he shouldn't be telling anyone. "Hello! How are you today?" Jamie was standing at the door waiting for the ritual hug that was required before anyone entered Berta's home. "I am just wonderful, so glad you could come over today. Now, give me a hug and come in here." Jamie stepped into the small living area of Berta's apartment, removing his coat. "It smells good in here, what are we having today?" Berta was heading into the kitchen. "I fried up some chicken last night, I thought we could have some chicken and potato salad." Jamie sat at his favorite spot, the counter looking into the kitchen. "Oh goodness, I haven't had your famous fried chicken in ages. That sounds amazing." Berta turned and gave him a big smile. "I knew you would like it. I'm going to have iced tea, would you like some?" Jamie smiled back. "There couldn't be anything better to go with fried chicken." Berta turned to the fridge and pulled out a pitcher. "Why don't you get us some glasses and pour this while I dish up the plates. While you're doing that, tell me what you know about that red car that was out here in front of the building." Most of the information Jamie would let loose was about older cases, however, today Berta did some extra prying to get this one out of him since it was so recent and so close to home. "I don't know, that's still a current investigation. It's kind of a sensitive subject." Berta pursed her lips and looked at Jamie from the top of her eyes. "What do you mean, sensitive? You already told me those people had been killed and it happened right in front of where I live. I think you can tell me about it." Jamie squirmed in his seat a little. "Well, I don't know what all you want to know. I interviewed a couple people but didn't find anyone that had seen anything." Berta set a plate on the counter for Jamie and walked around to the other side to sit next to him while they ate lunch. "Did you identify who was in the car?" Jamie was getting himself ready to dig into the chicken. "No, at least I haven't heard if they figured it out yet. They looked homeless so it could take a while to identify them." Berta hadn't started eating yet, she was holding her iced tea while listening to Jamie. "You didn't tell me the other day how they were killed. Are you going to tell me?

Or do I have to make that part up on my own?" Jamie finished chewing his first two bites of chicken then looked at Berta to see if she meant it. "You really want to know?" Berta adjusted her plate in front of her trying to decide what to eat first. "Yes, I want to know. I've seen enough crime shows on TV, I think I can handle it." Jamie shrugged and took another bite. "It's not the same, but I'll tell you." He paused to eat some more before diving into it. "Those people were attacked, person to person. Whoever did it, tied them up, gagged then suffocated them with a plastic bag. I'm not sure how he took on 2 people at once and was able to overpower them, but he did. Must be a pretty big person to do that." Berta thought about that for a moment. "You don't think it was more than one person?" Jamie shrugged again and shook his head. "I don't really know, there isn't any evidence that points either way. At least not that I've seen, maybe the detective knows something else." Berta continued to eat while she processed the information. "Do you think he will come back?" Jamie got up to get more iced tea. "Not likely. It depends on whether he was targeting those two or if it was random." After he sat back down, he paused thinking about the case. "I heard about another murder last week from a couple of guys at the station. It appears there were some squatters living in an old mobile home parked out in the woods above the lake that were manufacturing drugs. Looked like a dispute had taken place and one of the squatters shot the other one and left him there to rot. He said some kids riding ATV's found the place out there and were poking around, looking in the windows, and saw a guy laying on the floor. They called the police. Looked like the guy had been dead a week or so." Berta always seemed to take the information in stride, never showing any judgment or too much shock at the things Jamie would tell her. She would just ask questions and nod. Sometimes she would pry for more information if she thought it was interesting. "Do you think they're connected?" Jamie shook his head as he wiped his fingers clean from the chicken. "No, they're so different I wouldn't put those two together." Jamie wasn't aware that Berta really liked knowing all these things, it gave her something to talk about with her friends. "Well, you've had an interesting couple of weeks." Jamie smiled at her, "That I have. This was a really good lunch. I'm going to have to come over more often if you're going to feed me like this." Berta smiled and patted him on the shoulder. "It's a date! You come over any time, I love cooking and you love eating so that works out pretty great."

Katy and Jesse went out for breakfast Saturday morning before meeting with a realtor that was going to show them a couple of houses. "Have you heard any more about the police activity?" Jesse asked as he was sipping his coffee, waiting for breakfast. "No, I haven't, but if Berta hears something, I know she will want to share it." Jesse smiled, "She does like to spread the gossip." Katy laughed a little too, "Yes, she does, but she also gets the good info from her nephew." Jesse sat across from Katy, thinking intently about the murders. "Yeah, I suppose that's true, so it's not all bad gossip. Keep me posted on what she finds out." The conversation turned to the houses they were going to look at. Katy had to work at 2:00 that afternoon and Jesse was going to his parent's house to help his dad with a home project.

John avoided the trail on his way to work again, deciding that he'd had a close enough run in with rodents for a while. As he was passing, he did look over the area to see if he could spot any of the rodents he'd had contact with, either the scruffy guy or the caveman he had seen the day before, even though it was seemingly too early for any of the rodents to be up and moving about. John's mind was more clear that morning, he felt like he actually got some sleep and was on time for work. With any luck, things would be turning around, he really didn't like feeling so groggy and tired the way he had the day before.

About mid-way through his shift, John spotted Scruffy walking past the station with a garbage sack slung over his shoulder. *'I wonder if he has his life's possessions in that sack, what they could possibly be.'* Clint noticed John standing there watching. "What are you looking at?" John looked over at him, "I was just watching that guy, I've seen him before on my way home from work. Wondering what he has in the bag." Clint came over and stood next to John and they both watched Scruffy shuffle his broken, stiff body slowly past. "Probably cans for recycling, he's heading over to the recycle center to collect some money." John nodded as they watched, "Didn't Jesse say the guy he pulled out of the truck was a 'scruffy' guy?" Clint nodded back at John. "Yeah. I wonder if that's the guy, pretty hard to know, they're all really scruffy." Both of them were still standing at the edge of the station's islands, Scruffy was far down the street disappearing past the buildings, they had a feeling it was the same scruffy guy.

7

Sunday

John sat in his apartment on Sunday morning enjoying a fresh coffee and some eggs with toast for breakfast. He turned on the TV and flipped through a few channels until the news caught his attention. The newscaster was on the screen with a picture next to her, as he stared at the image the news lady went on in her solemn, newsworthy voice about the story. "Some local area hikers made a gruesome discovery yesterday while on their Saturday morning hike. We can't disclose the location as it is under an ongoing investigation, however, we do know that they discovered the body of a person encased in the burnt remains of the tent he had been sleeping in. Police reported that the victim had been bound and gagged, then possibly suffocated with a bag before the tent was lit on fire and collapsed over the body. The tent burned quickly and melted the fabric over the body encasing it in a melted shell." While the news channel didn't say the location of the crime scene, they did show a picture from the trail head that John had been at on his hike. The photo showed where the homeless camp had been. He recognized it immediately. There was that feeling again, that feeling of deja vu, but why? He knew he had been to that camp when he was on his hike but this feeling was different, it was more personal but he couldn't put any of the details together.

John nearly dropped his plate when he saw the report, he was entranced by his racing thoughts. *'I was just out there!'* John was considering things he had seen over the last couple of days. He went hiking and found the camp, he was disgusted with the mess the homeless rodents had left behind. He found that his shoes were covered in mud and his truck had mud all over it, but he didn't know how it got there. He discovered that he had gone out when Steve told him that he saw him late at night driving on the edge of town. Things were starting to add up in John's mind, his thoughts were getting carried away, he was frozen with the thought that he might be responsible for what he just heard. *'Oh Shit! Oh Shit!'* John again thought of the mud on his shoes and his truck. *'Could I have done that?! Is that where I went the other night?'* He got up and went to the window and looked out at his pickup. It was still in the same spot, it hadn't moved since he noticed that it was 4 spots away from the dumpsters. He went back to the couch and sat down hard, the couch cracked, nearly collapsing under his weight. His mind was reeling, spinning things out of control, a feeling that this could be his doing was growing, he thought, *'What do I do? This doesn't seem real, I can't have done this. I don't like those rodents, but I wouldn't do that. Would I?'* Just as that thought finished, another came into his mind, *'The officer told me that those people in the little red car were bound, gagged, and suffocated with a plastic bag too! Did I do that!?'* His face was blank, but his mind was racing with all the what ifs. Sunday was John's second day off during the week. He had planned to take another hike, this time along the river that skirts the edge of town. Now he wondered if he should just stay home and hide out. *'If I did this, did I leave anything behind? Did I leave evidence? Did I touch that car? I need to wash my truck, I need to wash my shoes! All of my clothes!'* John took his plate to the kitchen and washed it off, setting it in the dishwasher with three other plates from the week. He went to his room and picked up all his clothes and dumped them into the washer that is tucked into the hall closet, he threw his sneakers in on top, added detergent, a little more than usual, and started the load. After getting dressed, John spent the rest of the day washing the outside of his truck and the floor mats. He was taking every precaution he could think of just in case he was responsible for what he had seen on the news.

Sunday morning, about 8 AM, Berta called Katy, "Good morning Miss Katy, I hope I didn't wake you." "Good morning Berta, no I've been up for a bit now, just getting ready for the day." Berta, sounding hopeful, "Good then, do you work today? The reason I ask is, I have some news about that police activity we had." Now Katy was a little excited, "I don't work until this afternoon." Berta was excited but almost whispering into the phone. "Do you have time to come over for some tea? I've got some more details about those dead folks in the car."

Katy went over to Berta's apartment about 10 AM, Berta was excited to see her, with her normal hug for a greeting, she invited Katy right in. "I've got the water almost hot, we'll have some tea here in just a minute." The tea was really just a formality to all the gossip that Berta wanted to spill. They sat in Berta's living room, crowded with a sofa and a reclining chair.

"I talked with my nephew last night. He said that those people in the car had been killed the same way as each other. Looked like someone had wanted to get rid of them. He didn't really want to tell me because it's still an investigation and he didn't want me to worry about being safe and all that. But I kept on pestering him, I told him I needed to know what's going on in my own neighborhood." Katy was leaning toward Berta, listening intently. "That is kind of scary, those people were killed right there in front of our apartments, I mean I am a little worried about that."

Berta got up to get the hot water and pour their mugs for tea. "Well, he said that it looks like someone was targeting those people and that it's not likely that it's going to happen here again." Katy got an inquisitive look, "What do you mean, targeting them?" Berta was nodding her head, "I had the same question. He said that the way they were killed made it look like they were exactly who he wanted, not just random people." Katy still had not relaxed but was trying to take it all in while she sipped her tea. "I'm not sure I want to know now, but I'm going to ask anyway. How were they killed?" Berta sat back down and still hadn't touched her tea. "He said they were suffocated, I guess I said that already, but he also said they had their hands tied behind their backs and they had rags stuffed in their mouths. I haven't a clue how one person could do that to 2 people, unless maybe there were 2 people that did it to them." Katy had a worried look on her face, "This is all too much, I don't like it at all." Again, Berta was nodding in agreement, "Did you watch the news this morning?" Katy had a strange look on her face, "No, I'm not much of a news watcher, what did you see?" Berta almost rolled her eyes, "There was someone killed out by the lake, I just saw it on the news! They said the body was found yesterday, but the thing is, the guy they found was bound, gagged and suffocated with a bag just like those people in the car." Katy was making a face, "Oh my gosh, Berta! Do they think it was the same person?"

"The news report didn't say anything about the one that happened here. Jamie said that the news doesn't know about that one, it never got reported to them. It's very concerning, a lot has happened in the last week. There was something else that Jamie had told me. He said that they found some homeless people shot to death in an abandoned mobile out in the woods. It was a wreck of an old place, one of them mobile types that someone pulled into the property and eventually just left it to rot. Apparently, the homeless people found it out there and since no-one was living in it, they took it as their own. Jamie said they were making drugs in it and it looked like things must have gotten out of control, or they had some disagreement, and one of them ended up shooting the other one. He said that once they found out it was drug related and a shooting and all, the DEA came in and took over the investigation." Katy was feeling overwhelmed, she had a look of disbelief on her face. "Did he say where that was?" Berta shook her head, "No, he said it was up in the hills a bit, made it sound like it wasn't all that close to town, maybe out by the lake?" Now Katy was shaking her head, feeling like she'd had enough of the bad news for the day. "This was harder to hear than I thought it would be. Do you have any good news?" Berta brightened up and told her about seeing some friends of hers on Saturday and that she had plans to see them again the next week. They chatted for another 30 minutes before Katy decided it was time to go and get ready for work. As she was walking back to her apartment, she was thinking she couldn't wait to tell Jesse what she had heard, but it would have to wait until later. Jesse had left just before her to go help his parents with something at their house, and she was working late.

8

Monday

When John woke on Monday morning, he checked the room for signs that he might have left the apartment the night before. He was on high alert and pretty scared that he wouldn't be able to tell if he had been out or not. He checked his previous day's clothes, still in the hamper. He checked his shoes, dry and in the same place. Looked out at the lot to see if his truck was in the same spot, it was four spots over from the dumpsters. He felt a little better after that, however the nagging feeling of, *'What have I done?'* wouldn't go away. Aside from checking everything in the apartment from the day before, he went about his same routine of getting ready to go to work. Coffee, shower, toast, jacket, shoes, keys, out the door. John decided it was best to keep to his same routine, he didn't want to raise suspicions by changing things up. Not that John had a lot of things that he could or would change, he didn't have a lot of options on his route to work and he didn't do much with his free time. John was feeling very paranoid on his walk to work, he kept his head down most of the time, just walking his one speed along the white line. He didn't bother looking at the rodent camps as he passed them though, if he had, he may have noticed that the camp had gained a new tent since he went by the night before. It was placed just 10 yards off the edge of the road where the cut across trail from Ted's Grocery merged back to the roadway. It was a 2-person tent, there were a couple of trash bags stuffed with who knows what, and a bicycle flopped on top of them right next to the tent. Just a short way up the trail the caveman that John had words with on his way home was sitting in a lawn chair outside his tent, no doubt pondering life's bigger questions like, where his next meal would come from. John just kept moving steadily down the white line as cars passed him, whipping him with cold air, other people on their way to work with no idea they might be passing a killer on the side of the road. As John was nearing the GasNGo station he started to look around, checking who might be watching him or might be at work already. He could see that Clint just walked into the break room as he got close, Clint was always a few minutes early while John was right on time today. He could see a couple of cars at the pumps, morning was usually pretty steady with people headed to work. John spotted Scruffy at the edge of Ted's Grocery as he passed it. Scruffy was headed around the corner of the store, it looked to John like he might be headed to the back of the store where the dumpsters are. Ted's Grocery was known to throw out stale bakery items on Monday mornings and Scruffy was sure to get the best pick of what was there early in the day. When John reached the break room Clint was coming out with coffee in hand. "Good morning John!" Clint is a morning person which is the exact opposite of John. "Good morning Clint, why are you so chipper in the morning?"

Clint turned and smiled, "Awe I don't know, it's just another day and I like that I made it out of yesterday alive." John looked at him for a moment considering what Clint had said. "What do you mean happy to get out of yesterday alive? Did something happen to you?" Clint chuckled a little, "No, nothing out of the ordinary, but if you think about it, you could meet the end at any time. There have been some murders around town lately, you could get in a car accident and not survive. Heck! You could fall in the bathtub and die! At least, that's what I've heard." John was again silent for a moment in thought. "Yeah, I guess all that's true, good for you to have a positive outlook. I just can't seem to do that, I always feel like there is a cloud over my head." After helping a couple of customers, Clint brought the subject up again. "What is it that weighs you down?" John stood still looking at Clint for a moment, thinking about how to answer the question, *'Do I trust him to tell him I don't know where I've been the last couple nights? No, I can't bring that up.'* "Well, have you heard about the murders in the area? That stuff is really heavy, but maybe what bothers me more is the rodents, and they are the ones being targeted. I just don't have any sympathy for them and I feel like maybe I should." Clint's face turned more serious, "What rodents? What are you talking about?" John stammered a little bit being called out for calling the homeless people rodents. "Uh, Oh, did I say rodents? It's the homeless people and their camps and stuff, they remind me of rodents, so whenever I think about them that's what I call them." Clint shook his head a little but didn't respond to the explanation. "I've heard about the murders," he acted casual about it, "I guess there have been a few. I don't know that it's so strange that you don't feel bad about it. There is no connection between you and them, so why would you? Most

66

people hear about news like that then go about their own day and not give it a second thought, except since this is so close to home, maybe they protect themselves a little more or pay attention to their surroundings a little better." John nodded a bit on his way to help a customer, "Yeah, I suppose they do, not sure that helps me, but thanks for trying."

John didn't feel any remorse for the rodents that had been killed, and he considered this frequently, wondering if there was a way to get rid of them. He didn't think that was something he would do, but he just couldn't explain what had been happening around him. He didn't feel comfortable talking any further about it with Clint. Not feeling sorry for them actually made him believe that he had done it, plus the mud on his shoes and on his truck was hard to explain. He still wasn't sure where that had come from. John kept moping about the rest of his shift, trying unsuccessfully to let go of his gloomy feeling.

Jesse got home around 4 on Monday, Katy had worked an early shift and came home about 5, Jesse went to greet her at the door. "Hey sweetie, good to see you, it feels like I haven't seen you in days. I hate it when our shifts don't line up." Katy dropped her things and gave Jesse a hug and a kiss, "I know, I don't much like that either. How are you? How was work?" Jesse helped hang up her coat. "Work was good, we are keeping busy, just a steady flow of trucks in and out all day." Katy listened as Jesse told her about helping his Dad with the deck project over the weekend and that they want to have a barbecue when it's all finished. "Hey, did you hear any news about that car and the police activity we had here last week?" Katy perked up a little bit as she started to get things ready for dinner. "I did!" Jesse came into the kitchen and grabbed a beer from the fridge, offering one to Katy. "Really? Do tell. What did you hear?" Katy accepted the beer and dove into the story as told by Berta. "I got all this from Berta downstairs, who got most of it from her nephew Jamie, who is a cop." Jesse was sipping his beer and watching Katy pace in the kitchen, half the time getting things for dinner while the other half was just pacing and thinking as she told the story. "Okay, yeah I think you mentioned that she had a cop nephew, go on."

"Right, so the little red car that was here last week belongs to the Perkins family, they live here in the complex, I don't remember which building. They were or are on vacation, and Berta saw their car was gone, then it came back. Did I tell you this part already?" Jesse nodded his head, "Yeah, I remember that part." So, Katy kept going "Alright, well, it turned out that someone stole the car and brought it back, but then it wasn't clear to me if the people that stole the car were still in it, or what, but there were people killed in the car! That's why the police were all over the place! They were investigating a murder." Jesse's eyes got wide, but he didn't say a thing. Katy continued, "Actually, I guess it would be a double murder because there were 2 people in the car." Jesse set his beer on the counter and rubbed his face with both hands, "Wow! That's pretty crazy! Are there any leads to who did it?" Katy shrugged "I don't know, Berta didn't say anything about that, but I would guess that maybe Jamie didn't or couldn't tell her any of that information. But here's the thing, there was another murder a couple days ago where they killed the guy the same way as the people in the car!" Jesse's hands were still on his face "What! No way! Where did that happen?" Katy took a long sip of her beer and grimaced a little at the sour taste. "Out by the lake, Berta said it was on the news Saturday, some hikers found the body." Jesse was shaking his head and seemed to be thinking about the whole thing. "Did she say how it happened? How were they killed?" Katy had stopped moving around the kitchen and was nodding at Jesse, "Yeah, they were all tied up and gagged, then suffocated." Jesse grunted and just stood there leaning against the counter with a blank look on his face, processing. Several minutes went by, Katy went back to meal preparations, then she spoke. "I'm not sure what to think of all this. It scares me, it makes me nervous. Jamie told Berta that he didn't think it would happen around here again because he thought those people were targeted, but I don't know if I believe it. Not after the second one just happened." Jesse looked into Katy's eyes and said calmly, "The second one didn't happen here, so he was right about that." Katy didn't agree with the logic, "Well, not exactly right here but pretty close by. It's in our area." Jesse conceded, "Yeah, I guess so. I want you to be safe, always check your surroundings, always lock the doors, don't go out at night by yourself if you don't have to. When you leave work have someone walk out to the car with you. Be careful!" Katy nodded her agreement and hugged Jesse for a good long time.

Jesse pulled away, "Make sure you let me know if you hear anything else, I don't hear much information from the guys at work and I'm interested in what's happening." Katy was looking a bit somber "Okay, you will be the first to know. I start a late shift tomorrow and it goes through Sunday." Jesse sneered at that, "How late?" "6 to midnight, I hate that shift, but at least we rotate it, so I don't have to work that one all the time." Jesse took a deep breath and let it out slow, "No, that's true, that stinks though. You need to be super careful when you get off work that late." Katy gave him an awkward smile, "I was hoping you would drop me off and pick me up from work." Jesse was taking a swig of his beer and nearly choked on it, "What! That's kind of late. I have to be at work by 5." Katy came in closer and gave him a pouty face, "Please? I really don't want to be out there alone, it would mean a lot to me." Then she kissed him. "You really know how to work me over don't you? Okay, I'll do it. It's going to be rough, but I'll do it." Katy smiled big and gave him another hug and kiss. "Thank you so much." Katy returned to prepping dinner, they chatted and drank beer, then sat and watched TV before going to bed.

9

Wednesday

John's nerves settled some over the next few days, he thought he had been watching his surroundings closely on his way to and from work. He couldn't really know if that was true, but he hadn't noticed anyone watching him, he was starting to feel comfortable again in his daily routine. Wednesday afternoon on his way home John saw the caveman and cave woman that he'd had a run in with, he made eye contact with Caveman as he passed. It was an eerie feeling. John had looked over as he was walking and they locked eyes, he couldn't look away for some reason. No words were spoken between them but John could feel himself slow his pace, in his mind it was that slow motion feeling you get in the movies, there was something about the look in Caveman's eyes that said *'I know what you did.'* Caveman's face was stone cold, he made no expressions, much like John. The years of living outdoors made him look older than he was, his face dirty and wrinkled from exposure to the sun and rain. His hair and beard were dark and matted, it changed color as the light changed, shining off the dirt and grime as though he had highlights. His clothes tattered, well used and dirty, hung off of him like loose fitting rags. John's heart raced a bit in his chest and he could feel a cold sweat break in the palms of his hands. John was finally able to break the gaze with a hard blink. When he turned his head and looked away, he noticed the new tent in the rodent camp. He was stunned that he hadn't seen it before, it was so close to the road, the pile of rubbish was already substantially large. There didn't appear to be anyone there at the time, John kept his slowed pace as he passed, marveling at the mess that had appeared, seemingly so quickly that he hadn't noticed it showing up. He had gotten a hundred feet or so past the camps then stopped, turned part way around, and looked back at what he had seen. He looked at the new tent and pile of trash resting between large stands of brush, then past that he could see Caveman still sitting in his lawn chair and Cave Woman, just as dirty and well used as the man she was with, fussing with what looked to John like a pile of trash, but was surely some possession she couldn't be without. Past them and farther off the road, deeper into the bushes was another tent and a broken pop-up with its torn blue cover that appeared to be over a pile of broken bicycles and maybe a barbecue. The tops of 2 more tents could be seen farther past that, obscured by the heavy brush farther off the road. John made a mental note of everything he could see there, frustrated with the fact that he hadn't seen it when this new one arrived, he would keep a closer watch from here on out to see if more camps popped up in the future. John turned back the other way and looked across the road where the scruffy man's tent was, along with 4 others spread farther apart. He couldn't see anyone from where he was and only part of the piles of trash that were strewn between all the tents. John took a slow deep breath, held it a moment then let it out just as slow. He turned toward home and continued his walk along the white line, cars rushing past, some giving him plenty of room while others seemed to be close enough to brush him with their mirrors as they went past. John didn't react to any of the cars, he just kept on walking at his steady, slow pace. The sun had come out again the last couple of days causing the temperatures to get up to the 80-degree mark, a late September heat wave. He could feel the heat on his face, it burned a little bit as he looked west into the sun.

The bright orange-white glow of the sun was low on the horizon, it made it hard to see where he was going, he squinted into it as he neared Fir Street. Looking away from the sun, John could see into some of the neighborhoods near his apartment, glancing between houses and down long empty yards of groomed green grass as he strolled past. Something caught his attention just as he turned onto Fir, someone had emerged from behind a house. The figure was moving stiffly around the yard, then he recognized the figure, it was Scruffy. *'What on earth is he doing back there?'* John stopped a moment at the corner, from there he could see Scruffy carrying a backpack, it looked like it had a little weight to it just by the way he was carrying it. *'Oh, that's not good.'* He stood still watching for a few moments as Scruffy went across the lawn to the next home and around the side of the house. John started walking again in the direction of Scruffy, his apartment was across the street from the houses and a little farther down the lane. As John got closer, he could make out Scruffy leaning into a gray trash can rummaging for treasures. He didn't notice John on the street, at first John didn't let on he was there. John clenched

73

his teeth, *'This has gotten out of control.'* "HEY!" John yelled. "You shouldn't be here!" his voice came out rough as if he hadn't spoken to anyone in days. Scruffy scrambled, his head popping out of the can, looking back for where the voice came from. Scruffy froze for a moment, seeming to consider his options and wonder what the guy yelling at him was going to do. Scruffy pulled a plastic bag from the trash and emptied two aluminum cans from it and plopped them into his backpack on the ground. John stood still, just watching. Scruffy replaced the trash can lid, gathered his backpack up, and walked to the sidewalk. He looked at John, put his hand up in a single wave, in a low quiet voice partly incoherent, "I'll go. Just looking for some recycles. I don't mean any harm." John didn't trust him, he felt very uneasy with someone poking around outside houses that he shouldn't be at. "You can't be doing that. You don't belong over here, you can't just go into people's yards and dig through their stuff." Scruffy went wide around John not saying anything else, his eyes down on the street looking right in front of him, but walking as quickly past John as he could. John turned and watched him pass, then started walking behind him, Scruffy picked up his pace even more, heading toward Route 18. John hadn't walked this fast in years, possibly since he was in high school trying to walk between classes on the verge of being late and getting yet another detention. John could smell a sour something in the air as he followed, surely due to the heat and lack of cleanliness of the rodent ahead of him. Scruffy broke into a jog as best as he could, seeming to limp along. It looked difficult for him to move, something between being old and broken, and just having not jogged in a very long time. His baggy ratty clothing swishing around, backpack bouncing over his shoulder as he went as fast as he could. Once Scruffy reached the corner and turned east toward his camp, John broke off his pursuit and stood watching as long as he could see Scruffy jogging down the road. Once he was out of sight, John turned and walked back toward his apartment, looking at the neighborhood houses again as if he would see someone else in between them that he could chase out and do another good deed. John actually felt satisfied that he had removed a possible threat from the area. He knew it wasn't much, but he was satisfied nonetheless. He also considered that since he knew where Scruffy's camp was, if anything happened in the neighborhood, he would pay him a visit. John's concern for the safety of the local homes made him feel the anger and disdain for the rodents rise up in his chest again. John climbed the 3 flights of stairs to his apartment, went inside and kicked off his shoes, threw his keys on the table, then grasped his head with both hands, closed his eyes tight and shuddered with anguish. *'Oh man I just don't know what to do about the rodents!'* He pulled the curtains over the 2 small windows in his unit, he was determined to shut out the outside world for a while. He clicked on the TV in the dusk of his apartment and slumped onto the couch to try and clear his head, to focus on nothing important.

10

Thursday

When John woke on Thursday he felt a little better about the previous day's encounter, but it was still dwelling in his subconscious, somehow, his mind was still cloudy. John didn't think that he had left his apartment at night for unknown excursions in the last week, checking his clothes and shoes and car placement every morning for signs that he might have gone out without knowing it. It had only been a few days since he saw the news story and put together that he might have killed those people. Freaking him out, but not to the extent that a normal person might freak out. John was feeling the paranoia lift off his shoulders but didn't realize what *was* there, there was still a cloud but not about looking over his shoulder, being worried that he would be caught, that had faded into the background. He wanted to put that feeling behind him and decided he had laid low long enough, even though it had only been 4 days, it felt much longer to him. Thursday, being one of his days off, he decided to get outside. The weather had been great most of this week and he wanted to take advantage of it. He slept until 8 AM, which felt surprisingly good. He got up and started his coffee, then decided to go out and walk the trail along the river since he had enjoyed being outside the last time he took a hike. As John packed a lunch for his hike while making some breakfast at the same time, he remembered the last hike he took, discovering the rodent camp at the end of the hike. He was hopeful he wouldn't find anything like that along the river trail. After finishing his breakfast, he dug his hiking boots out of the closet again, John checked them to see if they were clean, wondering yet again how he had gone out in the middle of the night and gotten all muddy in his street shoes, he slipped them on and left the laces loose. He checked his watch, 9 AM, *'That's perfect, it will still be a good temperature outside.'* He threw on a sweatshirt, filled his backpack with a couple of waters and lunch, then left the apartment. John checked over his truck before throwing the backpack in the passenger seat. Still unmoved from the fourth spot over and no mud anywhere. He was sure he hadn't driven it since he washed it. He drove slowly out of the apartments and made a loop around the block of houses that he had seen Scruffy at the day before. Performing his own neighborhood watch, he didn't see anything suspicious, then continued into town passing the GasNGo station on his way to the bridge that crosses the river. There is only one bridge in town to cross to the other side of the river, the next bridge is 8 miles downriver. About a half mile down river from the bridge at the edge of town there is a pull out off the road that many of the locals use to hike the trail and fish from the banks. John pulled his truck into a spot between a few other pickups and parked. He gathered his pack, cinched up his shoes and headed for the path that leads through the poplar trees toward the river. There are several trails leading from the parking area to the river, the trail John chose was about a half mile before the actual river trail, he felt the cool morning air on his face as he pushed past branches and brush hanging close to the trail. It was about 60-degrees but would heat up later in the day without a cloud in the sky. As John reached the T in the trail right at the edge of the river bank, he looked up river and could see a couple of fishermen trying their luck from the banks. John turned downriver and walked at a meandering pace. John's footsteps were heavy at first as he found his pace on the uneven dirt path, that wanders between outcroppings of rocks and roots exposed from nearby trees that had been flooded over time as the river would rise and fall with winter storms. He spent some time on his walk looking at the river, then back at the trees as the river trail meandered along the twists and turns of the river itself. At times the river was within a stone throw of the road and houses on the other side, then it would pull away from the road and feel very secluded. It's a 2 mile hike down river to where there is a footbridge that crosses the river. John was feeling good and decided to stay on the path, not crossing over for now, maybe he would cross on his way back. It wasn't much past the footbridge that John spotted a rodent camp far to his left up in the poplar trees. There was an opening in the trees elevated above the river banks, somewhat protected from potential river flooding. 3 tents stood spread-out around piles of trash that they had discarded. A fire pit in the center was smoldering while a disheveled man sat on a sofa in the dirt, facing the burning embers. Several lawn chairs sat around the fire pit with no one in them. It was after 10 now, it was likely that the other rodents were still in their tents with no reason to get up. The man on the sofa didn't look up as John stood there taking in the scene, he didn't seem to be aware anyone was there at all. John couldn't tell if his eyes were open or closed from the distance he stood away from him. He was feeling that rage in his stomach, it was clenched just like his jaw, his whole body became tight with anger as his mind raged. *This just isn't right, should I yell? Would it do any good? Go home! Don't you have somewhere to go?* It was during these thoughts that John made the realization that they might not have anywhere to go, *'Could they have exiled themselves from everyone they had ever known? Was this the end for them? The best they could do? Why wouldn't they try to do better?'* His frustration grew deeper and deeper until he let out an audible groan of anguish. The man on the sofa jolted, sitting up straight, looking around then spotting John. John caught his look, an impulse without thinking he yelled, "I don't know what to do!" He paused with the realization that he had yelled that allowed, staring right at sofa guy. The man on the sofa leaned forward as if to say, what are you talking about? John realized his spontaneous comment was valid, he yelled it again. "I don't know what to do." The man on the sofa raised both hands with a shrug, then dropped them and with a defeated posture sulked back into the sofa, he yelled back, "Keep walking." John hung his head, not sure what he thought would come from that interaction, his body still tense as he turned to face the trail down river. He had no idea what to say next or what to do, deciding that there was nothing, he started to walk away. The best thing he could do would be to keep moving. He felt frustrated, his mind confused and cloudy, he could still feel the tension in his body as he walked down river. John continued down river for another hour, seeing a few fishermen along the banks on the other side of the river as well as 2 more tents on the same side as him, presumably with rodents living in them. He was somewhat pleased that the last 2 tents he came across didn't have as much trash scattered about. Either they were fairly new to the area or they just didn't bring as much crap back to their site. John found a tree that had fallen across the river at a narrow spot and thought crossing here and going back up the other side would be better than doubling back on the trail he had already been on. John climbed up the roots carefully, standing on top of the downed tree, bouncing to test the security of where it had landed, wanting to make sure it wouldn't roll over while he was trying to cross. He made his way across carefully one foot in front of the other holding limbs that stuck up for balance. The tree got down to only about 5 inches in diameter by the time he got to the other side, it was very bouncy by then, as well as having many more limbs in the way as he tried to find a spot to dismount at the other bank. He spotted a landing area where he thought he could jump to the ground and possibly others had already done it, judging from the broken limbs. It was about 4 feet down, this would do, so he jumped. Crashing through the limbs of the downed tree, John landed solidly on the bank with his left foot but his right foot came down on the edge of a river rock rounded off by years of tumbling over and over as the river pushed it down stream, causing his ankle to roll outward, pushing his ankle toward the ground and his foot inward. John's body went crashing all the way to the ground with the instant searing pain to his ankle. He ended up on his knees in a pile of branches broken into splinters by the falling of the tree. He stayed there on his hands and knees for a minute, staring at the ground, holding his breath, waiting for the pain to subside, not believing what he had just done.

Just as he thought the pain wasn't going to go away, he tried to move his ankle and the pain subsided slightly. He let his breath out in a gasp after realizing he had been holding it. He looked up from the ground and could see a hole through the brush, instead of standing up he crawled his way out of the limbs until he was clear of the downed tree. His ankle was throbbing and had a stabbing pain when he tried to lift his toes to the air. John saw an outcropping of large rocks and pulled himself up on his left leg, moving tenderly with his right foot on the ground. He made his way to the boulders and sat down. He pulled himself farther up on the rock and sat for a moment, then pulled his right foot up to him so he could inspect the damage. He pulled his jeans up and sock down, he couldn't quite see his ankle below the top of his hiking boot. John pulled the shoe off, then pulled the sock from his foot. The outside of his ankle was very red but no visible bruising yet, he felt lucky to have worn his hiking boots, it would have been much worse had he not had them on. He glanced back over his shoulder to see how close he was to the river. It was just to the other side of the boulders he was sitting on, spinning around to the other side, he eased himself down to the next rock, pulled up his pant leg and eased his foot into the cold water. It was shockingly cold but he knew it would be good to keep swelling down. He pulled his backpack off and decided now was as good a time as any to have his lunch.

John soaked his foot and ankle for about 15 minutes until it was completely numb from the cold water. Inspecting it when he pulled it from the river, he couldn't see any bruising and it wasn't throbbing too bad. John worked it back and forth for a while, testing the flexibility, then sat and ate the rest of his sandwich while his foot dried off. When he was done, he massaged his ankle a little after putting his sock on, then slipped on the boot. He gingerly slipped off the rock where he was sitting and tested his footing, putting some weight on his ankle, then off again. It didn't feel too bad with weight on it. *'Wouldn't that be something, come out here for a hike and break my ankle, not be able to walk back to the truck.'* John started making his way up the bank, carefully picking his way around rocks and river scrub. Once he got to the trail, he didn't feel too bad, he was hoping it would hold up so he could make it back to the truck without too much trouble. He had a bit of a limp as he walked up river, following the trail on the opposite side he had come down on, the trail was not as well-worn on that side, it was narrower and there were more roots and underbrush growing over the trail that John had to push through. He was getting used to the feel of it, his boot was getting tight as his ankle swelled up, but it didn't hurt too bad. His progress was slow but steady. He stopped for a few minutes where the fishermen were and watched them cast out, hoping to get a lucky bite. After drinking some water from his pack, he kept going up river, it was taking longer now, his mood had spoiled when he came across the rodent camp and now being injured, he was ready to be done. When he came to the point that he could see the 3 tent campsite on the other side, the fire had been stoked up and there were a couple of other people sitting with the guy on the sofa. John stopped where he could see the camp and stared across the river at them. Sofa guy spotted John and raised a hand in a wave, John mumbled to himself, *'I don't know you. Don't act like I do.'* He turned and kept walking slowly, gingerly, starting to feel the swelling stiffen his ankle until it didn't want to bend.

It was another 30 minutes before John made it back to the

footbridge and crossed over to the side that he had started. The fishermen that were on the same side of the river earlier were no longer there. It was nearly 3 PM when John finally made it back to his truck, the parking area was empty, his ankle was extremely sore, and John was ready to go home. He climbed into his Ranger with a sigh, glad to be off his feet, *'That wasn't so successful was it?'* he said to himself, exasperated. He cranked the little pickup to life and started for home.

As he pulled onto Fir Street John spotted Scruffy walking toward Route 18 and recognized him immediately, *'Prowling through the neighborhood no doubt.'* John was upset with Scruffy but his ankle hurt so much he didn't even think about confronting him. John was turning into the lot as Jesse was getting out of his truck, they both gave a friendly wave, John was going fairly slow through the lot and Jesse waved him to a stop. "Hey John, how are ya? What are you up to?" John wasn't really in the mood for small talk but didn't want to seem rude, "I'm okay, just got back from a hike down by the river, how are you?" Jesse was leaning down a bit looking into John's window, "Yeah I'm good, that must be why I didn't see you at the GasNGo today. Anyone out fishing on the river today?" John checked his rear view to see if anyone had pulled in behind him since he was blocking the drive, "Yeah, I have weird days off, but it works for me. There were a few guys out fishing from the banks, I don't know if they were doing any good. Then there are the homeless camps out there too, some guy sitting on a couch looking dazed and confused." Jesse nodded "Oh good, good, I'm going to have to get down there and check out the fishing. Seems like the homeless are popping up everywhere, not sure what anyone can do about it." Jesse changed the subject, "Hey, this is a nice truck, I've seen it a couple of times but didn't know it was yours." John just looked out at Jesse, "I don't drive it much, I walk to work every day." Jesse nodded some more, "Oh that's right, I think you told me that." Just then another car pulled in behind John and he was relieved that it did. "Hey I need to get out of the way, I'll talk to you later." Jesse backed up so John could drive away, "Sounds good, see ya later." John was in luck as he drove in front of his building, he saw that his parking spot by the dumpster was open and pulled in. He limped his way up the 3 flights of stairs, unlocked the door and dropped his things in the entry. He pulled his shoes off and went to the kitchen for an ice pack. After gathering the pack and a glass of water he collapsed on the couch and put his foot up with ice on it. He turned his leg one way then the other to have a look at it, still no bruising to speak of, but it really hurt.

Jesse went up to his apartment, Katy was there waiting for him with some food ready. "Hi Love, good to see you. How was your day?" Jesse has been eating early when he gets home then taking a nap since he hasn't been sleeping through the night this week while taking Katy to work. "Oof, I am wearing down a bit, the late nights are getting to me. I got really tired driving the lift today, I almost fell asleep behind one of the trailers waiting for the driver to get it opened up." Jesse smiled and faked falling asleep at the wheel with his head cocked to one side. Katy led him to the table where she had a sandwich waiting, "Only 2 more days, then you can sleep in." Jesse dug into his sandwich like he hadn't eaten all day. "I ran into one of our neighbors today in the parking lot, his name's John, I talked to him for a few minutes. Clint works with him over at the GasNGo, I'm not sure that guy is all there." Katy sat down across from him, "What makes you say that?" Jesse swallowed and took a drink of water. "He just has no expression at all, he acts a little off. I mean he seems nice enough but there's something strange going on in his head, or maybe there's nothing going on in his head, hard to tell which." Katy made an expressionless face, "You mean like this?" Jesse chuckled at it, "Kind of, but it's hard to explain. You know how when you talk to people their expressions change depending on what you're talking about? He doesn't do that, it's just the same flat expression. Kind of like a monotone face." Katy laughed, "Monotone face. Does he have a monotone voice too?" Jesse had to think about it a little bit, "No, not really but maybe a little bit, I think there is some inflection in his voice, but I was having trouble reading his face, so I didn't really pay attention. Anyway, I never even knew the guy existed until Clint introduced us and I just talked to him in the parking lot. He's a little strange, that's the only reason I brought it up." Katy nodded, "What did you guys talk about?" Jesse shrugged and finished off his sandwich, "Nothing much, I was just saying hello since I recognized him, he said he was out at the river hiking today." Katy went expressionless again "That doesn't seem too weird." Jesse laughed a little, "No it doesn't, I need a nap. Do you want to sleep some before your shift?" Katy thought for a second, "No, I slept in, I think I'll just read for a while. I'll wake you up at about 5:30." Jesse got up and cleared his dishes, "Sounds perfect." He kissed Katy and went to get some sleep.

At 11:20 PM John rolled out of bed, stretched and yawned. He pawed through the laundry basket for his jeans that he'd thrown down, not bothering to turn on the light, he slipped them on. He found his t-shirt on the bed, then walked the 12 steps into the front room of his apartment, stopped at the front door and put on his hiking boots. He grabbed the sweatshirt he left hanging by the door and his keys from the table. As he headed down the 3 flights of stairs putting on his sweatshirt, he didn't even notice the pain in his ankle, or that it was raining a little bit. He got into his Ranger, not aware of where he was going because he wasn't conscious. John was pulling out of the lot when Jesse was leaving to pick up Katy. Jesse pulled out right behind him and recognized his truck. *'Where the hell is he going?'* Jesse's curiosity was on high alert. John was going the same direction so Jesse hung back a little and watched as they got into town, John was heading toward the river bridge, then turned before crossing. Jesse made a snap decision to follow him for a while, he was early to pick up Katy so he had some time. They were headed out of town, Jesse thought at first John might have been going out for a late-night booty call, but now he wasn't so sure, the farther out of town he drove there are fewer houses and they are farther in between. He had backed his following distance off from behind John's truck, there were very few cars on the road and he could see John's tail lights from a long distance away. Jesse was going to have to turn around soon or he would be late, Katy would understand, it's hard to get up in the middle of the night, *'I overslept.'* It's easy enough to explain. It was almost 11:45, Jesse was about to give up when he saw that John was making a turn, *'What the heck? He's going to the lake? Man, this guy is strange.'* Jesse decided he had seen enough and turned around before he got to the road leading into the trail head parking area. He stepped up his pace back to town trying not to be so late picking up Katy, Jesse didn't want her to be standing around for too long.

86

When he got there, she was waiting inside, looking out the window. Jesse flashed his lights when he pulled in and Katy came out. "Hi, thank you, I know this is tough coming to get me late like this." Jesse leaned in for a kiss, "You bet, sorry I'm a little late, it was tough to get up." Katy smiled, putting her hand on his cheek, giving him another kiss, "You're amazing." Jesse smiled and started out of the parking lot. "I saw that neighbor guy again, John, when I was on my way to pick you up." Katy turned sideways in the seat, "Really? This late? Where at?" Jesse glanced over and could see Katy's eyes in the street lights going by, "He was heading through town, went to the other side of the river on Bridge Street, that's where I lost him. I thought maybe he was going out for a booty call or something." Katy laughed and reached over, giving him a shove on the shoulder. "Maybe so, good for him if he is, after you told me how weird he is, that just proves there is someone for everyone." Jesse laughed too, "Oh for sure, good for him. On another note, I have to start a little early this morning, we have a couple of early loads to take care of today, so I will be leaving pretty early, but I'll be home about the same time." Katy put on a pouty face, "Oh that's going to be tough to do, I'm sorry, please be careful. No sleep driving the forklift." Katy pretended to sleep drive, making fun of him. "I'll be careful, I promise."

John pulled into the trail head lot and stopped in the middle, he sat there looking around at the dark, no movement anywhere. All he could see was the gravel in his headlights and the edge of the boat ramp. To his left he could see the trail head sign and the darkness of the trail next to it. After a couple minutes he cranked the wheel hard left and drove to the trail, stopping just in front of it, lights shining down the path, tree branches hanging over the edges, looking like long arms dangling in the air ready to grab anyone that dared to walk through. After a couple more minutes he drove ahead down the trail dragging the long branch arms down the side of his truck, they screeched and scratched making screaming sounds as they ran along the paint as if to say, 'Please stop, no you shouldn't come in here.' He bounced along over roots and rocks bending around the corners in between the trees with just enough room to not get stuck, tires spinning in the mud and sliding over wet rocks, wipers on low pushing away the water, pine needles and leaves that had fallen from branches above. He crawled along for about 5 minutes until he could see what he was after in the headlights. Just yards ahead of the truck stood the site where the rodent camp had been burned and the rodent exterminated. Crime scene tape wrapped around the trees encompassing the site. The tent was gone, it had melted to the body and went away when the body was taken. The rest of the mess was still there, the trash, the bicycles, a mattress, piles of clothes, rags, towels and indiscernible trash. John worked his truck in a circle getting it turned around and backed in close to the scene. He got out of the truck and walked to survey the scene by the light of the taillights. There wasn't enough light to see what he needed, so he went back to the truck and rummaged behind the seat for a few moments. He emerged with a 3D cell flashlight and a pair of gloves. He turned it on and set it on top of the truck, shining it over the area. John set to work. He started by pulling down the crime tape, then picking up the larger trash bags strewn about, throwing in the bicycles and gathering loose trash bit by bit, throwing it all in the back of his truck. He topped it off with the heavy wet mattress, it was floppy and soggy and he got dirty and wet wrestling it into the truck on top of all the other trash. He went back into the cab, rummaged behind the seat again producing a rope and tied it all down. John was messy, wet, and cold, but completely unaware of it. He drove back up the trail, wipers clicking back and forth, more needles and leaves falling from above, the hood now getting covered by them as if he had parked under these trees for a week. The Ranger was getting better traction on the way out with the heavy load in the back, but bounced heavily over the rocks and roots. In minutes he emerged from the end of the trail and went directly to the road, not stopping in the lot to look around. John drove straight to his apartment, keeping to the speed limit, taking the most direct route straight through town. He parked in his spot next to the dumpster like he had never left. While he climbed the stairs he was limping slightly, but the pain didn't register in his brain. John opened the door, kicked off his hiking boots and removed his clothes, leaving the dirty wet pile in front of the door. It was 1:30 AM when he dropped back into bed, closing his eyes, having no idea what he had done or that he had ever left.

11

Friday

When John's alarm went off Friday morning, he had an extremely difficult time getting his eyes open. He swung his legs off the side of the bed and sat up with his head hung down, still sleeping in the upright position. John stretched, trying to relieve the tension he had built up in his body from the fitful dreams he had the night before. His body felt like he had worked out in his sleep, his muscles were sore and his hands hurt. He stood up slowly like he had aged 10 years overnight and zombie walked into the bathroom, noticing that his ankle felt terrible, it was much more sore than the night before. He switched the light on in the bathroom to have a look and found that it was solid purple from the top of the ankle to the bottom of his foot. *'Wow I didn't expect it to get that bad.'* He poked at it and bent it this way and that, trying to test how much it could take, then got in the shower. After a too long hot shower, he was awake but didn't feel rested at all. Managing to pull on clean jeans, a t-shirt and a sweatshirt in his half awake state, he made his way out into the living room heading to the kitchen, and noticed his pile of clothes by the front door. He stopped, dumb founded, *'What the hell?'* He walked over and picked up the wet sweatshirt, turned it over in his hands and noticed that it was very dirty, wiped with grime across the front. *'Ho no!'* John pulled open the front door and went to the edge of the stairs where he could see his truck in the lot. It was raining lightly and still not light out at 5 AM. He could see the truck with the help of parking lot lights nearby. It was covered in leaves and pine needles all across the hood and top of the truck, the back was filled with trash topped with what looked like a soaking wet mattress. *'Oh no! What did I do? What did I do?'* He hobbled back inside, grabbed the pile of wet clothes and dropped them into the laundry basket in his room, then went to the door again, pulled on his shoes, grabbed a jacket, his keys and went gingerly down to his truck. John stood by his truck surveying the pile of junk in the back as well as the marks running down the sides. *'What did I get myself into? Good grief, it's no wonder I'm tired.'* Then another thought occurred to him, *'Ugh, I hope no one is dead.'* This thought had him stunned, he stood there by his truck staring into the pile of rubbish with thoughts of dead rodents running through his mind, he closed his eyes and tried to focus on remembering where he went. His mind was fogged, he couldn't picture anything clearly in order to recognize what he had done, it was hazy and dark, nothing recognizable, not even the pile of garbage in his truck could spark a memory.t He heard something behind him and snapped out of his trance, looked over his shoulder to see someone across the lot getting into their car, heading off to work. John looked back at the truck, then at the dumpster it was parked next to and started to unload the trash into the apartment dumpster. It was a dirty mess to unload but he made it all fit except the mattress which he left sitting beside it. John was sure that it was early enough that no one had seen him unloading everything. His ankle was throbbing horribly when he finished and his clothes were wet and dirty, he would have to change again before going to work. He limped his way up the 3 flights of stairs back to his apartment to change his clothes. *'Oh man, I am so late, no way I can walk on this ankle this morning, I'm going to have to drive.'*

As John drove to work, he was hoping that some of the mud and tree debris would wash off in the rain and wind of driving, but it wasn't very effective. He parked beside Clint's C10, hoping it wouldn't be too visible to anyone. John was a little over 20 minutes late to work and Clint saw him limping in. "Steve is pretty upset, you might try to avoid him if you can." John made a move toward the break room to punch his time clock and twisted his ankle nearly taking him to his knees. "Holy crap that hurt!" Clint made a move toward him as if to help, "Dude! What happened?" John waved him off, "I rolled it yesterday, it's all purple and swollen, hurts like hell." Clint had a wincing pain look on his face, "Damn okay, let me know if you need anything. At least you have a reason for being late." John nodded, thinking to himself, *'Yeah at least I have that.'* He walked into the break room, Steve wasn't present, thankfully, *'I'll get to deal with him later,'* and clocked in, then headed back out to get to work.

It was a pretty rough day for John, his ankle swelled up even more but he toughed it out. It rained off and on all day, temperatures in the 50s but the wind was blowing, keeping the temperature feeling like it was in the high 40s. Steve eventually called John into the break room to talk about his *'Showing up on time'* problem. "John, I really need you to be here on time, I just can't have an empty shift, it slows things down too much and I don't want to pay overtime to the overnight crew to cover you." John leaned on a chair to take weight off his ankle, "Yeah, I know, I was up on time but I rolled my ankle yesterday and I almost had to call out today, it's in pretty bad shape." John put his foot up on a chair, pulled up his pant leg and forced his sock down to show Steve he wasn't joking. Steve could see just at the top of John's shoe the ugly black and purple bruising on John's ankle, "Oh crap, that looks really bad. Are you sure that's not broken?" John put his sock and pants back in place and put his foot down, "No, I'm not too sure, it sure hurt when it happened but I was able to walk on it afterward so I don't think that it broke. If it doesn't get better in a day or so I'll go have it checked." Steve nodded in agreement, "Okay, well I can see what you're dealing with here, but you have to understand that since this isn't the first time, I had to say something. I'll let this go, you take care of that leg and try to be here on time even with the bum ankle." John agreed and went back out to finish out his shift. He wanted to tell Steve about the truck full of crap but decided that was a bad idea at the last second.

After his shift John limped out to his truck and had forgotten about the pine needles, leaves and mud all over it. He collapsed into the seat feeling grateful to be off his feet. *'Oh I need to get this thing cleaned up, best not to be seen though, since I have no idea what happened.'* Not really feeling like being on his ankle any longer, he gave in and drove 20 miles to the neighboring town to find a drive through car wash. After going through the wash, *'Best six dollars I ever spent.'* John returned home, stopping at Ted's Grocery. Since he was driving he bought extra items that he doesn't like to get when he's walking, forgetting though that he still had to carry them up 3 flights of stairs until he arrived home. *'Oh shoot, I'll just leave it in the truck for now.'* John carried only the soft food up, making it in one trip, leaving the extra water bottles and case of soda in the truck. It was almost 6:00 when he finally got home and was ready to settle in for the night. It had been a long, exhausting day.

Friday morning was a popular time for fishing on the river, often there would be construction workers on the banks pretty early in the morning since they work a 4 / 10 shift the first part of the week, giving them Fridays off. There had been a few rain showers moving through the last couple of days causing the rivers to come up a little bit by then. The locals knew that if they got to the river just after a small shower the fishing would still be alright, but if they waited too long the river would rise too much and be too muddy to be any good. The rain had let up early in the morning, the skies were clear when the sun came up. The morning sun was glistening off the wet leaves. Friday would be a good day to fish. Morning temperatures were cool, in the low 50s, but it would warm up later in the day.

Thomas Dean and Adam Stevens, were out looking for a good fishing hole when they hiked down from the footbridge along the river trail. As the 2 of them scouted the trail they climbed up onto an embankment to get a better look at the trial ahead, trying to spot good fishing areas. Once on top of the bank they noticed 3 figures sitting on a sofa in front of the smoldering embers of what used to be a camp fire. The smoldering left a smoke plume hanging in the air above the camp, the smoke gathered in the trees around the clearing where 3 tents were set up hanging like fog in an arena made of trees and leaves. Adam looked at Thomas. "I didn't know camping was allowed out here." Thomas was looking at the camp with a bewildered expression on his face, "It's not, take a closer look at the camp." Adam moved to the side a little and squinted his eyes as if that would help him see farther, "Oh shit, it's a homeless camp." Thomas moved over a little bit as well and stood on a rock to help look over some of the Scotch broom, "Yeah it is, what a mess. Looks like there are some people sitting on a sofa. Something doesn't look right though." Adam came over to the rock Thomas was standing on, "Let me have a look." Thomas jumped down and Adam took a turn. "They don't look like they're moving, I can't make out their faces from this far away but something doesn't look right." Thomas stood looking up at Adam, "Should we take a closer look?" Adam was still watching the 3 on the sofa, "Yeah... they still haven't moved. They could be asleep but they're all sitting upright like that, it just looks weird." The air was cool and damp, the sound of the river slapping at the rocks in the background, there was just the slightest smell of smoke in the air even though there was a fog of it over the camp. They looked at each other both thinking the same thing. *'This is a little creepy.'* Adam jumped off the rock he was viewing from and they started making their way farther up the bank toward the camp, pushing through the stiff brush, holding their fishing poles above their shoulders, trying not to snag lines on the limbs. They made it about 25 yards from the camp before they realized that the people on the sofa were definitely not moving, Adam stopped first, "Am I really seeing this? Do those people have bags over their heads?" Thomas was standing right next to him, in a quiet voice, "Yeah I think you are really seeing that. Do you have your phone with you?" Adam started searching his pockets, "Yeah, here it is. I'll call now." Adam called 911, "I need to report

95

um, we found, um we found some bodies. Yeah I'm pretty sure they're dead. They haven't moved in a while and it looks like they have bags over their heads." Thomas could hear the mumbling of the operator on the other end of the connection, but not well enough to make out what she was saying, just hearing Adam's side of the conversation was enough. "No, we haven't touched anything, we can just see them from a distance." Adam listened to instructions, then gave her their location as best as he could, describing where the homeless camp was in relation to the road and the footbridge. "Okay, we'll wait for them to arrive." Adam disconnected and put the phone back in his pocket. "They should be along pretty quick, she said we shouldn't touch anything and the police will likely have some questions for us." Thomas looked away from the bodies long enough to look at Adam, "Man this is weird, I've never seen anything like this before. Should we meet the cops at the parking area?" Adam nodded. "Yeah that's probably best, then we can lead them into the spot." They worked their way back to the main part of the river trail and back to the parking area. The police had arrived before they had gotten to the lot and were starting to gather their equipment to check out the scene. Adam and Thomas explained what they had found and where the camp was. The police decided to try and come into the camp from the trails on the road side of the clearing, there were several trails leading into the area, probably used by the homeless to access the camp rather than hike down the rougher river trail. Officer Jamie Roak had taken their ID's and run background checks on them. "Would you two please wait here until we locate the site, just in case we have any other questions? We will let you know once we have secured the area when it's okay to leave." Both Adam and Thomas were nodding, Thomas turned around and pointed toward the river upstream from the footbridge, "Do you mind if we go over that way and do some fishing while we wait? That is what we came out here for and as long as we are waiting anyway we may as well do something." Officer Roak thought about that for a second, "Sure, that will be fine, I'll have someone come let you know if we need anything." They both thanked him and started walking toward the river with their poles in hand. "Isn't this just the most bizarre thing that has ever happened?" Adam looked at Thomas with wide eyes, "Yeah it is! That's some crazy stuff." Officer Roak went back about his duties securing the area for the investigation team. He didn't know it yet since he hadn't been to the crime scene, but there would be FBI all over the area very soon.

Friday evening Jesse was taking Katy to work just before 6, they drove past the intersection that crosses the river bridge when 2 police cars and an investigation vehicle were crossing the intersection coming across the bridge. Katy's eyes were glued to them, "What's that all about!? Have you heard anything?" Jesse gave her a weird look. "Why would I have heard anything? I've been at home sleeping." Katy had a sheepish look on her face. "Oh yeah, I know but that's a lot of cops coming from the same direction and that investigation truck isn't something we see out here." It was raining hard, the wipers of the truck were banging back and forth, not keeping up with the water hitting the window. Jesse pulled through the intersection after the police vehicles had gone through, looking toward the river but unable to see what the action was about. "I can't see anything, and really who knows how far they came before getting into town." Katy made a sideways smirk and slumped into the seat, she was hoping for a better explanation. "That's true, I guess I'm on edge with all the stuff that has been happening around here." They drove in silence the rest of the way to work, Jesse focused on keeping the truck on the road in the pouring down rain. Katy just watched out the side window as they passed the buildings in town, seeing the water rush down the sides of the road washing away the leaves, piling them up in the drains. Jesse rolled the truck into the parking lot, dropping Katy off at the front door so she could stay dry, "See you tonight, I love you." Katy leaned over and kissed him, "See you at 12, sleep good." She jumped out and hurried to the door. Jesse rolled slowly away but didn't drive straight home. At Bridge Street he made a right turn, went across the bridge then turned down the river, he was looking for the police activity. As he neared the lot where all the fishermen park he saw that there were still several police cars parked there but it looked as though they were getting ready to leave. They were all trying to take cover from the rain and keep their equipment dry as they loaded things in their cars. Jesse cruised by casually, windshield wipers flapping back and forth on his C10, he watched them load their equipment as he rumbled past. He noticed 2 more SUV investigation units and a black SUV farther down the road, it looked like they were blocking off a trail that led into the trees. There wasn't anyone near those vehicles, *'They must be back in the trees still.'* Jesse's curiosity was satisfied for now, he didn't want to drive back by the officers so he made the 8 mile trip down to the next bridge and looped back on the highway to get home. It took an extra 20 minutes to go that route but it was worth it to not be noticed driving by again.

12

Saturday

Saturday morning Jesse and Katy were up by 8, even though they didn't get to sleep until about 1 AM Friday night after Jesse picked her up from her last late shift of the week. Katy made a nice breakfast for the 2 of them, bacon, cheese and mushroom omelets with bacon and toast on the side. They sat and ate breakfast in their kitchen and drank coffee for a little over an hour while chatting about this and that, what their last week looked like and what the coming week would bring. The subject of police cars didn't come up, Jesse thought about it and decided to let it go. Katy wanted to get outside for a while so they made plans to take a walk out on the river trail. It had rained off and on over the last couple of days but Saturday the skies had cleared and it promised to be a beautiful fall day. Jesse was interested to see if the fishermen on the river were having any luck and maybe he had a little interest in whether the police were still around. Katy just wanted to get out for some fresh air. They drove out in Jesse's truck and parked along the road where the fishermen left their trucks, there was no sign of police cars when they pulled into the parking area. They walked the muddy trail towards the river, the grass was heavy with rain from the previous day's showers, it brushed against their pants leaving them wet and heavy. They skirted the larger puddles on the trail, trying not to get their shoes muddy. As they got close to the river, they could hear the pounding of the water over the rocks, the river was much higher than the days before, all the rain had raised its level by a couple of feet. Jesse was a bit disappointed, "Oh the river is so high right now, it would be tough to catch anything, but the salmon run will be coming in soon." Katy stood looking at the rushing water, "Yeah its really fast, it seems like it would be tough for the fish to stay still." She looked at Jesse with a smile. Jesse looked at her with an *'Are you serious'* look on his face. When he could see she was kidding he just laughed. "Which way would you like to go, Goofball?" Katy pointed down the river, "Let's go this way, towards the foot bridge." Katy led the way, carefully picking her steps between puddles, roots and rocks. The trail was a little slippery but not so bad that she couldn't walk it. Jesse was right behind, mostly watching the river crash past them. "It's so loud today! A person could scream and no one would hear you." Katy looked back at him, "It is very loud, and I think you're right, you would have to be right on top of someone to hear them screaming." They continued walking, enjoying the fresh air, Katy looking at the trees and the sky and sometimes the river, Jesse watching mostly the river as it raged past, occasionally looking at the opposite banks to see if anyone was trying to fish from it. Some of the trees were starting to turn to fall colors, a light breeze in the tree tops made the leaves shimmer from green to silver and orange to brown. Altogether the sight was glorious and relaxing for Katy, Jesse didn't seem to notice. Katy wanted to cross over at the footbridge so instead of following the path underneath they veered off to the left to join the trail that goes over the footbridge. At the top of the bridge in the middle they stopped to take in the view of the water rushing past underneath their feet. Katy couldn't quite believe what she was seeing. "We only had 2 days of rain, kinda crazy the river came up this much." Jesse nodded as he looked up the river. "Yeah, it doesn't take much for this river to get pretty crazy, it's a short river and all the fields run off into it." They turned around to look down river, then after a moment of looking down river Katy turned and continued across the bridge. Reaching the end, she looked down the trail, "It doesn't look very good on this side, it's crowded with limbs." The branches of the brush on that side were heavy from rain as well as being overgrown on the less used side of the river, Jesse was standing looking down the trail with his hands in his pockets. "No, it's not as good on this side, it doesn't get used as much over here." Katy shrugged, "Okay, let's go back to the other side and go down that way." She was pointing down the river, looking to Jesse for approval. "Yeah, sure, that sounds good." They walked slowly back across the bridge, Katy just enjoying the outdoors, looking at the fall colors as they transitioned back to the muddy path being careful not to tromp through the puddles. As they walked down river Katy looked side to side making sure not to miss any of the scenery, something yellow caught her eye. The yellow was a little brighter than the turning of leaves from the fall colors. She kept walking, but her eye was still drawn that direction trying to catch that hint of yellow again and identify what it was. Several minutes went by before she spotted it again, this time she stopped and craned her neck a bit to try and see the bright yellow flash over the ledge on the high side of the bank, "What's that up there?" She pointed the way she was looking, then looked over at Jesse to see if he was looking in the right direction. "Jesse stood up on a rock to get a better look, "Looks like some caution tape or something." Katy made a questioning face, "Oh that's weird, can you see why it's up there?" Jesse jumped down from his vantage point, "No, I can't tell what it's for. Probably just marking a sink hole or something so no one falls." They continued to walk down the trail for another minute when the trail opened up and Katy could see exactly what was up on the elevated bank surrounded by the yellow tape. She was astonished, once she came to a good view point, she stopped with her back to the river taking note of everything she could see. The yellow tape was crime scene tape, it surrounded what looked like a campsite, but the site was a disaster. It looked like 3 tents with piles of trash, clothes, bicycles and random junk strewn everywhere, at the center of it was a large fire pit with several broken-down outdoor lawn chairs and right in the middle, a sofa facing the river. "What do you think happened here?" Jesse stood next to her, surveying the scene. "I don't know, maybe a giant homeless camp? Maybe the cops came and just ran them off? I don't really know." Katy shook her head, "I don't know, there has been so much weirdness happening around here lately, this just freaks me out a little bit. Do you think they will come clean it up? It's such a mess and so sad to see it here where everything else is so pretty." Jesse shrugged, not really interested in whether it would get cleaned up. "I don't know for sure, I would guess eventually the parks department will clean it out of there." Katy turned to Jesse, "I'm ready to turn around, I don't want to go any farther."

Jesse took her hand, "Okay, we can go back." He turned and started to lead her back up the river. "Maybe we can go to my parents' place for a barbecue tonight, they wanted to have us over and the weather looks like it will be good all day." Katy squeezed his hand before dropping it to keep her balance on the trail. "Yeah, that sounds good. I haven't been over there in a while. Can we go home and take a nap first? I'm tired all of a sudden." Jesse laughed a little at that, "Yeah that sounds amazing."

Katy was thinking right away that she wanted to talk to Berta to see if her nephew knew anything about what the police were doing at the river. When they got back to the truck Katy pulled out her phone and made a call to Berta, Berta picked up with a question in her voice. "Hello? Miss Katy, is that you?" Katy giggled a little, it was funny to her how older people answered cell phones. "Yes Berta it's Katy, how are you doing today?" "Oh girl, I'm doing just wonderful, I'm about to get my hair done up, then go out for a late lunch with my daughter." Katy got a big smile on her face, "That sounds just wonderful Berta, I won't keep you long, I just was wondering if you were available to talk in the morning? There's been some police activity that I was hoping you had heard about." Katy could hear Berta take a gasping breath, "Oh goodness, no, I haven't heard anything new from Jamie in a few days, is it close by?" Without waiting for Katy to respond Berta kept talking. "I haven't seen anything on the news either. I could give Jamie a call tonight and see if he has heard anything. He's not much of a phone talker though so he might not tell me much if I call him." Katy was a little disappointed to hear that but didn't give up on it. "It's close by, we just saw some crime scene tape stretched around an area in the trees out at the river. Do you think I could come by around 9? I have to work at 12, but we could have some coffee or tea in the morning before I go." "That sounds just fine Katy, it will be good to see you, I need to go, it's my turn, I'll see you tomorrow." Berta broke the connection without waiting for Katy to say goodbye.

Katy sat back in the truck, thinking about seeing Berta tomorrow, Jesse was looking at her waiting to see what Berta had said. Katy looked at Jesse, "She hasn't heard anything yet and might not have anything tomorrow, but she is going to call her nephew and see what he has to say." She turned and looked back out the front window. Jesse started the truck and rolled slightly forward, the gravel crunching under the tires, the motor rumbled, vibrating through the seats of the truck, he sat there, just looking at Katy, contemplating what to say. *'Was she concerned? Yes, I would think so.'* "Are you okay?" Katy straightened up and looked at Jesse, "Yes, I am, this is creepy though. I haven't heard anything on the news or even from the people at work about what has been happening with these murders. I feel like people should be more concerned about it." Jesse nodded a bit and looked back out the front window himself, "Well I haven't seen any news about it either, I feel like it is being kept pretty quiet, or the police just don't care since it's happening to homeless people." Katy grunted a little at that, "Why would they not care? they're still people!" Jesse backed down on the subject right away, "I don't know, it was just a thought, doesn't mean that's what is happening at all." Katy was shaking her head, "That would be awful, lets go, I'm tired. We will see what Berta can find out, maybe that will shed some light on it." Jesse started driving out of the lot, slowly rolling through the gravel, waiting for a couple of cars to pass before merging onto the road. "Be sure to let me know what you find out, I am pretty interested in what's happening as well." Katy reached over and grabbed Jesse's hand, holding it, resting their intertwined fingers on the seat, "I will, I don't work too late tomorrow so I'll fill you in when I get home." With that they drove home holding hands, not speaking another word with only the sound of the motor rumbling and the wind passing by the cab of the truck.

When John woke up Saturday his ankle was still the color of blueberries. It was also extremely stiff. He sat on the edge of the bed with his right leg crossed over his left, he massaged his ankle and moved his foot in circles trying to get the joint to loosen up. He could feel the crackling in the joint as he moved it around. After getting out of the shower and dressing, he looked around the apartment for signs that he might have left in the middle of the night. Nothing seemed to be out of place. He made some lunch to take with him and some toast to go. He sat on the sofa to put his shoes on, it was too hard to do it standing on the bad ankle, then put on his jacket and went to leave. His keys weren't on the side table, *'What the heck? I always put them on the table.'* Automatically he started patting his pockets to see if he had them on him already. Nothing there, he turned to look around the room but still didn't see them. John started to panic a little. *'I can't be late for work, this is no good.'* He had been sleeping in a little since he was driving to work. There was no reason to get up so early. He went to the kitchen looking for keys, checked his pockets again, then spotted them sitting next to the refrigerator. *'Oh that's weird, why did I put them here?'* Satisfied but bewildered by it, he headed back to the door, on instinct he reached for the deadbolt to unlock it. *'It's not locked, wow, I'm losing it. Didn't*

105

lock the door, put my keys in the kitchen. What next?' Again John shrugged it off and left the apartment. He struggled down the stairs feeling that crunchy feeling in his ankle as the blood moved around with each bend, and made his way out to his truck, still parked in the normal spot. He did a once over check, it seemed to be clean. As he pulled out of the lot he noticed the fuel was very low, maybe low enough that he might not make it to work. *'I swear there was more fuel in this thing last night.'* John coasted into work, the truck on fumes. Just enough to pull into a parking spot next to Clint's truck. He walked across the parking lot gingerly and into the break room just in time to clock in. Steve was there making sure the shift change went well. "Good morning John, thank you for getting here on time, I do appreciate it." John filed his time card back in the slot. "You're welcome, it was a close one this morning, my truck is out of gas and I lost my keys this morning." Steve chuckled, "Glad you're here." John turned around and went to get coffee, it was almost gone. He poured himself the half paper cup and started to make a new pot. Steve moved that way and waved him off. "You go ahead and go out to the pumps, there is a bit of a backup right now. I'll make another pot, should be ready by the time those customers are taken care of." John set the pot down and moved to the door. "Thanks for doing that." It would be several hours before John would make it back into the break room for his second cup of coffee.

13

Sunday

Katy slept in on Sunday morning, not getting up until 8, her sleep schedule was still off a little from working the late shift. Jesse had left about 7 to go back out to help his dad with some chores they had talked about the night before at their house. Katy didn't have to go to work until noon but wanted to go see Berta before she went. Katy got ready for her day fairly quickly then went downstairs to Berta's place. When Berta came to the door, Katy could hear the TV on in the background. "Good morning sweet girl, good to see you this morning." Katy came in and gave her a hug. "It's good to see you as well. I see you've got the news on, anything interesting today?" Berta was headed to the kitchen, "Yes there is, but first, would you like coffee or tea this morning?" Katy followed her to the counter, "I'm feeling like coffee would be great, it was hard to get up. I think I need that extra boost." Berta had already made coffee so she grabbed a couple of mugs and poured one for each of them. She opened the refrigerator giving Katy a carton of creamer. Katy took the creamer happily, "That's perfect, you know what I like." She poured it generously into the mug and swirled it around with a spoon. "So, what did you see on the news this morning?" Berta started heading back to the living room, "I think that the police activity that you asked me about was just on a news report that said there was a murder out there, but they really didn't give any details. They said something about an ongoing investigation, the same old thing they always say." Katy made a fist and bumped it on her leg. She sat down on the edge of the sofa. "I knew it! I knew it was something awful! It was quite the mess out there, piles of garbage and stuff strewn all around. It was a homeless camp. It had all that yellow crime scene tape all the way around it." Berta had gotten comfortable and set her coffee down, "You saw it up close?" Katy shook her head a little bit, "We didn't get too close, it gave me the creeps. Did you talk to Jamie about it?" Berta picked up her coffee again and took another sip, "No, I called him right after I got my hair done, and just like I thought he didn't want to talk about anything on the phone. He is coming over for dinner tonight though, and I'm sure we will be able to talk about it then." Katy sat back on the sofa and sipped her coffee, thinking. "I'll have to touch base with you about that, for some reason I feel like I really need to know what happened out there." Berta looked at her, concerned, "Is everything okay? You seem to be a little wound up about this." Katy tilted her head to the side trying to shake free how she was feeling. "Yeah I think everything is fine, I can't put a finger on why this has got me wound up." Berta started to get up for more coffee, "Well you just sit and relax for a bit, I'll get us some more coffee, then we can talk about something else for a while." Katy handed over her mug and waited for the refill.

"Oh, that's probably a good idea, try and get my mind off of this for a while. I have a question though." Berta looked over at Katy, "What's that hun?" "Have you talked to the Perkins'? Did they come back from their trip?" Berta raised up her hand, "Yes they did, I talked to Janette earlier in the week. They had a wonderful time." Katy was watching Berta fill the mugs, "Did they know about their car?" Berta came back into the living room with the mugs and handed Katy hers. "Janette said that they didn't know until they had gotten back and the police had left them a message on their home phone to get a hold of them. That's when they found out that their car had been stolen." Katy was sipping her coffee, mostly listening to what Berta was saying. "I haven't seen their car in the lot, are they going to get it back?" "Janette said that the police still had it, and they wouldn't be getting it back any time soon. But she did say that their insurance company was renting them a car until theirs was returned." Katy winced a little at that, "I don't think I would want the car back after those people were killed in it." Berta made an 'oh' face, "I hadn't thought of that, maybe I should ask Janette if she had talked to the insurance company about that." Katy was feeling like it was time to go, "Berta I'm going to go get ready for work, I have to be there in an hour and I still need to fix my hair. I'll check in with you later this week to follow up, I want to know what Jamie saw out there." Berta got up with Katy and set their coffee mugs on the counter. "That sounds good hun, now you be safe out there and I'll talk to you later." Berta gave her a hug as Katy was standing at the door, then watched Katy walk down the sidewalk towards her apartment until she couldn't see her anymore.

While Katy and Berta were going onto their second mug of

coffee, John was sitting in his apartment wearing sweat pants and a t-shirt, glued to the TV news, hoping to catch another news story about the murder by the river bridge. He had caught the tail end of the first story as he sat on his sofa to have breakfast on his day off. He only heard that there was an ongoing investigation as they showed a photo of the parking area with police cars gathered in it. The same lot where he had parked on Thursday to hike the river trail. *'There's been another murder? When did it happen? Come on, tell me when it happened.'* He frantically flipped through several other channels trying to catch another news story about it, but it was too late, most of the stations were off the local news now. Before making breakfast, he had gone through his new morning routine of checking his clothes, for either dampness or that they were piled on the floor by the door, as well as going out to look at his truck, making sure it was in the same spot and not muddy. Nothing seemed to be out of place but he was quite worried that he may have done something that he didn't remember. John was limping back and forth in his living room, starting to sweat with nerves, the TV was still on but had gone away from the news and was just starting a home improvement show. He decided it was best to just sit tight today, he needed to keep his ankle up anyway. *'I need to let this blow over and see what happens with it. Maybe there will be more news about it later.'* With that thought, he went and got a new ice pack for his ankle and a fresh cup of coffee. He sat back on the sofa and started changing channels to try and find something that would take his mind off all of this and hopefully make the time pass a little easier.

Sunday night Jamie arrived at Berta's about 6 PM, he had come straight over after work but had already changed into his street clothes. Berta greeted him at the door with her standard hug. "Good to see you young man, how are you doing?" Jamie took off his jacket as they walked into the small living area. "I'm doing fairly well, things have been quite busy at work lately, can't say that I don't like it. It's been very interesting. Not that I like what has been happening but it makes the work days go by fast. What are we having for dinner?" Berta got a big smile, "Always one for a good meal aren't you? There's a meatloaf in the oven and some baked potatoes in the microwave." Jamie rubbed his belly, "Yes I am, that sounds great. Nothin' better than home cooking. Anything I can do to help?" Berta shooed him with her hand, "Nah, it's all just up to the oven at this point, you go ahead and get comfortable." Jamie went and got comfy in a puffy chair near the window. "So, I know you're keeping track of what's been happening around town, with all the murders and whatnot. Pretty unusual stuff for around here. What have you heard lately? News reports and all?" Berta took a seat on the sofa, a lovely flowered piece that you would expect to find in a grandmother's house. She looked at Jamie as though this was an odd question. "Don't you watch the news?" Jamie smirked a bit, "I thought you knew me better than that. I don't watch the news, at least not much. I see enough of the real news right in front of me every day, I don't need to see the exaggerated news on TV." Berta rolled her eyes at that, "Oh well, it might be embellished news but it's all I've got to know what's happening out there." She made herself a little more comfortable, sliding back from the edge of the seat and leaning against the arm of the sofa, "I heard there was another murder out by the river, they didn't say where exactly, something about ongoing investigations and such. Is that fake news?" Jamie looked down at the floor, seeming to study the patterns in the carpet, "Well, not exactly, I suppose it would be nicer if it were fake." Berta felt justified about watching the news, "Okay, so they got it right then?" Jamie pursed his lips, looking back at the carpet again, "Sort of? There was another murder, actually the part they got wrong is that there were three more murders." Berta got a surprised wide eyed look on her face staring straight at Jamie, "THREE!? Well that's the first time the news has under-told a story! It's quite usually over blown." Jamie chuckled, "Yeah you could be right about that. I can tell you this stuff and you won't let it get out, right?" Berta gave him a big emphatic nod, "Yes, of course! You go ahead, I would like to know the real story." Just then a timer sounded in the kitchen. Berta started to get up, "Let me check on that, see if it's done. You go ahead, I can hear you just fine." Jamie leaned forward in his chair, putting his elbows on his knees.

"I'm just going to start from the beginning if that's okay with you." Berta looked over the counter at him from the kitchen, "That's the best place to start." Jamie felt like he was too far across the room so he got up and moved to the stool at the other side of the counter from the kitchen. "That it is. Yesterday morning, I had only been on shift for less than an hour, I heard the call from dispatch that some fishermen had found some bodies, the call was from out on River Road just down from Bridge Street. There were four of us that responded. There wasn't anything to see when we first got there, the fellas that called it in weren't there at the lot where all the fishermen park. There were a few trucks in the lot though so we figured they should be there somewhere. They came along shortly after we got to site and I started talking to them, trying to find out what they had seen.

Turns out, it was a bit of a hike down to where they had seen the bodies. One of the other deputies, Mike, likes to fish and had been to the area so after the guy described where it was Mike knew a better way to get down to the site. He led us to a trail that cut through a large stand of poplar trees into a clearing that was about a quarter mile into the trees. I don't think any of us thought that these guys really found dead bodies so we all went in there like we were on a Sunday hike, just tromping through the woods." Berta was getting plates out for dinner, so Jamie got up to help set the table. "Now we didn't disturb anything, we just walked in there single file and came into the clearing. There were 3 tents in there and a bunch of trash spread all over the place. Some shopping carts and whatnot. What got me though, was the sofa sitting in the middle of their camp, right in front of a fire pit. The fire was still smoldering, so it hadn't been all that long before we got there, heck there was still smoke in the air hanging in the clearing." Jamie got them both glasses of water and put them on the table, then they each served a plate in the kitchen before sitting down. Berta had stopped in the middle of fixing her potato, "There was a fire still burning when you got there? Was there anyone there?" Jamie was nodding, then shaking his head one right after the other. "Yeah, well, sort of, they were there." Berta continued fixing her food as Jamie was headed to the table. "Go ahead, you've got my attention." Jamie sat down and looked back at Berta, "Oh, it gets more interesting. From where we walked into the camp, we couldn't see where the fire pit was or see the sofa that well, so we split up a bit, 2 went around each side of the camp making our way a little slow, just not sure what we were going to find. I think Mike spotted

113

A SLEEPWALKER'S NIGHTMARE

it first and stopped, he caught my eye and gave me a head nod
to look over toward the sofa." Jamie paused for good effect, he
liked telling the story as much as Berta liked to hear it. "Well
go on! What was it?" Berta pushed him to continue. "There
were 3 guys sitting on the sofa, just sitting there straight up
facing the fire pit like they were just enjoying the view. All 3
of them were dead." Now Berta had an astonished look on her
face, "Oh goodness! Oh now the news just said a murder. It
was 3?!" Jamie nodded his head as he dug into the meatloaf.
"This is really good by the way. Yeah it was 3 all in the same
place." Berta was eating slowly, thinking about it. "Isn't that
something, what on earth is happening with these people?"
Jamie wasn't sure if that was a rhetorical question or not. "I'm
not a trained investigator, but it looks like the same guy is
doing it to all of them. They were all killed the same way."
Berta looked at him with a question on her face. "All of them,
meaning all 3 of those guys?" Jamie shook his head, "No, I
mean yes, all of them, but also the last few that have been killed.
The little red car and the one out at the lake, all the same."
Berta took another bite, and chewed it slowly. Jamie could
tell she was thinking it all through. "What are you thinking?"
Berta took a sip of water, "Tell me what it looked like. What
happened to them." Jamie was hungry, trying to tell the story
between bites of food. "Okay," Jamie paused thinking of how
best to formulate what he wanted to tell her, "We went over to
the bodies sitting on the sofa, we couldn't touch anything of
course, but from what I could see, all 3 of them were sitting on
their hands, I presume they were tied behind their backs. They
all had bags over their heads. Now the last few, those other
victims, had rags in their mouths too, I couldn't see through
the bags on them, but I would bet these guys had rags in their

mouths too. Again, I'm not the investigator but that all seems pretty easy to me." Berta was giving another big nod, "Yeah that seems pretty straight forward. Were you out there all day?" Jamie got up for a second helping, "Yeah, it took all day and I was just the clean up crew. I drew the short straw, and had to get first contact with the finders and secure the site while the investigation team was on route. Then I had to do standby all day, making sure no one entered the site that wasn't supposed to be there." Berta was just finishing her meal, she was thoroughly enjoying the story. "You got to talk to the people that found the bodies first? What was that like?" Jamie had slowed down on the second helping, he continued eating while telling the story, "They didn't know much, said that they spotted them from a distance and something didn't look right. They spotted them sitting on the sofa but the people weren't moving, and couldn't tell that they were dead from the distance they were at, until they had gotten closer. That just created a lot of paperwork for me, I have to write up their statements and turn it all in." Berta started clearing the dishes, "If it's the same person doing the killing, do you think he will do it again?" Jamie got up with his dishes and went to the kitchen as well to help clean up. "Yeah, it's looking highly likely, unless they catch up to him first. I'm not sure how they're going to do that, it all seems darn random to me right now." Berta looked a bit concerned to Jamie, "I wouldn't be too worried about your own safety, I mean, unless you're wandering around outside late at night. You're not, are you?" Jamie was smiling at her. "No, I've got nothing to do out that late." Jamie was washing dishes as Berta dried and put away. They had some dessert and talked more about recent events, as Jamie was getting ready to leave he had to reassure himself that it was okay to share this with Berta. "Now promise me, you won't go telling people about this stuff. I don't want any trouble if it gets back to the wrong people." Berta waved him off, "No, I won't let it out. My friends aren't interested in this stuff." Berta gave him a big hug, "You should come by again next week for dinner, this was nice." Jamie agreed and pulled the door closed on his way out.

After John spent all of Sunday in his apartment, wondering what had happened at the river and if he was to blame, he saw a story on the evening news that gave him barely more than he heard on the morning news. The news station nearly passed right over the story, all they said was that there was another murder, this time out at the river. They didn't say when it happened, they didn't say how it happened, just that there was an ongoing investigation. John was pacing the floor, limping back and forth, he was frustrated, and angry. *'How can they just skip over it?'* He was having a fit of anger, barely noticing the pain in his ankle, pacing this way and that, wearing a path into the carpet. It was only 4 steps, then a spin around and 4 steps back. He came to a point that he was holding his head in his hands, his face bright red, holding his breath when a thought came to him. *'The news stations were letting it go, they didn't care. They weren't even interested in covering the story anymore.'* As he considered this, he was talking himself out of the fact that he might actually be responsible for the murders, and even if he was, no one was interested anymore. Leaving him feeling free to do whatever he felt he needed to do, to take care of the rodents, without the need to look over his shoulder in fear that he would be caught. The weight was lifting, his mind cleared almost instantly with this realization. *'I'm fine, no one is even interested in what's happening to these rodents.'* His pacing slowed until he was just standing in the middle of the room with his hands on his face. He rubbed his face vigorously as if trying to wake himself from a hard sleep. He realized that his ankle was throbbing again, he limped his way to the kitchen for another ice pack before returning to the sofa, feeling reassured that he wasn't going to be caught up in the investigation of the rodent murders.

14

Monday

Jesse was driving home after work on Monday when he stopped at the GasNGo for fuel. He had gone into the mini mart and grabbed a fountain soda as well, then chatted with Clint for a few minutes in the parking lot. "Did you do anything good this weekend?" Clint was standing with his hands buried into his coat pockets trying to stay warm, having been outside all day. It had turned cold and rainy again. It was drizzly rain and a little windy, maybe 50 degrees, one of those dreary gray days in the Northwest. "No, I stayed home most of the weekend, I went grocery shopping but that's not classified as good or fun. How about you?" Jesse smiled standing there shuffling his feet around, he set his soda on top of one of the pumps. "No, I suppose not so much. Me and Katy went for a hike out on the river trail. There was a bunch of police activity out there this weekend. We saw where they had all their crime scene tape strung up all over the place." Clint had an interested expression on his face, "Another crime scene? Where was that at?" Jesse couldn't stand still. "It was just down river from the footbridge. Katy was all upset about seeing it, and wanted to know what happened out there. I think she's been worrying a lot about the murders that have happened lately." Clint bobbed his head back and forth, "Can't say that I blame her for worrying at least a little bit about it. It's kind of a big deal. That kind of crap doesn't happen out here." Jesse stopped moving for a moment, then went back to shuffling his feet back and forth, he was staring at the ground, then looked up at Clint. "Well, I suppose that's true. I told her she shouldn't worry about it, she's staying safe. Doesn't go out at night by herself and stuff like that. Besides, it seems to just be homeless people that are getting whacked." Clint gave him a sideways look, "Yeah, I hadn't really considered that it has been only homeless people, rodents as John calls them. That's a little strange, I guess. Still it doesn't mean that it won't be someone else next time. Unless he gets caught." Jesse stopped moving again and looked Clint in the eyes. "Unless he gets caught? I wonder if he'll get caught." Clint returned his stare, "I would suspect that he will at some point, there are some of those people out there that never do though." Jesse moved over and picked up his soda looking back at Clint with a smirk. "John calls them rodents? I guess that's kind of fitting." Clint shrugged. "It's kind of fitting, kind of rude but it's not completely wrong." Jesse nodded, "I'm going to head out, call me later this week, we should go do something." Clint gave him a wave, "Will do, talk to ya later." Jesse got in his truck and fired it up, he drove out of the lot onto the main road without so much as a look for oncoming traffic. He was just past Ted's Grocery when he went to grab his soda out of the cup holder and the lid popped off, the cup collapsed in his hand, spilling the fizzy, cold drink all over his leg and the seat of the truck. It surprised him and he dropped the rest of it into the passenger seat. Within a second he realized what he had done, he lunged over to grab the cup before it dumped completely out onto the seat. It was too late, when he lunged he pulled the steering wheel hard to the right making the truck veer off the road diving down into the ditch with a whoomph and a thump. His truck bounced through the ditch, crashing over the overgrown Scotch broom bushes and through the blackberry vines, he was headed directly for a pile of garbage and a shopping cart. Jesse was trying to get control of the truck, turning the wheel hard to the left while stomping on the brakes. He couldn't avoid the garbage pile smashing through it, sending debris flying every direction, then he hit the shopping cart at the right front of the truck, it flew through the air sending rubbish exploding everywhere, like shrapnel from a bomb. The cart was flying, tumbling, airborne, Jesse watched it happen in slow motion as it flew toward the tent owned by the caveman and cave woman couple that John had interacted with. Jesse was still trying to get the truck to stop or turn with no luck, the ground was wet and muddy. The tires wouldn't get traction on the greasy clay. He was headed straight for the tent. His eyes were huge, his heart racing out of control. The shopping cart crashed down on the tent pushing half of it to the ground then tumbled past it, landing in a heap of tangled metal against a Scotch broom bush. The truck was sliding in the direction of the tent that the shopping cart had just crashed into. Jesse was unable to make it turn. Skidding over the muddy ground like the tires were on ice, he was sure he was going right over the top of the soggy tent in front of him when he hit something very hard with the right front wheel. It made a terrible crunching sound, but the truck lurched to the left, just clipping one of the tent poles as he went past. The other half of the tent collapsed in a wet pile as Jesse regained control of the truck, smashing over more brush, narrowly missing another tent closer to the road, driving back in the direction of the roadway. Jesse glanced in the rear view mirror unable to see the tent, wondering if anyone was inside. He stepped on the gas, giving it enough to keep moving through the bushes and back up the ditch onto the road. Once Jesse had gotten onto the road, he stopped and sat dazed for a few moments to catch his breath. He looked back at the tracks he had left from his off-road excursion, he could see the tent in a pile, sopping wet and tangled in the poles that must have caught on the truck as he went by. There were 2 people trying to crawl out, working at getting through the twisted fabric and poles that were tied in knots. He stepped out of his truck to get a better look. The caveman and woman appeared to be unhurt, they were standing, and didn't seem to be tending to any injuries. They turned around and looked directly at Jesse, they started making familiar hand gestures, shouting something indiscernible. That was enough for Jesse, he hurried back into the truck and drove away before any other cars could come by the incident. When Jesse parked in the lot at his apartment, the first thing he checked was the damage to his truck. It was minor, a slight dent at the front right wheel well and a scratch on the wheel itself. A few dings in the front bumper and grill but there was already damage there from a different run in. There were bushes hanging from underneath and stuck to the bumper in several places. He pulled those loose and deposited them into the dumpsters. He would have to come back out and clean up the seats after changing his pants. Jesse was feeling quite proud of himself, no one saw what happened, except 'the rodents' as John called them. *'That shouldn't be a problem.'*

John noticed the tracks going through the campsite on his way home from work. They were on the same side of the road that he normally walked the white line on. He slowed his truck down to get a better look. He could see exactly where the vehicle had left the road, and the path that it followed. The tires had dug into the soil trying to get purchase to stop and steer away from the pending collision, plowing over bushes, leaving stumps and broken limbs behind. The tent that was damaged was still laying flat in a wet tangled mess, right next to the tire tracks. There was a shopping cart in a twisted heap just past the tent, and piles of trash that had exploded with the impact scattered everywhere, debris hung in the bushes and was strewn about the ground, soggy and weighed down by the rain. John couldn't take his eyes off the area, wondering what had caused someone to veer off the road, smashing through the rodent camp *'Or was it on purpose?'* If he wasn't careful, he would veer off the road too while he was gawking at the sight. He wondered to himself if it was him, he didn't really think so since there was no damage to his truck that he knew of.

Katy had to work a morning shift on Monday, she was anxious to talk to Berta again. It would have to wait until after 2 when her shift was done. She called ahead at her break, "Hi Berta, it's Katy, how are you this morning?" Berta was quiet on the phone but Katy could tell she was in a good mood. "Good morning Miss Katy, it's good to hear from you. I'm just doing lovely today. How are you?" Katy was standing in the back room of the restaurant trying to get some privacy, "I'm good, I just called to find out if you had talked with Jamie yesterday?" "I sure did," Berta sounded excited, "He was very talkative last night, and told me all about his day out at the river. It was very informative." Katy straightened up a little bit, "I can't wait to hear about it, do you mind if I come over this evening and we can chat about it? I can bring burgers." Berta cleared her throat, "Miss Katy, that would be wonderful, I haven't had a burger in ages. What do you think about 5 o'clock?" Katy was almost disappointed, she didn't want to wait that long. "That will be perfect, see you then." "Okay Hun." Berta broke the connection before Katy could say goodbye. Katy gave her phone a strange look as if it was the phone that broke the connection. She checked the time, *'Two more hours and I'm out of here for the day.'* At least that's what she thought at the time. When it came time to clock out, Katy had the opportunity to stay for another hour. One of the people on the next shift was running late so she covered it, thinking the extra tips would pay for the burgers she was getting for her and Berta, and the time would go faster. She called and let Jesse know she was staying late and then she was going over to Berta's for dinner with burgers. Jesse was feeling upbeat, "Bring me one too please, with fries and a chocolate shake." Katy couldn't refuse since she was skipping out on dinner with him. "Okay, I'll bring it to you before I go over there." There was a distinct pause on the line. "I could go with you. I would like to hear what she knows." Katy hmm'd, thinking about it. "Yeah okay, but I don't know if she will be as talkative with you there. We talk all the time and she has really opened up to me." Jesse hmm'd back at her, "Yeah, I suppose that's true but we have talked before, it's not like she doesn't know who I am." Jesse could hear the hesitation in Katy's voice. "I'm just saying you might not get all the information she has if you're there." Jesse harrumphed, "Okay, you go ahead, but you have to tell me everything." Katy giggled. "Yeah, okay, I'll be there soon." On her way home Katy stopped at The Burger Joint, to pick up burgers and fries. Milkshakes too, why not? The service was a little slow, it took 20 minutes to pick up the food, but it would be worth it. When Katy passed Ted's Grocery she noticed the tire tracks heading off into the ditch, and all the trash scattered through the bushes. She didn't see there was a tent laying in a heap next to the tire tracks, she didn't take her eyes off the road long enough. She was watching the road as the wipers flapped back and forth and the smell of the burgers and fries made her very hungry. She parked in front of the apartment and hurried up the stairs to drop off the food for Jesse, she was a little late getting to Berta's place. "Hey sweetie, here's your burger and fries. I'm a little late so I'm going to hustle down to Berta's, I don't want to keep her waiting." Jesse took the bag and gave her a kiss. "Thanks for getting me one too. Do you think you will be long?" Katy made a pursed lip face. "Maybe? I don't know for sure, it depends on how deep we get into it. Oh! Almost forgot to tell you, I have to do the late shift again this week. Starts tomorrow night. Will you drive me again?" Jesse got an annoyed look on his face and hung his head. "That's so tough, I don't think I can do that. I'm sure you can handle being safe on your own." Katy clasped her hands in front of her chest in a pleading motion. "Please? It's just till Friday." Jesse tilted his head still with the annoyed look. "So, the rest of the week. I can't do it, I'll fall asleep driving the lift." Katy stopped pleading, but looked a little pouty. "Okay, I understand that it's super difficult for you. I'll be careful. I hope this doesn't become a permanent thing, I knew I would have to work some late nights but 2 weeks back to back is a little rough." She picked up the other bags of food and turned to go. "I love you, I'll try to be back before you go to bed." Jesse was already opening his bag, getting the burger and fries out. "Okay, see you soon."

Katy hustled down the stairs balancing 2 shakes in a drink tray with the burger bags in the other hand. She was 15 minutes late when Berta came to the door. "Miss Katy, I thought you were going to skip out on me." Berta said it with a smile "Come on in, oh those smell wonderful don't they?" Katy came in and set the food on the counter between the kitchen and the living room. "It does smell good, it made me so hungry in the car, I'm ready to eat. I brought you a shake as well, hope you like chocolate." Berta's eyes got wide for a second. "Like it?! It's its own food group that must be consumed daily." Katy laughed heartily at that. They both opened their bags and prepared to get comfortable and enjoy the burgers. Katy took a seat at the counter and spread out her food. "Well, let's get to it. What did you and Jamie talk about?" Berta sat down next to her. "Oh goodness, there is a lot, Jamie was very talkative last night. There were a lot of details that really don't matter much. Like what he did standing around out there putting up the crime tape and talking to the people that found the bodies. He said he had to guard the scene the whole day so people that weren't supposed to be there didn't get in." Katy was munching fries and listening, "Wait! You said bodies. As in multiple bodies?" Berta was chewing, giving Katy a chance to think that through. "And he got to talk to the people that found them?" Berta tried to wash her burger down with a sip of the milkshake but instead caved her cheeks in trying to get it through the straw. "Yes," Berta spoke in a ghastly tone, "He said there were 3 people out there that had been murdered. He talked to the people,

I guess he had to take their statements, I think it was about how they found the bodies and if they had touched anything. Stuff like that." Katy was still munching fries, but also eating up every word Berta spoke, as if they were even better than the fries. "Wow, that has to be sort of weird to do. Did he see what happened to the people?" Berta gave up being anywhere near formal and started talking with her mouth full, as politely as she could. "He did. He said that he and 3 other policemen went out in the trees where the guys said to look and found the camp. He said that all those guys were sitting on a sofa, facing a lit fire pit, and all 3 of them were dead." Katy stopped eating to let that soak in, then sucked on the straw in the milkshake. "That's bizarre, all just sitting in front of a fire, but dead?" Berta nodded, "Yes, that's what he said he saw. He also said they had bags over their heads, and he thought their hands were tied behind them." Katy had an astonished expression, "Just like the one that happened in the car?" Berta was still enjoying her burger, Katy had hardly touched hers but the fries were gone. "It sure seems like it was the same thing." Katy started on her burger, contemplating the news. She was silent for a while. "I have to work the late shift this week, it makes me a little nervous to be out late because of this stuff." Berta had been watching Katy trying to read her expressions. "I asked Jamie if I should be worried. He didn't think I had anything to worry about, but that's also because I don't go out at night. Can you have Jesse pick you up from work?" Katy was shaking her head before Berta had even finished what she was saying, "I asked him to do that, but he did it for me last week and it's just too hard because he works the early shift." Berta thought about that for a moment. "That's too bad, I'm sure you will be okay as long as you aren't walking around in bad areas. Stay away from the homeless camps." Katy laughed, "I don't make it a habit of hanging out in homeless camps." Berta laughed too, "That's good, you shouldn't. I was trying to think if I could have Jamie escort you home, but he works the day shift too. I think he might do it if I asked him to though." Katy held up a hand as she finished a bite of burger, "That's awfully nice but please don't ask him. That would be too big of an imposition. Besides he works the day shift, he doesn't need to be getting up in the middle of the night to escort me home." Katy smiled big at the thought. "I almost brought Jesse with me tonight." Berta looked at her inquisitively, "Why didn't you? I like to have the company." Katy wadded up her burger wrapper and bag. "I like to talk to you by myself, it's kind of nice to have someone different to talk to without the person that you're with all the time." Berta put her hand on Katy's arm, "You know, you're right, it is nice to have someone you can talk to other than your significant other. I'm glad that we can get together, I enjoy it too." Katy grabbed up Berta's trash too and cleaned the counter. "Speaking of significant others, I am going to go home so I can see him for a little while before our shifts are offset and I don't see him for the rest of the week." Berta got up at the same time Katy did. "It was so nice to see you tonight, and thank you very much for the food, it was great." Katy gave her a big hug. "I'll try to come by one day this week before I go to work." Berta went to the door with her. "That sounds great, I'll see you then." As Katy was walking away Berta called behind her, "You be careful out there."

When Katy got back to the apartment, Jesse was just turning off the TV and getting ready to go to bed. "Hey, how did it go with Berta?" Katy went straight to him and gave him a big hug and a kiss. "It went okay, she told me all about what happened out there and it's really not good. There is someone out there killing those homeless people, and it's pretty brutal." Jesse pulled back to look at her face, "Yeah, that seems to be true. It shouldn't be super concerning to you though." Katy frowned at that, "That's what Jamie told Berta too, 'Don't go out at night and hang out with the homeless and you should be okay.' It still makes me somewhat nervous. What happens when it's not homeless people anymore? It could be someone else at any time." Jesse got a thoughtful look on his face and held Katy tight. "I think you're going to be just fine. Tell me what happened at the river." They moved into the living room and sat down as Katy recounted the story about Jamie talking to the people that found the bodies, then walking into the camp and finding the 3 people sitting on the sofa with bags on their heads in front of a lit fire pit. "I do find it interesting and intriguing but also scary at the same time." Jesse was hanging on every word of the story. "They were sitting in front of a lit fire? Wow, that's crazy." Katy gave him a sideways look at his excitement. "Yeah, that's pretty strange for sure. I don't know if that means anything." Jesse smirked a little, "I don't know that it means anything either, just kind of a weird thing to see at a murder scene I guess. I mean, was the fire there when they were killed? Or, did the killer take the time to light a fire in the pit before he left? And how big was the fire to last long enough that it was still burning when the bodies were found? There are just a lot of questions about that." Katy's body language softened. "Yeah, I hadn't thought about that, you're right, that is kind of interesting to think about." Jesse grabbed Katy's hand and pulled her toward the bedroom. "Come on, I need to get some sleep."

15

Tuesday

As John drove into the lot of his apartment, headed for his parking spot next to the dumpster he noticed some movement at the dumpster bin. The dumpster bins sit inside an enclosure so the bins aren't always visible. His first thought was it was just one of the neighbors tossing their bags in. It happens daily, it wouldn't be anything new. He pulled his truck into his spot and got out after a moment. It struck him as a little strange that whoever was next to the dumpster was still in there. *'What could be taking so long?'* He stood outside his truck for a moment listening, there was a lot of rummaging happening in there. John walked to the back of his truck, he wasn't sure what he was going to find as he peered into the bin area. There were two legs and a butt dangling from the edge of the dumpster wearing grungy dark gray pants, a gray and black backpack sitting on the ground beside it. John stopped to watch for a moment considering his options. "HEY! Get out of there!" Scruffy froze, then slowly popped his head up, bringing his balance toward his feet, his dirty, dark green jacket flopped over his matted hair, He looked over his shoulder still leaning into the bin and spotted the person yelling at him. John had stepped back not sure what Scruffy would do once he yelled at him. Scruffy lowered himself onto his feet, his jacket flopped back down at his waist and put a can into his bag. John took another step back, sounding not that sure of himself. "You can't be here digging through the trash. Please leave and don't come back to this neighborhood." Scruffy picked up his backpack and looked at John, "I'm just trying to scrape enough together to survive." He sounded as if he hadn't spoken a word in months, his voice was low and raspy, in desperate need of a drink of water. John just stared at Scruffy, holding his breath for a moment, deciding if he really wanted to have this conversation. "I don't know what brought you to this point in your life that digging through trash bins is what you do to survive, I just know that I don't want you doing it here." John turned to his truck and opened the door, leaning in as he reached into a grocery bag on the passenger floor. When he stood back up he held out a bottle of water to Scruffy. "Here take this, you sound like you could use a drink of water." Scruffy paused, not sure if he should accept. He slowly stepped forward and reached for the water with a grime coated hand, taking it from John. "Thank you, I do appreciate the generosity." John closed the door to the truck. "You're welcome, now please go." Scruffy started shuffling away, headed for the exit of the complex, he glanced back at John to see if he was watching. He was, and would watch until Scruffy was well down the street.

John grabbed the rest of the water bottles and his soda from the truck and took it with him up to his apartment. He dropped his keys on the table by the door and hung his jacket. He took the water and soda that had spent several days in his truck into the kitchen and put it away.

Tuesday evening John was feeling pretty good about the progress his ankle had made. He sat on his sofa testing his range of motion, it still hurt when he bent it to the extremes of its range and the purple of the bruising was giving way to an ugly yellow-green color. He was feeling like he was missing his morning walks to work, plus he had been spending more on fuel lately, even one tank on his budget was too much. He decided to walk to work on Wednesday, his ankle was feeling better and he was thinking he could make it just fine. The weather over the next few days was supposed to be overcast but dry, it would be nice walking weather. He changed his alarm so he would have plenty of time to walk even if he was a little slower than normal, which was already pretty slow.

16

Wednesday

Wednesday, as John walked to work, things were going well, he was feeling good, his ankle hurt a little bit at first, but not so bad once he got it warmed up. He was on the side of the road that Scruffy's camp was on. He noticed how messy it was as he approached, piles of garbage discarded everywhere, it looked worse than he remembered, spread out like a garbage dump yard sale, he clenched his teeth, his face turned red and started to rage in his mind, almost to the point of shutting down. He had to stop walking. He stood on the white line with his eyes pinched closed like a toddler throwing a tantrum. He hadn't felt this way in years, he had been getting worked up over the rodents, and the messes, it was taking too long to come up with a solution, his mind couldn't take it anymore. He stood there breathing deeply, eyes closed, letting cars whiz past. After a few minutes his mind started to clear, he opened his eyes and just looked down at the white line. He stood still for another minute trying desperately not to think of the mess to his right. Finally, he looked up, *'Look straight ahead, don't look over. Don't do it. Don't look over.'* He turned to the right, even though he kept telling himself, *'Don't look at it, don't look at it, it will go away if you don't look at it.'* He looked, it didn't go away. He blinked hard again, still didn't go away. Then he noticed Scruffy was standing outside his tent watching him. It startled him to find he was being watched. Not wanting to interact, John took a step, then another. He paused, looked back over his shoulder toward Scruffy, he wanted to ask him, *'Is this the way you want to live?'* He didn't. He looked back at the white line and started walking. *'I have to get to work.'*

John ate an early dinner that night, finishing around 6, he cleaned the kitchen and sat in his small living room to watch TV. By 7:30 he had fallen asleep on the sofa. He heard a door shut and jolted awake, the neighbors had slammed their front door and shook the apartment with it. He felt groggy and didn't want to get up, he shut off the TV and forced himself to go to the bedroom. He was half asleep walking into his room, he took his clothes off and threw them in the basket, then collapsed under the covers of his bed, feeling perfectly comfortable under the heavy blankets. He was asleep again in moments. It was close to 10:15 when John got up again, he had been in a fitful sleep, dreaming. He hadn't turned on the lights, he went to the bathroom to relieve himself, but when he came out of the bathroom he sat on the edge of the bed for a moment, looking around the dark room as if it were clear as day. Then, John abruptly stood up, seeming perfectly awake and aware of his surroundings, he went to the laundry basket, picked out the clothes he had been wearing that day and put them on. He went into the kitchen, got a glass full of water and drank half of it, set it on the counter and walked to the front door. John picked up his jacket but didn't put it on, he slipped on his shoes, grabbed his keys, then left the apartment. It was a very dark night, raining lightly, cold and cloudy in the mid 40s. John wasn't dressed warm enough for the temperatures but he wouldn't notice in his state of mind. Wearing his light gray sweatpants and a hoodie, he went to his truck, got in, and threw his jacket on the passenger seat. He slowly drove out of the lot, John was heading the direction of work, something in his dream had sparked this mission. He was going to do something about the mess at the rodent camp. There wasn't anywhere to park his truck that was close to the camp so he parked it partway into the ditch, right in front of Scruffy's tent, it was set 20 or so yards away from the next tent. He got out of his truck and walked into the bushes, looking at the mess all around him as if it were daylight and he could see with no problem, it was time to take care of it. His subconscious was just done with the mess, this was the only way he could cope with it. Somewhere in the back of his mind he had to take it upon himself to clean it up. John started picking up the trash around the area, going from one pile to the next until his arms were full, then taking it to the truck and dumping it in the back. He walked back into the brush and did it again, and again, silently, taking care not to get too close to any of the tents. Each trip he made he was getting wetter and wetter. Each trip he got dirtier and dirtier, but he had no idea. He was there for 2 hours, he only stopped because the back of the truck was full. John pulled some ropes from behind the seat of his truck and lashed down his load of trash, then got in and drove his truck back to his complex, parked in his normal spot and went back upstairs to his apartment. He stepped inside the door, soaking wet, dropped his keys on the table, kicked his shoes off by the door and went to his room.

He took his dirty clothes off and threw them in the basket. He was very cold as he pulled the blankets up around himself and continued to sleep the rest of the night.

Jesse had been thinking about the little off-road excursion wondering if the caveman and cave woman from the tent would be turning him into the police for almost running them over. He didn't need that kind of trouble, it was an accident but he didn't exactly stop to see if they were okay. *'They did get a good look at me. I wonder if they saw my plates.'* Jesse was driving home, getting close to the off road excursion zone, he slowed down considerably below the speed limit. He checked the rear view mirror for any coming traffic. Seeing it was clear he nearly came to a stop as he passed the tire tracks that he had left through the bushes. He could see down the path where the tent still lay in a heap, just past it there was a new tent, not 10 feet away from the old one. Sitting in a lawn chair that somehow missed being twisted into a tangled mess by Jesse's truck, was the caveman from the tent. The caveman looked right at Jesse and stood up. Jesse saw him stand, *'Oh shit! He recognized me!'* Jesse stepped on the gas hard, his truck roared to life and accelerated away in a cloud of blue smoke. *'Oh, that's not good, now he really knows what I look like. He can't turn me in, can he? He doesn't even have an address.'* Jesse talked himself into feeling secure that the caveman wouldn't be able to turn him in for being reckless. He went home to spend a few hours with Katy before she went to work for the night shift.

Katy had to go to work at about 5:30, Jesse let her know he was going to go over to Clint's place to have a few beers and hang out with him after she left. "Oh, you're going to see Clint, but you won't take me to work?" Jesse had a sheepish grin on his face. "I would take you, I just don't want to pick you up. Besides it's only for a couple of hours. I'll still be in bed early." Katy smiled back, "Yeah, I know, I'm just giving you a hard time." It turned out to be quite a bit longer than a couple of hours. Even though he would have to be at work at 5 AM he felt that he hadn't seen Clint in a while and he could tough through being tired for one day.

As he was heading home from Clint's, he saw John's truck on the side of the road, he didn't see John though. *'What the heck is he doing?'* Jesse slowed down and turned the truck around, he had to go back and see what John was doing. Jesse slowed as he approached John's truck, looking for anyone moving, there wasn't much light, just the ambient light from his truck's headlamps reflecting off the rain in the air. It was very hard to see with the low black clouds making it extra dark. Jesse spotted movement 10 or 15 yards off the road, just the top of someone moving could be seen over the bushes. Jesse stopped. He hadn't quite pulled up behind John's truck, he was sure it was John out there. He didn't want John to see him, so he pulled out into the lane and accelerated, driving down to Ted's Grocery parking lot then turned around again. *'What in the world is he up to?'* He cruised by slowly, then saw John carrying something towards his truck. When he got to the side he dumped whatever it was into the back of it and turned around and walked back into the bushes. Jesse was extremely curious now but also didn't want to be seen, he could see headlights in his rear view mirror. It would have to wait, *'I'm going to have to keep an eye on him.'* With that, Jesse picked up his speed and went home. He got there about 45 minutes before Katy would be off work. He was asleep before she got home.

17

Thursday

John woke up late Thursday morning, when his alarm sounded he turned it off and passed out again without knowing it. 20 minutes later he jumped in his sleep, waking himself up. He looked over at the clock on his side table, *'Oh man, I hate it when I do that.'* John struggled to sit up on the edge of the bed, the heavy weight of his body was too much for his muscles to lift. *'Why am I so tired? I feel like I ran a marathon.'* He picked himself up and went into the bathroom to get ready for work. After his shower, while getting clothes out of the closet he noticed his sweatpants and hoodie in the basket, dirty and wet from the night before. *'Oh, what now?'* John was almost disgusted at the sight, *'This is happening too much.'* He finished getting dressed, then walked to the living room, his shoes were by the door, wet and mud stained. John was so tired he could barely react, he picked up his hiking shoes and put those on instead, then stepped out the door to take a look at his truck. It was there, in the right spot. It was hard to tell what was in the back piled so that he could just make out a heap above the top of the cab, there was not enough light to see it very well. He shook his head and came back inside. *'I'll have to deal with it later.'* He finished getting ready for work and made lunch before he left. In the kitchen he found the half glass of water that he had left the night before, he gave it a strange look as if it had put itself there, then poured out the water and put the glass in the washer. As he was going out the door, he grabbed his keys and reached for his jacket. *'Where did that go?'* It wasn't hanging on the hook by the door as usual. He went back into his room and checked the closet and the laundry basket just to make sure. After not finding it, he grabbed another sweatshirt and then headed for the door. John was calm this morning and almost frustrated with himself, he had dreamy memories of walking through bushes and splashing through mud puddles but he wasn't sure if it was a made up memory after seeing that his truck was full of trash. *'Is this my new normal, is this what it is going to be like going forward? I won't know from one day to the next if I am going to go out in the middle of the night and do who knows what?'* He went down to the lot passing by his truck, looking closely at the load of trash in the back. *'Where did this all come from?'* Glancing at the passenger side of the truck, *'My jacket!'* He opened the passenger side and swapped the sweatshirt in his hand for the jacket. *'All this trash, I can't deal with this right now, it will have to wait.'* He glanced at his watch, *'I am so late already. I could drive but I don't want to be seen with all this trash, people will ask questions.'* He shrugged, then continued his walk to work.

When he was a little less than halfway to work, as John followed the white line he noticed his mind was clear, that felt good. On occasion he would look up from the line, when he did he noticed the area around Scruffy's tent, *'It looks better, it's not perfect, but much better.'* Just then he realized what he had done in the middle of the night. *'That's what I've been doing! Have I killed those rodents too? I don't know, how do I find out? Is Scruffy still alive?!'* He stopped right across from Scruffy's tent, staring at it. *'Should I go to his tent and see if he's there? Maybe throw a rock? No. I'll wait, I'll wait until this afternoon, I usually see him in the afternoon.'* John turned and continued to walk. Now his brain was working over this new discovery, *'Have I killed those other people?'* He wasn't entirely sure. *'Maybe my subconscious is having me go clean up sites after I killed the people too. It doesn't all add up, there are too many gaps for me to fill in the blanks.'*

John was nearly 30 minutes late, but no sign of Steve when he went into the break room. Clint popped his head in while John was getting coffee. "Hey good morning. I covered for you this morning. Steve was here but had to take off, I told him your ankle was acting up again and you were on your way." John turned and gave Clint a blank look, "Thank you, I swear if I'm late too many more times he's going to fire me." Clint laughed, "I don't think he's going to fire you, he just likes giving you shit about being late." John made a move toward the door as Clint backed out of the room. "I guess I can take that."

As John was walking home Thursday after a quick stop at Ted's Grocery, he walked past the cut off trail through the mud, *'Not taking that chance again.'* John looked down the path left by Jesse's truck, it had broken the bushes off and cleared an alley between the other bushes and vines so that he could see straight to where the soggy tent still lay on the ground, all twisted into knots. He was dismayed to see that there was a nice, new tent standing not 20 feet beyond where the old one lay, that Caveman and Cave Woman had set up as their new residence. John stopped and surveyed the scene, with garbage hanging from the bushes, like ornaments lining their driveway at Christmas. *'Is it too much to ask that you at least remove the mess of your other tent?'* John answered his own question with a frustrated hard blink and shudder. *'I have to do something about these rodents.'* He continued along the white line, then looked across the road at Scruffy's side. It looked much better, but was still an eyesore. *'I haven't seen Scruffy today.'* John stopped, thinking about this morning when he passed by. He didn't throw that rock to try and get his attention, it was much too early. *'Should I do it now? No, I don't know. Maybe.'* He couldn't decide. Mostly John just wanted to know if he had killed Scruffy, the man did make him angry. *'What if I did? Do I want to know that for sure?'* He slung his backpack off his shoulders and reached in, rummaged for a moment and produced a bottle of water. He zipped the pack and put it back on, waited for a car to pass and crossed the road. John picked his way carefully through the brush headed towards Scruffy's tent. He stopped 20 feet short of it. "Hey! Are you in there?" John waited, listening for a reply. "Hey! Anyone home?" He waited longer this time, staring at the tent. *'Either he isn't here or he's dead. I guess that doesn't really answer my curiosity.'* John looked up from the tent and glanced around through the bushes. He heard something but it wasn't coming from inside the tent, it was behind him. He turned around to see Scruffy picking his way through bushes coming from the road. John felt relief at that moment, then panicked. *'What do I do? Do I say anything? Why am I here?'* Scruffy was almost on him, John held out the water bottle. Scruffy stopped and looked John in the face. "Thank you." He took the bottle, and without saying anything John walked past him through the brush back toward the road. Scruffy turned to watch him walk away. "Why?" he called from behind. John turned around and looked at him. "I don't know, Just wanted to make sure I didn't kill you." Then he turned back around and continued on his way. Scruffy had a bewildered expression on his face, but didn't say another word.

When John got back to his complex he walked past his truck again, looking at the mess in the back. *'I wish I didn't do that, now I have to clean it up. Can't let anyone see me dumping it, even though it will be obvious where it came from since it was in my truck all day. I don't need people asking questions.'* It was still early and he was tired from the lack of good sleep the night before, so he went to his apartment and napped while he waited until it was dark out. John set an alarm for 9:00 then went down and emptied the trash into the dumpster next to his truck. It had started raining while he was dumping the trash but a thought occurred to him in the process. When he was done he drove out to the river where the last murder was, fully knowing he was doing it. He looked at the trail that led into the trees and the rodent camp clearing beyond, dark and menacing, yellow crime tape strung from tree to tree, drooping with the weight of the rain. He sat in his truck with the headlights shining down the path but they would only penetrate the darkness a short distance before the light was swallowed by the limbs hanging low over the trail. He sat there thinking about going in and cleaning the site. *'I'll come back, I need to clean this up.'* His touch of laziness kicked in and he backed the truck away from the trail, turned it around and went home.

Jesse arrived back at his apartment after work around 3:30 that afternoon, he had been thinking about seeing John the night before. He noticed that the area where John was parked at the side of the road was much cleaner than it had been. *'Is that what he did? He went and picked up trash?'* After Jesse parked his truck he walked over to building B where John's truck was parked. *'Sure enough, there it is, full of trash. What is he doing? I can't explain that.'* Jesse glanced around the lot to see if anyone was looking his way. It was all clear. He passed by the truck a little closer, looking in the windows, for what he didn't know. Mostly just to see what was in there. Nothing, a sweatshirt is all he could see. Then he looked closely at the pile of trash in the back, tied down so nothing would fly out when John drove down the road. Random household junk, *'Not even sure what John's so called rodents do with all this stuff.'* Jesse looked around again, no one there. He walked back to his apartment eager to talk with Katy about his discovery.

Jesse walked into the apartment and greeted Katy with a hug and a kiss as usual. "How are you?" Katy smiled at the attention, she loved that he would always make sure that he paid attention to her when he got home. "I'm great, just getting ready for work. Anything new for you today?" Jesse took his work boots off and sat down on the sofa. "Not at work, but I think there is something weird going on with that guy, John, that I told you about." Katy came over to sit on the sofa with him. "What do you think is going on?" Jesse leaned back and thought about how best to phrase what he wanted to tell her, considering he wasn't going to be out that late last night, it just turned out that way. "Last night when I was coming home from Clint's I saw him at the side of the road at one of those homeless camps." Katy's eyes got wide, and her mouth dropped open a little bit. "What was he doing?" Jesse shrugged a little and shook his head. "I don't know for sure, but right now his truck is full of garbage from that campsite." Katy reached out and grabbed Jesse's arm. "What!? Why!? Why would he do that in the middle of the night?" Jesse was shaking his head. "I haven't any idea. It all seems pretty weird to me." Katy pulled away, with a more stern expression. "What time was it?" Jesse turned red a little bit. "Well, it was after ten." Katy didn't seem to care too much that Jesse was out later than planned. "He was out at a homeless camp after 10 PM? That's craziness." Jesse leaned back on the sofa and looked at the ceiling for a moment. "It is crazy, I don't know what he was actually doing besides picking up trash, but it doesn't seem like something a normal person would do." Katy still had a serious look on her face. "Do you think he has been killing those homeless people?" Jesse didn't respond right away, "What? Did he go in there and clean their campsite before killing them?" Katy shrugged slowly. "I don't know for sure, but maybe it's some kind of cover up for whatever he's doing to those people. He goes in beforehand and gets rid of things that could somehow link back to him?" Now Jesse had a stern look on his face. "Maybe he is the one, maybe you have something there. Or maybe whoever is at that campsite is dead now?" Katy jolted back a little bit. "Should we call the police?" Jesse got a smile at that. "No, I don't think we have anything to tell them that they would take seriously." Katy slumped down as she sat and thought about that. "I guess you're probably right, but maybe we should keep an eye on him a little bit. Something still seems strange with that." Katy got up and walked toward their room. "I need to finish getting ready. Do you want to have some dinner with me before I go?" Jesse got up as well. "Yeah. I'll get something going while you finish." They ate in the next hour and Katy was off to work for the evening, leaving Jesse on the couch watching TV.

18

Friday

Thursday night at 11 PM, just off of Highway 18 at the site of a homeless camp, there was a horrific flash of flame and a 'Whoomph' sound as the flames jumped to life and sucked oxygen from the air. The flames traveled from the roadway, out into the darkness of the rodent camp illuminating the fog with a bright orange and yellow glow. After the initial whoosh of the flames coming to life there was only the fading sound of an engine speeding away, then the crackling of the bushes as they caught fire and burned. The flames followed a trail of gasoline from where a vehicle was parked and a match was thrown to the ground, through the gravel, between bushes and vines, traveling 20 yards off the road before engulfing a tent with Caveman and Cave Woman in it. The flames burned steady for 5 minutes before anyone saw the them. They grew higher and higher above the tent, reaching 20 feet above the ground as the flames melted and burned everything they touched. Finally, someone passed by on the highway, seeing the flames and made the 911 call to report a fire. It was 15 minutes before first responders arrived on the scene and most of the flames had died down as the fuel had burned off and the tent, along with everything and everyone in it was burnt to a crisp. Police were the first on the scene followed by firemen, then EMTs after they discovered there was a tent in the middle of the flaming mess. The area was surrounded by police tape, emergency vehicles and people investigating the cause and death of the homeless people. Firemen stayed for hours making sure the ground and surrounding bushes wouldn't burn any longer, then packed their things and left. The EMT's had to wait for the police to check the area and take photos of the bodies, charred and black, melted into the fabric of the tent. Then they wrapped them into black bags and took them away. The investigators stayed all night, combing the area, looking for clues, spotlights were set up all around the camp, they roused other homeless people to find out what they had seen. "Nothing," was the common answer. Scruffy was the first to give the police anything to go on. "I've seen that guy over there a lot, he walks through here every day." Scruffy pointed to John as he walked the white line past the scene. Daylight was finally starting to take over, the light all around was flat white, fog had been stuck to the ground all night. John was looking the other way across the road from Scruffy's tent where all the action was. He couldn't believe what he was seeing, the scorched ground all around where Caveman's tent used to be, with a pile of ashes in the middle. There were lumps of burnt debris that used to be their personal effects, scattered in a tight circle around the epicenter of the melted mess. The torched and melted arms of the tent poles bent and twisted, leading out to fried ends that made them look like used Fourth of July sparklers sticking out of the ground at the edges of the circle. Officer Mike Halloway followed Scruffy's point and looked at John walking past. "Has he ever interacted with you? Why would you point him out?" Scruffy bobbed back and forth not seeming stable on his feet. "Sure, we have run into each other a couple of times, he's given me some bottles of water." The officer took that as a good sign, thinking to himself *'That's not the type of person that's going to burn out a homeless camp.'* "Okay, we'll have a talk with him. Thank you for your time." Mike turned to walk away, trying to look over the tops of the overgrown bushes and vines. "Hey, Roak!" he shouted, spotting Jamie as he walked away from one of the other tents. Mike pointed toward John, "Catch up with him." Jamie looked in John's direction and increased his pace. "Excuse me! Excuse me, Sir! I need to talk with you." John looked at Officer Roak and recognized him as the same officer from in front of his apartment and the little red car. John stopped and looked around on that side of the road, he spotted Scruffy as Mike was walking away. *'Oh, I see what's happening, Scruffy pointed me out.'* Jamie stepped up onto the road where John was stopped, "I'm Officer Roak, that's Officer Halloway, just want to ask you a couple questions." Jamie waited for Mike to get closer. John was looking back and forth between them then asked. "What happened out here?" Halloway pointed across the street. "There was an incident last night, we are just asking around to see if anyone has spotted anything unusual in the area. One of the residents here pointed you out, he said that he sees you every day." John looked past Halloway at Scruffy still standing by his tent watching the proceedings. "Yeah, I walk this way to work every day. I recognized some of the rodents, uh, residents." Halloway was checking John out, looking him up and down, trying to measure his body language. "Have you seen anything unusual out here lately?" John couldn't hold his attention on Halloway, he was looking across the street. "A new tent popped up a while back, I never saw anyone come or go from it. It just showed up with a pile of trash and a bicycle on top of it one day." Halloway followed John's gaze across the street. "Which one is that?" John pointed to the left of the burnt tent. "It's that one across from the burnt one by those tire tracks. The one closest to the road. Oh, that's something else. Those tire tracks happened a couple days ago. I didn't see it happen but they showed up and looked like the Caveman's tent was hit when whatever it was went through there." Halloway and Roak were both looking where John was pointing but looked back at him when he said Caveman. "Who's Caveman?" John looked down at the white line. "Sorry, that's just what I called him, he looked like a caveman. He lived in that tent, the one that's burned." Roak looked between John and the burnt tent. "Okay, you didn't see who drove through here?" John shook his head, "No, I just saw the tracks show up one day, I noticed them on my way home from work. Was Caveman in the tent?" Halloway turned around, seeming to check who was within earshot. "Yes, we believe so, there were two bodies." John stiffened at the news. "Cave Woman too, they were always together." Halloway was still checking John out closely. "You've seen the two of them together? Have you had interactions with them?" John noticed that Halloway was looking for reactions. "Yeah, I think they were a couple, just my assumption though. I spoke to them once when I was walking past, but nothing more then that. I really should be going, I'm late for work now." Halloway shifted and took out his notepad, "What's your name?" John was still looking at the white line, "John Dell." Halloway wrote it down, "Where do you work?" John looked down the road toward the GasNGo. "I work over there at the GasNGo station." Roak followed where John was looking, as did Halloway. "Oh sure, I thought you looked familiar. I'll bet I've seen you there." John nodded, "Pretty likely, can I go now?" Roak stepped back out of John's way. "Yes you can, we might be in touch." John stepped between them and continued walking down the white line. *'That was interesting. I really hope I didn't have anything to do with that.'*

John was 20 minutes late getting to work, Steve met him at the break room door. "John! This can't happen so often!" John pointed back at the activity down the road. "They stopped me, they were asking all kinds of questions." Steve looked down the road. "Yeah I saw that down there, why were they asking you questions?" John stepped into the break room to clock in before having the rest of this conversation. "I guess because I walk down that road every day and one of the rodents pointed me out to them." Steve smirked, "One of the rodents. Yeah okay, that makes sense." John didn't wait around for the conversation to go any deeper, after he clocked in he stepped past Steve and went back out to the pumps to help Clint catch up. Clint was busy filling a pickup. "Hey buddy, how are you this morning?" John gave him a look as he approached a car that was waiting. "I'm doing okay besides being late again." Clint laughed at him, "Did Steve give you crap again?" John nodded as he stuffed the fuel nozzle into the tank of a Subaru. "Without fail, at least he's consistent." Clint smiled even bigger as he went to help someone on the other side of the pump John was at. "What's happening down there?" Clint gave a head nod toward the police activity, it was about ½ mile away but still visible with all the flashing lights through the fog." John looked over at Clint and shook his head. "Someone had a barbecue. Toasted their tent." Clint had a surprised look on his face. "Oh shit! Really? Were they in it?" John hung up the nozzle he was working with. "Yeah they were." Clint gave a big shiver. "Damn, that's dark."+

Katy got out of work just after 12 AM Friday morning, she had the line cook walk her out to her car. He stayed at the door until she pulled out of the parking lot, he wanted to know that she at least made it out of the lot safely. Katy was tired, the week of working the swing shift had caught up to her. She was relieved that it was her last night on the late shift, at least until the new schedules came out on Sunday. Driving home was a slow process, there was a very heavy fog covering the area and sitting in the warm car, finally off her feet, Katy was getting sleepy. She was taking extra precautions due to both. When Katy passed the GasNGo station on Highway 18 she started seeing some flashing lights ahead. At first it looked like just a police car or 2. As she got closer, the scene became more vivid, she could see there were also fire trucks and an ambulance and 3 more police cars, all with their lights flashing, reflecting through the fog as if all the lights were underwater and muted by the silt that floats by in the current. A police man was directing traffic, the trucks were blocking the road, there was no shoulder for them to pull out on. She slowed down to wait for direction to pass through. Now she was wide awake, her attention focused on what was happening. She couldn't see past the trucks and police cars, they were doing a good job blocking the area. There was a strange smell in the air, she couldn't place it, something burnt, but it didn't smell like just wood. It was an acrid smell, fabric and rubber or plastic, something else she couldn't place. She got the wave to go through by the officer, she pulled into the oncoming lane and moved slowly through. At the other side she was free to go, but very curious as to what had happened. There were no clues that she could see as she passed, only people walking in and out between the vehicles, doing whatever their jobs were at the scene. She picked up speed but only a little, the fog was so dense her headlights could barely shine a few yards in front of the car. Katy made it home safely. The police activity was intriguing and she wanted to talk with Jesse about it but he was asleep when she got into the apartment. It would have to wait until Friday evening, Jesse would be leaving for work soon and be gone until that afternoon.

Jesse was up before 4 AM, he left the apartment at 4:15. There were still 6 or more police vehicles at the fire site, he had to wait to be waived through. The fire trucks had left but the ambulance was still mostly on the road. He tried to look into the scene as much as he could as he drove past, flood lights had been set up and there were police combing over the entire area. It was as foggy at 4:30 as it had been just after midnight. The heavy layer of fog covering everything gave the scene an eerie graveyard feel. Once past the site, Jesse accelerated away toward work, he was not one to be late. His day was just another day, driving in and out of trucks, off and on the train platform, moving precious cargo from one place to another so that people would get their shipments on time. All in all nothing special to report, he returned home just after 3:30 PM.

Katy did some grocery shopping and cleaned the apartment while Jesse was at work. She was still tired from the late shift but didn't have to work again until Sunday. She was anxious for Jesse to get home so they could talk about the firetrucks she saw on her way home in the early morning hours. They were gone by the time she went to the store, ther were just a couple of investigation vehicles left at the site as she passed. She saw a burned area in the bushes, some crime scene tape strung up around the area, hanging from the thin limbs of bushes, but she still didn't really know what had happened.

Katy had just turned off the TV when Jesse walked in, she jumped up to greet him. "Hi! I'm so glad you're home, I've missed you." She wrapped her arms around him and gave him a tight squeeze of a hug, then kissed him. "How was your day?" After their embrace Jesse took his work boots off and hung his jacket in the closet. "It was okay, just the same stuff really. Moving big boxes of stuff all day." Katy smiled at him. "You made it home safe and now your weekend begins." That made Jesse feel a bit better, "It's always nice when you get to the weekend." Katy turned to go into the kitchen, "Can I get you something to eat?" Jesse followed her, getting himself a glass of water. "That sounds good, just something lite I think. Hey, Did you see all the police cars when you came home last night?" Katy's eyes got wide. "I did! I was going to ask you about them. Could you tell what was happening when you went through? It was too closed off for me to tell." Jesse sat down at the kitchen table. "All I could see was the big lights they had set up and that there were a bunch of people out in the bushes looking around at stuff. Not sure what they were all doing." Katy slumped a little at the shoulders, looking at Jesse. "Awe, I was hoping you saw more than I did. There was a big burnt out area when I went by today going to Ted's, and there were still a few people out there looking around at stuff. Only 2 unmarked cars on the side of the road."

152

John and Clint watched the movement at the crime scene off and on all day, they saw police and investigation vehicles come and go. By late afternoon there were only a couple of unmarked vehicles left at the side of the road. The fog had lifted by mid morning, giving way to a partly cloudy day, John was enjoying his walk home in better temperatures. Following the white line past the rodent camps, crime scene tape surrounding the burnt tent, John stopped to take it in. Charred bushes mixed with whatever trash or clothing was strewn about the area, some blackened items hanging from limbs, presumably from the vehicle hitting rubbish and sending it flying every which way. The blackened area where the tent once was, thoroughly combed through for evidence of whatever other crimes had taken place. John could only imagine what else happened before the fire broke out. *'I wonder if someone killed them before burning them, like out at the lake. Do I have it in me to do this? I don't feel bad that they're gone but I just don't know if I could do that to them.'* He still had doubts about his involvement in the recent killing spree. John noticed one of the investigators looking up from what he was doing, watching John as he stood there contemplating the scene. He took that as his cue to move on, he turned and walked toward home on the white line. He looked past the burnt area, there were still several other tent camps with piles of trash strewn here and there. *'Too bad it wasn't all of them.'* His contempt for the mess hadn't gone away, he felt no sympathy for the rodents and the recent attacks on them. 40 minutes later he was walking into the apartment complex feeling tired and hungry. *'It's time to relax for a while, what a weird day.'* John made himself dinner early, real food, not out of a box for a change, then watched a movie until about 8 PM when he went to bed.

19

Saturday

John didn't stay in bed, he was up at midnight getting dressed for a night out cleaning up after the rodents. His subconscious was still working on the rodent problem and the extreme messes they make, he couldn't let it go until there was a solution. He put on the jeans he had worn Friday as well as a sweatshirt and his hiking boots, then left the apartment. His subconscious recognized that his truck was low on fuel. He stopped at the GasNGo on his way into town. The night crew let him fill his own tank since he worked there. Had they interacted with him more than just a wave of acknowledgment, they may have figured out that John was sleeping. When he left the GasNGo John drove straight through town on Bridge Street, once across the bridge he turned down River Road and into the gravel lot he had looked at a few nights before. He idled his truck across the lot, gravel crunching beneath the tires, he slowly backed in, close to the dark tunnel that led through the trees, giving himself enough room to squeeze behind the truck so he could walk down the trail. There was very little light to be used, the moon was waning at less than half and the skies were partly cloudy. At times the light from the moon showed through the trees, faintly casting ghostly shadows across the path as John walked into the clearing and gathered trash, then walked it back to his truck and dumped it in the back. The trail was muddy and slippery from the last several days of rain, John sloshed through puddles, slipping and tripping on roots and rocks, not really watching where he was walking. He trudged back and forth for over 3 hours, picking up all manner of debris left from the now deceased rodent campers. When he couldn't fit any more into the back of his truck, he tied it down with rope that he kept behind the seat. He made a surprising dent in the amount of trash that was left in the clearing but there was still plenty more to gather. John was muddy up to his calves, his sweatshirt was dirty with soot and mud from from wrapping his arms around the trash, hugging it to his chest. He pulled his keys from his pocket and fell into the seat of the truck, his body was exhausted even though he was in a zombie-like sleep. He drove away from the trail, flipping his headlights on, heading back to his apartment. When he arrived, he pulled into his parking spot and shut off the engine, he went to open the dumpster as soon as he got out of his truck. It was full, it hadn't been emptied since he filled it from the last outing. John turned around and looked at the size of the load he had in his truck, then looked across the parking lot at the other buildings. He spotted the bin area at another building then got back in his truck and moved over to the dumpsters at building C, he backed the truck right in front of the bins and got out. He lifted the lid to see if there was room for his load of trash. Satisfied with what he could see in the dark he thought it should fit. He flipped the lid open and it banged down on the back of the bin, making a very loud hollow banging sound.

Jesse Kohl was sleeping lightly at 4 AM since that's the time he usually gets up, his body said it was time to be awake. John went about untying the load and moving it to the trash bin. Jesse's body jolted with the sound of the trash bin lid slamming open. He laid there for a few moments as it registered in his brain what the sound was, then slipped out of bed, careful not to wake Katy, and looked out the window. Jesse could see John's truck in front of the dumpster and John moving back and forth from the truck to the bin. He stood and watched for a few moments as his head cleared away the sleep. *'What is he doing? This guy is hiding something.'* Jesse made the quick decision to go out and find out what was going on. He slipped on some sweatpants, a jacket, and shoes, then quietly tiptoed out the door. He moved quickly down the steps and across the lot toward John's truck. Jesse was watching John to see if he spotted him before he got there. John didn't see him coming. Jesse didn't want to startle him, he spoke in a loud whisper, "Hey John, what's going on out here?" John barely looked toward Jesse, then just kept moving toward the bin with an armload of trash. Jesse tried again. "Hey John, you need some help?" He was hoping he could at least get a response. Again, John glanced his way as he was gathering more junk from the truck. This time he said something, but it was gibberish. It didn't make any sense to Jesse. "What was that? Are you okay?" Now Jesse was actually a little concerned. "Dumping stuff... rodent...mess, mess, stuff burnt." He was saying words but very mumbled and hard to understand. Jesse started looking at John closely, he wasn't sure what to do, he wasn't sure what was happening. He stood there watching John move back and forth, he could hear him mumbling quietly but he couldn't make out what he was saying. Jesse moved toward the truck and looked closer at what was in it. Just trash, some of it burnt, most of it not. He knew it had come from one of the homeless camps, especially after seeing John at the side of the road. *'He's in some kind of trance or something, he isn't all there.'* Jesse backed away, keeping an eye on John until he reached the stairs. He went back to his apartment, quietly went inside and got back in bed after taking his jacket and sweatpants off. He laid there thinking about what he had seen until he heard John's truck start up and drive away, then he went back to sleep.

John parked his truck back in his spot by building B and went up to his apartment on the third floor. He kicked off his shoes at the door and dropped his pants on the floor. He threw his sweatshirt in the basket in the closet and laid down on the bed. His alarm would sound in an hour.

Katy woke up after 8 Saturday morning. Jesse was already up, he had the coffee made and was watching the morning news. There was a replay of Friday morning's homeless camp fire, but they didn't give too many details. 'Two people had died' and 'Under investigation' was all the information they would give. Katy came over and gave him a kiss. "Good morning, did you sleep well?" Jesse got up to get a refill of his coffee. "Yeah pretty good. Can I get you some coffee?" They both went into the kitchen, Katy sat down at the table. "Yes please." Jesse went to get another mug. "I was woken up at 4 this morning, it was weird." Katy's eyes lit up. "What woke you?" Jesse poured coffee with creamer and handed it to Katy then sat across from her. "I was sleeping a little light, and I heard a loud bang outside. I laid there a little bit but I got curious so

I got up to look out the window. It was John, that neighbor I told you about, the guy that picked up the trash off the edge of the road the other night." Katy had a confused look on her face. "At 4 in the morning? What was he doing?" Jesse was trying to sip his coffee but it was too hot. "He had a truck full of trash that he was dumping in the bin." Katy, feeling perturbed, "What? I mean the picking up trash is a little weird for sure and why this one at 4 AM? Why not the one by his apartment?" Jesse raised his eyebrows. "That's not even the weird part." Katy tilted her head. "It gets more weird?" "It does! He was moving back and forth, taking stuff out of his truck and putting it in the dumpster, so I went down there." Katy interrupted. "You went outside!?" Jesse was nodding, "Yeah, I wanted to find out what he was doing. So I went down there and tried to ask him what was going on, but he was...I don't know... Not there. He couldn't answer me, he was just mumbling and I couldn't make out what he was saying." Katy was trying to understand what Jesse was saying. "I don't get it, he was what? A zombie?" Jesse finally got a good sip of coffee, then bobbed his head side to side. "Sort of like a zombie, I guess. I've never seen anything like it. It was like he didn't register that I was there. I tried to talk to him a few times, but he never responded." Katy was amazed at what she was hearing, "Wow! That's super strange. So let me get this straight. He is out there in the middle of the night, picking up trash or whatever, but he's under some kind of spell or in a trance or something?" Jesse rolled his eyes a little, "That seems a little over dramatic, but yeah it seems like it. I wonder if that's what happened the other night when I saw him." Katy was sipping coffee and got a far off look in her eyes. A few minutes went by before she said anything, "What if that's not all he's doing?

What if he's responsible for the murders happening out there?" Jesse started nodding slowly, thinking about the possibilities, then recited his take on what's happening, "Yeah, he could be. He's a zombie and takes out the homeless population in the middle of the night." Jesse had a wide grin on his face as he was telling his rendition of John's outings, completely making fun of the whole scenario. "Then on his off nights he goes out and picks up their trash after they're gone?" Katy was still staring off into nothing but listening to Jesse's hypothesis. "Sounds a little fishy but I guess it could happen." She smiled and laughed at the absurdity of what they were talking about, "I don't know, it's all too weird." She laughed again, Jesse started laughing too, then got up from the table. "I'm hungry, would you like breakfast?" Katy leaned back in her chair as if thinking it over, "Are you cooking? If you are, then yes." Jesse laughed. "Okay, you asked for it. It might be terrible unless you just want toast, but I'll give it a shot." Jesse made breakfast for the 2 of them, as he did, Katy asked about the news story. "I saw you were watching the news this morning, was there anything new about the... I don't know what to call it. The site of the fire?" Jesse smirked, "They said 2 people died, but they didn't give any details. You know, 'ongoing investigation' they couldn't let out their secrets." Katy turned in her seat a little and had a scrunched look on her face. "2 people dying is news to me. Wow! I wonder what happened, with the fire and all, maybe they were trying to stay warm and things got out of control." Jesse nodded his agreement, "That sure could be, I can't imagine living in a tent in this area."

John's alarm went off an hour after he'd laid down. He rustled in bed some but didn't reach for it, trying to block it out. Finally reaching toward the nightstand, fumbling for the switch. *'This can't be real, I feel awful.'* Everything felt heavy, arms, legs, even his face. *'Why do I feel so bad?'* He forced an eye open and looked at the time. 5:05 AM. He pulled the covers to the side and tried to swing his legs over the edge of the bed but they didn't want to move, they were too heavy and he couldn't seem to force his will over them. *'I feel like my body was pulled through a knot hole.'* He put both hands on his face to try and rub his face awake. *'What the heck?'* His hands were rough and scratchy, he rubbed them together, it sounded like sandpaper. He reached over and turned on the bedside light then looked at his hands. They were caked with dirt and grime, stained black in places from the soot of burnt materials he had loaded into his truck. *'Oh no!'* He sat up forgetting how heavy his body just felt, swinging his legs over the edge of the bed. He went to the closet looking into the laundry basket at his sweatshirt. It wasn't wet but it was filthy, then he went out to the living room. At the front door his muddy pants were there in a heap and his hiking boots caked with mud sat next to them. *'Oh my gosh, what a mess. What have I done?'* John's heart had picked up the pace, he wasn't feeling the weight of his tiredness, now it was adrenaline. *'I hope I didn't do anything bad.'* He wanted to go check his truck but he didn't have any pants on. *'I'll just shower and get ready, there's nothing I can do about this right now.'* He picked up his muddy pants and threw them in the basket on his way to get ready for work. After his shower and getting dressed, John put some lunch together and dropped it into his backpack with a few water bottles. He had to put on his sneakers that were dirty, his hiking boots were worse, and put on an extra sweatshirt because his jacket was a mess. It was just getting light out when he got down to his truck, John was surprised that there wasn't anything in it. *'Why were my clothes so dirty? There's no trash. What else could I have done?'* He walked past his truck on the way out of the lot, wondering if he had done something more sinister than pick up trash in the middle of the night. He stood there for a moment to consider what he might have done. *'I don't have any dream like memories of it, hmm. Maybe one, I feel like it was at another dumpster.'* In John's faint memory he could see himself moving from his truck to the dumpster bin but it wasn't the one in front of his apartment. John looked across the parking lot, he could see the dumpster bin at building C. *'In that one?'* He detoured across the lot on his way to work to check the bin, as he got closer he could see that the lid wasn't closed all the way, the bin was over full. *'That's where it is, at least I did it last night instead of waiting. I hope no one saw me over here.'*

It was another cool fall morning, no rain, just some high clouds. John was plenty warm with just a sweatshirt and his backpack. The walk to work was easy considering the lack of rest he had. John had no idea how late he was out the night before, just that it was extremely hard to get out of bed in the morning. He spotted Scruffy standing outside of his tent as he neared the rodent camps, Scruffy gave him a head nod, he acted as though he didn't see it. Looking at the white line, seeing the toes of his dirty shoes with each step. John glanced over at Scruffy a couple of times before he passed him just to see if he was being watched. Scruffy had gone about his own morning routine, getting ready to dumpster dive at the nearby stores. John looked across the road at the crime scene, yellow tape still strung between bushes, it almost looked worse than before the fire. There were still 4 other tents that he could see from the road that had piles of trash pushed into the bushes next to them. *'They need to light a fire in the middle of all the tents and burn all that trash.'* John thought that would help, *'It would be easier than picking it all up.'* A few minutes later John was punching his time clock to start the day of filling fuel tanks and mind numbing conversations that meant nothing to him. *'At least Clint is working today, he's not so bad.'* John got a cup of coffee and went right to work checking the pump readings, he was on time. *'No drama from Steve, win win.'*

Berta was in the middle of making pork chops and cheesy potatoes with apple sauce on the side when Jamie knocked on the door. She hustled to answer, "Hello handsome, come on inside." She gave him a big hug. "How are you doing this fine evening?" Jamie stepped in and shut the door behind him, took his coat off and laid it over the back of a chair. "I'm doing well, it was a beautiful day today and I didn't have to work. That always feels pretty good." Berta went back into the kitchen to tend to the cooking. "Oh, that is a good feeling, I can remember when I had to work every day, I always really looked forward to the weekends. Having those days off to just do whatever I wanted always felt so good." Jamie sat at the counter to watch Berta in the kitchen and chat from there. "Work has been crazy lately, I can't believe all the weird stuff that's been happening." Berta looked at him with a raised brow, "Is that right? Something else has happened since last week already?" Jamie dropped his head low, acting exhausted. "Yeah just yesterday, well it was actually early morning Friday. I wasn't on shift yet when it happened, I got called in early to go help out. More crime scene protection, I don't get to do the investigating, but my goodness it was pretty gnarly." Berta was stirring potatoes looking sideways across the kitchen at

Jamie, "You want something to drink, while I finish this up? I bought some beer last time I was at the store." Jamie looked up and over at the fridge as if he could see through it. "You know, that sounds pretty good, I'll have one of those." Berta stopped stirring and went to the fridge to retrieve the beer, she set it on the counter in front of him with a bottle opener. Jamie had a fake impressed look on his face making fun of Berta's beer choice, "Wow, look at you getting the fancy beer. No twist off tops around here." Berta dried her hands off on a towel before going back to stirring. "Nothing but the best for you. Now what were you saying about Friday morning?" Jamie adjusted himself to be more comfortable on the stool and took a swig of beer. "Something happened around midnight Thursday, rolling into Friday morning. I got called about 2 AM to come help secure the scene and direct traffic around it. I had to set up lights and crime scene tape. Just the basic stuff like I told you last time. I did a couple interviews again in the morning. You know, trying to talk to some of those homeless people can be tricky. Their minds aren't all together most of the time and you just don't know if what they are saying is real or not." Jamie paused to take a drink. Berta had covered the potatoes and put them in the oven. "No, I suppose there is a reason those people are out there on the streets. They lost their minds someplace along the way and that's a tough thing to get back." Jamie set his beer down and folded his hands across one another. "Well you're right about that. Some of them seem pretty 'with it', and some not so much. Anyway when I got to the scene there were a couple firetrucks and a few other cruisers, there were already some of the investigation units on site. You could smell something burnt in the air. It was a harsh smell, it stung in your lungs for a while. I didn't know what I was smelling, I couldn't put a finger on it for a minute. Then it occurred to me, I had smelled that before. It was out at the lake when that guy had been killed out there and the tent was set on fire and it burned up all around him. It was the same smell. It felt stronger this time, I feel like it's burned into my nose." Jamie paused to scratch his nose and take a drink, talking about it made his nose itch. Berta was leaning on the counter listening, "Do you suppose it's the same person doing it?" Jamie raised a hand up, "Absolutely, yes I do! I can't say what the investigators think, but I don't see how it can't be the same guy. Also I am sure it was the same guy we talked about last week out at the river. These people had their hands tied behind their backs, deader than dead. This time the guy burnt the tent they were in like the other guy at the lake, instead of posing them on a couch. I got a look at these 2 before they bagged them up. They had rags stuffed in their mouths, the rest of them was so burnt up you couldn't know if they had bags over their heads before it happened or not. Just gruesome." Jamie sat for a moment, his eyes went blank, he was seeing the sight in his mind and not seeing what was in front of him. He snapped out of it and took another drink. "There doesn't seem to be a whole lot to go on as far as catching the person doing it." Berta had turned around and pulled the potatoes and chops out of the oven. "Looks like this is ready, if you're ready to eat." Jamie stood up and moved around the counter to help set the table. "I am ready, It smells wonderful." Berta set everything out on the counter to serve. "Does it bother you to see those things?" Jamie paused for a moment to consider it, "Not really, what's done is done. I'm sympathetic to the people but the reality is, I can't help them by the time I get there." Berta let Jamie serve first, standing to the side. "Well

I suppose that's a good attitude to have in your line of work. You said they had their hands tied behind them, but they were all burnt up. How did you know they were tied up?" Jamie moved over to let Berta serve her plate. "Their hands were tied, but they were laying on them so when the coroners moved the bodies we could see that their hands were bound." Berta heard him say it but didn't react at all, just served some food and went to the table. "Do you think it's just one person? How does one person kill and tie up two people, especially if they're in the same tent?" Jamie had sat down across from Berta and was already eating. "You know, I've been working on that one in my head. I haven't figured it out yet. Even though one of them this time was a woman, I don't know how someone could take them by surprise and overpower both of them, get them tied up, bound and gagged, pull a bag over their heads without help. I just don't see it. There has to be a part I'm missing." Berta was eating slowly, she was very interested in this part as well. "That is interesting, it seems nearly impossible, the struggle with one person alone would be a lot, I would think. Do you think that they may have known the person? So they didn't feel threatened?" Jamie was savoring the pork chops and thinking about Berta's theory. "That is a good thought for sure. That would allow the person to get close to them without being alarmed. Then at the right moment take advantage of a separation or something between the two people. Maybe if I get a chance to talk to one of the investigators I will run that by him and see what he thinks." Berta nodded her head as she was eating, "That would be good." The two of them enjoyed their dinner, talking about crimes, Berta relating it to things she had seen on TV, and Jamie telling her how some of that wasn't exactly the way it worked in real life. They talked about

Jamie's future, if he would ever want to be a detective. "Maybe someday, I like the idea, it takes a lot of school though and I'm not sure I want to go back to school." Berta brought out apple pie and ice cream for dessert before Jamie went home. He left about 9 o'clock, it was one of his longer visits with Berta. He had been enjoying coming over more frequently, especially for dinner. It seemed as though this would be a standing get together, at least for the near future.

20

Sunday

Sunday morning John had slept in trying to recover from the late nights he had endured. His body was tired, it wanted to give up most days, but he pushed through making it to work mostly on time. John rolled out of bed just in time to catch the Sunday morning news. He had gotten into the habit of watching with breakfast. He turned it on and went to the kitchen to make coffee and French toast while listening for news of last week's local happenings. The coffee smelled wonderful, just the fragrance of the fresh ground beans filled the kitchen and made him anxious for that first sip. He was whipping the eggs in a bowl when the news he was wondering about came on the TV. He went in to see the story, bowl in one hand, whisk dabbed in eggs in the other. "Investigators are still trying to piece together what exactly happened early Friday morning at a homeless camp off Highway 18. Two homeless people perished in a tent that caught fire. It is unclear whether the fire was set intentionally." John stood watching, hoping there would be more to the story. That was it, they moved on to other things he didn't really care about. *'Gripping. Thanks for nothing.'* He went back to whisking ,sauntering back into the kitchen to finish breakfast. *'Judging from the news story, they don't know what is happening any more than I do, but maybe the police are playing it close to the vest. Was that possible? Were they capable of keeping things secret even from the media? Then again, maybe this is old news, it isn't exciting to the media outlets, just like the last one, they've moved on.'* John was fine with that, inside he wanted to know what information they had but he knew there was no way he could find that out. Mostly he wanted to know if they suspected him. *'I guess if they suspected me, they would be knocking at my door and I haven't seen anyone come knocking.'* John relaxed and finished making his breakfast. He watched an old TV show called Andy Griffith, a sort of old time cop show as it turned out. Then he went about cleaning his apartment from top to bottom. It had been at least a week since he had done it and all his clothes needed to be washed. By mid-day he was getting a little tired of seeing the inside of his apartment. Things were picked up and cleaned, it doesn't take long, it's never really that far out of sorts. The laundry was still running, on its second load. He wanted to get out of the apartment, at least for a while. *'Maybe I should go for a drive.'* John peeked out the window to see if it was worth it to go out. It was a nice fall day, coming into October, mornings were cool, some days it rained, others it was nice. Sunday was a patchy day, some rain, some sun. *'If you don't like the weather, wait five minutes.'* John hadn't had lunch yet, so he packed a sandwich and snacks to have in the truck. Making lunch for a road trip always reminded him of his mother making lunch to go for a drive to see relatives. They would never stop to eat out, it cost too much on a tight income, but Mom would always make sure there were things to eat in the car. He put his food in the backpack with some water bottles and headed for the door. He had cleaned his hiking boots, as well as his sneakers, for the second time. He chose hiking boots, *'Just in case.'* His jacket was yet to be washed so the hoodie he had on would have to do. Out the door and down the 3 flights of stairs to his truck he went, without thinking about his ankle. His ankle was feeling much better, he had almost his entire range of motion back, it would hurt just at the end of motion if he pushed it too hard. *'Hiking might not be out of the question.'* He started driving without thinking about where he was going, almost going in an instinctual direction. He checked his fuel, *'¾ tank, that will do.'* He turned left on 18, drove slowly past Scruffy's tent, then looked the other way where Caveman's tent used to be, *'Oh that mess! It's getting worse.'* Past Ted's Grocery, then the GasNGo where he works, his instinct was taking him out Bridge Street, across the bridge to the stop sign. He sat at the stop sign until someone beeped their horn behind him, *'Make a decision.'* He turned right, down river. The parking area where the fishermen gather was just ahead on his right. A few trucks in the lot but no people there. He pulled in hesitantly, something inside didn't want him to, but also did. His mind telling him not to, but his body following some other direction. He drove to the far end of the lot, slowly at idle speed, his tires crunched through the gravel, the truck jostling left and right as he drove through the potholes filled with rainwater. He stopped at the end near the trees that lined the outside edge of the clearing where the rodents met their demise sitting upright on the sofa, unable to see all the way through the thick trees into the clearing, but able to imagine what it looked like when he was there last. *'Why do I know what that looked like? I wasn't ever really there, was I?'* That deja vu feeling came over him again as he sat in his truck staring at the stand of trees in front of him. He felt like his subconscious had been there but didn't think he should be able to recall that from memory. He hadn't planned to hike into the clearing but here he was, stopped in the lot, the trail just steps away from where he had parked. John sat in the truck not thinking about where he was, just letting it happen. He munched on snacks and drank water from one of the bottles. He had eaten his sandwich on the drive over without thinking about it. Sprinkles of rain wet the windshield of the truck as John sat munching on chips. He folded the top of the bag and set it aside, opened the door and stepped out. The air felt better than he expected, it was refreshing. The clouds moved across the sky rapidly but he couldn't feel the wind from the ground. He thought he might feel strange getting out of the truck in this spot, knowing what had happened beyond the trees, feeling that his subconscious had been there before. It felt fine, he raised both hands above his head and stretched leaning back, feeling his back pop and align itself. He closed the door and began to walk toward the trail, taking in the rustling of the fall leaves, watching some of them fall in the slight breeze that hushed through the tops of the trees. At the beginning of the trail he stood looking into the tunnel of branches that bent and arched over the path. It had looked black and menacing when he was there in the dark, the sense of deja vu pulled the feeling of dread up in his subconscious that was telling him to stay out that night, but that didn't deter him from his mission and he moved into the darkness anyway. Now as the sun came out, peeking through the limbs, leaving a latticework of shadows on the dirt, it was inviting John to walk in, he agreed and moved forward. The path was well worn, but just wide enough to walk single file between the limbs that reached out and brushed his shoulders as he walked through. John felt a pleasant warm fall breeze pass his face as the sun reached in between the trees. He felt strangely content with his decision to walk into the clearing where the 3 rodents sat dead on the sofa only a week ago. He was satisfied in knowing they were not there and now he was sure he had cleaned away much of what they left behind in the middle of the night, helping put nature back in order. He came to the end of the trail, the arms of the trees giving way to an open clearing from where John could see all the way to the river. He had expected to see some debris still in the clearing, he knew he couldn't have gotten everything picked up in his little truck, he was there alone after all, how thorough could he have been? As John walked past the last trees that flanked him on the trail, he was astonished, there was nothing left. It had been cleaned of every last piece of trash, every piece of furniture, every discarded piece of clothing, right down to every scrap of paper had been picked up, even the sofa had been removed. He stood at the end of the trail looking from right to left, from his feet to the distant banks of the river. *'Clean.'* He was overjoyed at the sight, a smile spread across his face. *'I couldn't have gotten it this clean, someone has been here since I was. It's wonderful.'* This is what he had wanted since he had started seeing the rodents take over. *'I just want it clean; I just want it to be nature, not to be tarnished by human rodents with all of their filth and uncaring.'* It finally struck John what had been eating at him about the rodents. It was an, 'Ah-ha' moment. He started to walk into the clearing, still looking left to right, amazed that it was all gone. When he got to where the fire pit was, he noticed even the ashes had been raked away and the rocks that surrounded the pit had been removed. It was no longer a rodent camp. John walked all the way through the clearing to the bank that was high above the river, he stood looking out at the rushing water. He looked up the river and spotted two fishermen on the banks hoping to be lucky enough to bring home dinner. John took a deep breath; the air was fresh with the scent of water and fall leaves. He held it for a moment before releasing it, his head was clear, it was time to move on. He turned back the way he came in, crossing the clearing as the wind rustled the trees above his head and fall leaves fluttered down around him. He felt a small victory, not fully knowing if it was his victory, if he had gotten rid of the rodents and then cleaned the area of their filth, but he was happy with the result no matter how it came about. As he walked back out through the tunnel of branches the sun had gone behind yet another dark cloud, the branches looked angry in the shadow of the clouds, dark gray and stormy, ready to reach out and pull John into their arms, not letting him go. He escaped their clutches just as raindrops started to fall, big sloppy drops, the kind that soak through your clothes the instant they land on you. He retreated to the cover of his truck, saving himself from being soaked. *'That was close.'* John started his truck and backed out of his spot, splashing through the puddles in the lot on his way to River Road. His trek into the clearing had made him curious about the camp at the lake. *'Do I dare? I would be disappointed if it hasn't been cleaned.'* It was getting late in the day, but John wanted to know if that site too, had been put back the way it should be. Across the bridge he took a right off Bridge Street onto the highway, heading out to the lake. *'I just need to see it.'* The wipers on his truck were flapping back and forth until he outran the storm, and the pavement became dry, it was a short shower passing overhead with the speed of the wind high above. Minutes later John slowed on the highway, the parking area coming into view. He pulled in slowly, seeing a handful of trucks and boat trailers in the lot. A few other cars, maybe fishermen or hikers out to enjoy the trail. He parked near the trail head sign where he had driven his truck in to clear the camp of its debris. He stepped out of his truck and looked around the lot. No one to be seen, just the evidence that they were there somewhere. He closed the door and looked toward the trail, right next to the trail head a new sign had been posted, 'NO CAMPING'. John stopped and considered the sign, *'Not sure that would have stopped them from camping here in the first place.'* He walked past the sign, ducking branches hanging over the trail, they were not as menacing here, not in the daylight, the trail was wide and covered with leaves that hid roots and rocks and other things to trip over. John walked hesitantly toward the camp that was once there. He didn't want to be disappointed but needed to know if it was clean. The trail snaked back and forth through the trees, coming closer to the waters edge then leading away, it was farther than he remembered. *'Just keep going, it's up here somewhere.'* The trail started to curve to the right, following the inlet of the lake. There, to the left, the small clearing in the trees. *'That's where the tent was set up. There were piles of trash here and over there. Now it's gone. It's wonderful, it's all gone.'* John was not disappointed; this area had also been restored to nature. No sign remained that there had ever been a rodent camp here. Again, a smile drew across his face, *'This has been an amazing day.'* He was satisfied that someone besides himself must care about keeping nature clean. He turned to walk back to the truck

173

when something caught his eye, some color that didn't belong. He stopped and backed up a few steps looking to his right. There. Caught in a bush, bright yellow with black lettering, 'Crime Scene Do Not Cross'. John looked around; it was the only piece of evidence he could see that something actually did happen right here in this beautiful park. He couldn't leave it there so he walked off the trail, picking his way between trees and low limbs and snatched the tape from the bush. It was only about 3 feet in length but it didn't belong out here anymore. He wadded it into a ball and stuffed it into the pocket of his hoodie. He picked his way back to the trail and continued walking back to the parking area. He stumbled on hidden roots and a rock or two that the fall leaves had hidden from view, it reminded him of his weak ankle, he needed to be careful not to re-injure himself.

Katy had to work Sunday afternoon, she preferred the after-noon shift, the tips were always better for the dinner crowd and she could sleep in mornings. She checked the coming weeks' schedule as soon as she arrived. She would be working evenings all week. *'Much better, I don't like working til midnight.'* The part she didn't like about working evening was being the opposite shift from Jesse, that made things hard at home. She was very much in love with Jesse and couldn't wait to get married. This job was only temporary, she would find something better one day. When she did find something better, then their shifts would line up, but for now it paid the bills. Before Katy went to work, she paid a visit to Berta for a morning chat and a cup of coffee. Berta was very happy to see her and full of the newest information that Jamie had shared with her. "Katy darling, it's so good to see you. How has your week been?" Katy hugged Berta and stepped inside. "It has been okay, really not bad at all. Work went pretty fast even though I had to work the late shift." Berta ushered her in and motioned for Katy to sit at the counter. "I'll get some coffee, I just made a fresh pot." Berta pulled the creamer from the fridge and set a couple of mugs on the counter. "Did you hear about that incident Friday morning?" Berta was trying to play it cool, even though she wanted to get right down to the dirt of it. She poured coffee in the mugs, Katy poured creamer. "I actually saw something going on when I was coming home from work Friday morning, I couldn't tell at the time what it was, but then we saw it on the news Saturday, well, Jesse saw it and told me about it." Berta added creamer to her coffee and stirred, "Yes, I saw the news story too, they didn't do it justice. Jamie came over last night for dinner and we talked all about it." Katy's eyebrows raised, "Oh good, all they said on the news was two people had died, but not what they died from. It was an awful lot of commotion for the news story to be so lacking." Berta hadn't even tried to sip her coffee. "Yes, they did say that two people died, did they mention there was a fire? I can't recall now since I spoke with Jamie and got the whole story." Katy set her coffee down, "Tell me what happened." Berta dove into the story, "Jamie said that he was called out in the middle of the night. Someone had reported a fire. It turned out there were two people in a homeless tent that was burnt up in the fire. Well, Jamie isn't one of the investigators, but he pays attention to all the stuff they find, kind of looking over their shoulders and seeing what's going on. He said that those people in the tent were killed the same as that one out at the lake and the ones out at the river. They had hands tied up and rags in their mouths. He said these ones were burnt like the one at the lake, so he doesn't know for sure if there was a bag on their heads or not, but he supposed that there was just because everything else looked the same." Katy was in shock just a little bit, she slowly sipped her coffee again. "Berta, it's so close to home. Does it worry you?" Berta shook her head right away. "No Hun, we went over that. I have no reason to think whoever is out there killing those homeless folks is going to be coming after me, and you shouldn't either." Katy pursed her lips, wondering if she agreed. "This was the same as the one in the car too." Berta nodded a little. "It was the same kind of thing." Katy remembered what Jesse had told her Saturday morning. "Did you hear anything outside your apartment Saturday morning? Maybe about 4 AM?" Berta got a glassy look on her face. "Hmm, well actually I did hear something, but I don't know for sure what time it was. I heard a bang, it jolted me awake. Then I realized it was the dumpster lid, someone had dropped it back. I didn't even consider what time it was and why someone was out there in the dark. Why do you ask?" Katy shrugged, "I'm not sure it's anything, just a guy from building B was dumping trash in the middle of the night, I guess his dumpster was full. Anyway, Jesse got up and went out there to see what he was up to. Jesse has met the guy, talked to him a couple of times, so I guess he felt comfortable going out and seeing what he was doing." Berta was leaning in on the counter listening intently. "Well, what did he have that needed dumping at 4 AM?" Katy shrugged again. "That's kind of what I thought, why 4 AM? Can't it wait? But Jesse said the guy was in a trance or something, he tried talking to him and the guy just mumbled back, he couldn't understand what he was saying. Jesse said he tried several times to talk to him and find out what was going on, but the guy just kept going back and forth from his truck to the bin dumping in trash like he was a zombie." Berta sipped again, looked at the ceiling and made a thinking face. "Could be nothing, maybe the guy works really early and just had to get it done?" Katy pressed her lips together hard. "Maybe, like I said, it's probably nothing but what is sort of weird about it, is that last Wednesday night at almost 11 PM Jesse saw the same guy at the side of Highway 18 picking up trash at the homeless camp. I am just guessing, but I would bet that's why the dumpster in front of his apartment is full. Like I said, I thought it was weird. Especially with all the strange stuff happening with the homeless. Jesse and I were joking around that he was the killer and after he did the deed, he cleaned up the campsites to cover his tracks." Katy laughed a little at herself. Berta smiled and laughed. "Wouldn't that be something?" Berta held up two fingers on each hand in air quotes, "The Cleanup Killer," then they both laughed. Katy smiled and drank more coffee, "It's funny but not funny at the same time." Berta drank and nodded as well. "That does seem to be a strange time to be doing roadside cleanup, though it seems like a good deed on the face of it." Katy made a funny face at that. "It does seem that way, people are strange, that's for sure." Berta rolled her eyes and nodded vigorously. "That they are, it takes all kinds. As far as that killer goes, I think he'll mess up soon and they'll catch him." Katy agreed, "I hope so, while this is interesting to think about, it gives me the creeps." Berta reached out and put her hand over Katy's. "I think you're going to be just fine, you just take care of yourself and don't go hanging out with homeless people." Katy laughed a little. "I have no plans of doing that." Berta stood up from her spot leaning on the counter, "Miss Katy, I don't mean to rush you out, but I have plans today with my daughter. We're going to get our nails done and have lunch out." Katy smiled a happy smile. "That's wonderful, I hope you have a great time." Katy stood and started moving to the door. "Thanks for taking the time to talk about this scary stuff with me, I think it helps to have all the details about what's going on out there." Berta came around the counter. "You know you can come talk with me any time. Now give me a hug before you go." They hugged tightly and Katy left so that Berta could get ready for her day out.

Jesse had made plans with Clint to go fishing out on the lake Sunday. They met at the boat ramp around 9 AM. "Hey Clint, how are you today? Did you bring snacks and beer?" Clint was walking down to the boat and held up a cooler in one hand with his fishing pole in the other. "You bet I did, I won't leave home without them." Clint laughed and tromped down the ramp to the boat Jesse had already put in the water and where he was waiting at the dock. "I also brought a thermos of coffee cause it's a little early for the beer." Jesse reached out and grabbed the cooler and thermos from Clint, helping him put things in the boat. Clint stepped in gently, trying not to upset things too much. "Are we ready? I'll cast off those lines if we are." Jesse gave him a thumbs up, and Clint untied them from the dock. Jesse fired the motor up and started to make way out to open water. "I was thinking we would head down to that cove on the south end, we haven't been down there in a while." Clint gave an okay sign and pulled out the thermos. "You want some coffee?" Jesse reached for his to-go mug and handed it to Clint. "Filler up please." Clint filled Jesse's mug and one for himself, then watched the shoreline as they motored past. It was looking to be a nice day on the water, no wind and patchy blue skies. The leaves turning orange and yellow lined the lake, the colors exploding brightly when the sun came out from behind the clouds. The water was glassy, reflecting the sun and trees from the shore along with white puffy clouds floating easily high above, the light smell of lake water mixed with clean morning air was calming. Clint sipped at his coffee then struck up a conversation. "Did you see that mess off Route 18 on Friday? There were cops everywhere." Jesse was checking their heading then looked back at Clint. "Oh yeah I saw it. I came through there at about 4:30 and had to wait for the police to let me through, looked like they had some kind of fire happen in the rodent camp." Clint laughed a little bit, "Did you get that from John? He calls them rodents." Jesse chuckled, "Yeah, I liked it and it stuck. I heard on the news that two people died, burnt up in their tent." Clint nodded a little. "That's what I heard too, me and John watched them investigate all day out there from the GasNGo. The police cars came and went all day long, they were still there when I got off work. I've seen a couple unmarked police cars come in and out of there a couple of times since." Jesse checked their direction again and made a small correction, he took another swig of coffee. "That place is such a mess, it wouldn't hurt my feelings if they all got burned out of there." Clint didn't have an outward reaction to Jesse's comments. "Yeah, they are making a pretty big mess out there. It's sort of a black eye coming into town." Jesse slowed the boat a little, directing them into an inlet by the shore. "That guy you work with, John. He is an interesting dude. I saw him the other night, out at the rodent camp. Looked like he was picking up garbage off the side of the road." Clint was looking toward shore then snapped his head toward Jesse. "What?! He was doing what?"

Jesse chuckled at Clint's reaction. "He was picking up trash at the rodent camp. The other night after I left your house, I saw his truck parked half in the ditch. I didn't see him right away, but I turned around and drove back. When I pulled up behind his truck, I could see him out in the bushes picking up trash or something and I watched him bring it back and put it in the back of his truck, then he went back out in the bushes. It was super strange." Clint was staring at Jesse with his mouth hanging open. "What side of the road was he on? Same side that burned?" Jesse shook his head and pointed at the anchor for Clint to drop it over the side of the boat. "No, he was on the other side. He could have gone to that side at some point, I didn't stay around. After I saw him out there, I watched for a minute and then left." Clint laughed almost to himself, as he dropped the anchor over the side. "What do you think brought that on?" Jesse was getting his pole situated to throw his line out. "How would I know, you know him better than I do, I just met the guy. But if you think that's weird, there's more." Clint straightened up a little as he grabbed his pole. "Okay, what else is there?" Jesse flipped his line out and got it set for a moment. "Saturday morning at about 4 AM, I heard some noise outside my apartment, so I got up and looked out the window, he was out at the dumpster just down from my place with a truckload of trash. So, I went down there cause I recognized him and I wanted to see what he was up to." Clint was dazed with this new story, just sitting there holding his fishing pole, not moving. "Wait... He was at the dumpster at 4 in the morning? What the heck?" Jesse held up his hand, palm to the sky. "I don't know where he got the garbage but when I tried to talk to him, he was absent, not there, it was like he was in a trance or something." Clint again sitting, staring at Jesse with his mouth agape, "In a trance? What did he say when you talked to him?" Jesse shrugged and checked his pole for tension on the line. "He just mumbled, I tried a couple of times to get him to talk to me but he just kept going back and forth from the dumpster to the truck. I gave up after a few tries and went back to bed." A big knowing smile came over Clint's face. "That's crazy, you know, he has a hard time getting to work on time. A week or so back he came in late and Steve, our boss, was giving him crap because Steve had seen him out driving in the middle of the night off Bridge Street, or someplace like that. So, John and I were talking about it and he didn't know where he was." Jesse had a confused look on his face. "What do you mean he didn't know where he was?" Clint was tapping his finger on his head. "It's all coming together now. I was giving him crap because he couldn't remember where he went the night before, I told him he must have had a great time if he couldn't remember it. I thought maybe he had gone out for a booty call or something and gotten a little carried away. Seems like maybe he really couldn't remember what he was doing. You said he was in a trance or something, so I wonder if it was the same thing that day that Steve saw him." Jesse got a face of realization for a moment. "This might be a recurring thing for him. Going out and not knowing it. Do you think he even knows the next day that he has been out in the middle of the night?" Clint shook his head, and finally cast his line out into the water. "He didn't know that time, he was adamant that he hadn't been out, or at least had no idea where he had been." Clint let his line settle then took another sip of coffee. "Damn Jesse, what if it's bigger than going out and picking up trash in the middle of the night? He obviously knows where the rodent camps are. What if he is the guy killing them?" Jesse looked out at his line and started reeling it in slowly. "Katy said the same thing, she thinks he might be the guy. I don't know, maybe he is, but how do you find out?" Clint watched as Jesse reeled in his line and saw the line go tight for a split second, then tap, tap, tap. Jesse set the hook and started reeling faster. Clint grabbed the net and scooped up their prize as Jesse pulled it in close to the boat. "Bottom feeder, might want to bring that line up a little bit." Clint took the fish off the hook and threw it back. "Follow him." Jesse looked at Clint, "What?" Clint shrugged, "That's how you find out what he's up to, you follow him." Jesse got a thoughtful look on his face as he prepared his line to go back in the water. "Yeah, I guess you could do that. Seems like it might be a lot of work or time to make that happen. I mean we have no idea when he is going to leave his place and go do whatever he does." Clint nodded and started to reel his line in to check his depth. "Well, you have a good point, but still, I think if you happened to see him at an odd time of night, you could follow him."

21

Monday

When Clint arrived at work he immediately thought of John. He hadn't put much thought into it since he and Jesse had talked about him the day before. Clint liked John, thought he was a bit of an odd guy but nothing wrong with him, they always got along well at work. Clint was feeling a little uneasy about him now though, since Jesse told him that he was out wandering around at night in a trance picking up trash at homeless camps. At least that's what it seemed he was doing. Clint wasn't sure what he should do, *'Should I say something to John? Maybe that would help the guy out, maybe this is really a problem for him. Or is he doing some nasty shit that I don't want to have anything to do with, maybe I would be better off trying to catch him doing something wrong?'*

Clint let it go for a while, just acting like he didn't know anything at all about what was happening. After John had checked in, Clint had already taken the pump readings and was ready for the shift. "Hey John, how was your day off?" John was feeling good, he had found that some of the camps had been completely cleaned out and that made him happy. "Good morning Clint, it was good. I went for a drive yesterday and cleared my head . It was a relaxing day." Clint was moving between two customers but trying to keep a dialogue going with John. "Nice, did you go anywhere interesting?" John was looking at Clint between two of the pumps. "Not really, I drove out by the river. I looked at the area where those rodents were killed." Clint got a serious look on his face not expecting John to bring that up. "What? Why would you go out there?" John was waiting for a pump to finish so he stood up between two of the pumps to get closer to Clint so he wouldn't have to talk too loud. "I wanted to see if the area was cleaned up." Clint cocked his head to the side. "Really? Why?" John was starting to get irritated with the questions. "It's important, I can't stand seeing all the trash out there all the time, it needs to be cleaned up, it weighs on me, it's important to me. I wanted to see if that had been cleaned up since those people weren't living there any more. They're ruining our natural area, everywhere you look now it seems like there are rodents piling their trash." Clint could sense the irritation in John's voice. "Oh, sure, okay. Yeah it is important. I don't like seeing all the trash all the time either." Clint turned to hang a pump back in the cradle, then had to move to the other island to help another customer. He didn't bring it up the rest of the day, figuring he had pushed the subject far enough for now.

John decided to walk the dirt trail home after stopping at Ted's Grocery for some fresh fruit and frozen pot pies. He was able to tuck it into his backpack so he didn't have the bags banging on his leg all the way home. He was walking slowly past the burnt out remains of Caveman's tent. Caveman wasn't there to bother him and he wanted to get a better look at the area. There wasn't much to see, the police had picked through all of his remaining belongings, burnt or not, the ground looked like it had been scratched by chickens pecking for bugs. The black, burned, sooty area had been turned over by the police searching for evidence. There were still piles of garbage strewn everywhere, it actually seemed that the mess had gotten worse. Some of the rodents had packed in more garbage and sifted through it in front of their tents, leaving the piles of unwanted remains laying in heaps where they would have to step over it coming or going from their tents. John was startled to see the new tent that he had never seen anyone in or around was being stood over by a lone man. He was clean shaven, tall and thin, with very long, straight black hair. He was wearing green pants that didn't make it past his ankles, and sticking out above the tops of his high top Converse John could see he was wearing wool socks. He had on some type of wool sweater with horizontal red stripes on a blue background, all very clean. He looked more like a hipster college student than a homeless person, he had an arrogant mannerism about him, *'Very Portland trendy, hmm yes Trendy is your name.'* John thought. He was standing just outside the tent, after crawling out of the flap. John looked him up and down, for some reason he seemed familiar. Not so much that he knew him but his presence was recognizable. *'Where have I seen you before?'* Next to his tent one of Caveman's lawn chairs was waiting to be used, it was singed black on the bottom of one of the back corners but was still in working order, it had been captured by Trendy, taken as his own. *'I'm sure Caveman wasn't gone a day before the rest of them pilfered through all they could find for anything that might be worth holding on to.'* The thought repulsed John,

'They are rodents. As soon as one dies, the rest of them squabble over everything the dead one had as if the living have rights to it.' Trendy watched John walking towards him but didn't seem to care, he wasn't watching him in fear or curiosity, but just because John was there, moving and upright. The trail passed at what John felt was a safe distance away from Trendy so he didn't stray from it. Rather, he kept his pace, glancing around the area, following the burnt trail with his eyes, seeing that it ran from where Caveman's tent was out to the edge of the gravel in the ditch. *'That's where it was lit. I'm not a detective but I can see what happened here. How did Trendy guy not get burnt up?'* He looked back at Trendy, still standing at the front of his tent scratching his head looking completely lost, then back where he was going, up the ditch to the white line that would take him the rest of the way home. *'I wonder if he had anything to do with it? How did he not catch fire?'* That played over and over in his head while he walked the white line and cars whizzed past him within an arm's reach. *'Was he just lucky? Is anyone that lucky that lives in a tent?'* He was shaking his head in disbelief. John looked up from the white line as another car passed by going the opposite direction. Scruffy was walking the white line on the other side of the road. When Scruffy saw that John was looking he lifted his hand in a gesture to say, 'Hello, I recognize you.' Just a single raised hand, no waving motion. John instinctively did the same in return. *'Why did I do that? Before you know it he will be having dinner at my house. I can't be doing that.'* John put his hand down as quickly as it went up, then stuffed it in his pocket and looked at the white line. *'Just keep walking, almost home.'*

Monday night John had fallen asleep on the sofa watching TV, he was fully dressed except his shoes. It was nearing 11

PM when he got up and put his shoes on. He had cleaned them some after he had returned home from work, he didn't like to wear dirty shoes, it made him look and feel sloppy about his appearance. John never considered himself good looking or thought that he had to wear overly nice clothes, but he didn't like to look like he didn't care. He often wore sweatshirts and jeans, but they were always clean and never tattered. All his clothes had been washed on his day off work, he had made a mess of everything over the last week, going out in the night picking up after the rodents. Monday night he went out with just a sweatshirt and jeans, wearing his sneakers. He got in his Ranger pickup and drove out of the lot. It was a short drive to the rodent camp where Caveman once lived and now Trendy was sleeping in his new tent. John slowed as he approached the area, looking for the spot that Jesse had driven off the road. He saw it and turned left, leaving the highway, driving down into the ditch, following the path Jesse left when he plowed over the bushes and vines towards Caveman's tent. John drove his truck past the burnt spot of the tent and parked next to a pile of trash, left there by the police and added to by the other rodents inhabiting the site. He was stopped just a few yards from Trendy's tent and shut the engine off. John didn't know if Trendy was there or not, it didn't matter to him, that's not why he was there. It was a cool night but dry. The moon was almost gone, just a yellow sliver when it was visible between the clouds. John got out of the truck and immediately started to work, picking up bags of trash, putting them into the back of his truck, robotic in his movements, one bag after another, then on to the trash that wasn't in bags. He was working around Trendy's tent, not caring that some of the piles might be things that he wanted to keep. There was a rustling sound that came from Trendy's tent, then ziiiip, and Trendy's head popped up above the tent. Trendy looked around and spotted John. "What's going on out here?" John didn't respond, he kept moving spot to spot grabbing garbage, loading his arms up and moving to the back of the truck, dropping it in. Again, Trendy tried to get his attention. "Hey, what are you doing?" Trendy's voice was crisp and clear, not the voice of someone that had spent years homeless, fending for himself out in the cold and elements every day. John paused as if he had actually heard him this time, but he hadn't, he returned to picking up trash. Trendy disappeared back into his tent, he rustled around for a few moments, then crawled all the way out this time. "Who are you? What are you doing?" John dropped his armload of trash into the truck and looked at him. "Disgusting!" Then went back to work. Trendy just stood watching John's shadowy figure move about the site bending here and there, picking things out of the bushes and off the ground, returning to the truck and dropping it in. Bewildered, Trendy moved toward John, wanting to get a better look at who this was. "Why are you here? Why are you picking up trash in the middle of the night?" John didn't respond at first, he walked past Trendy, going to put more items in the truck. After dropping his armload of trash, he turned to looked at Trendy, "Help, mblme membsh." 'Help' was all Trendy could make out. He turned and looked behind him as if there might be someone else that John was talking to. Finding no one there, he looked at his surroundings and then started to gather some of the trash and put it in Johns truck. The truck filled up quickly with the extra help. Trendy was confused, he had tried to talk to John but could get little more than mumbling and a clear word or two that didn't make any sense. When the back of the truck was clearly stacked above the rails, John produced some rope from inside the cab. Trendy stood and watched as John tied it all down. John opened the passenger side of the truck and rummaged for a moment, then walked over to Trendy and handed him a bottle of water without saying a word. He returned to the truck, got in and started it. John gave him a wave that Trendy could barely see in the dark and shut his door. He drove away, out the path that Jesse had left, following the tire tracks up the ditch and onto the road, headed back to his apartment. John parked in his normal spot, checking the dumpster, he found this time that it had been emptied, so he filled it more than halfway up with the load from his truck. He worked silently, except the first couple of bags hitting the bottom of the bin. No one came out to see what he was doing in the middle of the night this time. It had become routine at this point and he entered his apartment, kicked off his shoes and dropped his pants by the door. He shut the TV off and the lights in the living room, then went to bed.

22

Tuesday

John got up tired again, this time he knew from the moment the alarm went off that he had been out in the night. He was tired, didn't want to move, his body was heavy, and his hands were dirty. *'I've got to start washing my hands when I get back from picking up trash.'* He went straight to the shower to wash and get ready for work. After showering and getting dressed, he picked up his dirty laundry and put it in the basket. He looked at his shoes before going into the kitchen to make coffee and breakfast. They were clean enough for today. *'Wherever I went must not have been too muddy this time.'* John still wasn't sure that the only thing he was doing was picking up trash, his truck was empty the last time he came home with muddy pants and shoes, but he hadn't heard of any murders happening where there would have been a lot of mud. He ate some toast and put coffee in a to go mug, sacked his lunch, and left the apartment. He checked his truck as he walked out of the lot. *'Empty. Hmm. What did I do?'* He walked to the dumpster and peeked under the lid. *'There it is. Smart. I unloaded before going back to bed. At least I know I was picking garbage and not killing someone. I guess I don't know that for sure.'* He dropped the lid and continued on his way to work. There was high fog floating above the road as John walked the white line, he could see breaks of dark blue above the fog where it was thin. The sun wasn't fully up yet, it was casting a glow from the east, orange on the horizon, white above that and dark blue to the west, it looked like it would be a nice day. John looked into the rodent camp where Scruffy lived, it had become routine for him to check on Scruffy, not close up, just as he passed by daily, walking to and from work. Scruffy's site hadn't gotten any worse but it wasn't looking better either. *'It could use a good cleaning.'* John looked across the road after he passed Scruffy's camp, peering down the new path created by the off-road excursion. It was better, there was less trash, *'That must be what I did last night. Right next to other rodents. Not smart, too close for comfort. I wonder if any of them saw me.'* John kept staring across the road, looking for movement, *'It's too early, maybe I will see someone this afternoon.'* He was almost at work, the GasNGo station loomed in the distance, the lit island cover's lights glowed like watercolor paints, yellow and red in the fog. He was on time, he could see Clint's truck already in the lot, *'Always the early bird. Suck up.'*

That afternoon an investigation unit stopped at the roadside in front of Trendy's tent. The detective stepped out to take another look at the scene of what was Caveman and Cave Woman's murder. He wasn't pleased to see that the area didn't look the same as it had when he left it. Trendy was sitting in his lawn chair next to his tent, watching as the detective wandered around the area. Eventually, the detective made his way over to talk with Trendy. "Hello, I'm Detective James Milkey, do you mind if I ask you a couple of questions?" Trendy stood up and reached out to shake hands. "Hi, I'm Jake Jefferies, people call me JJ." James was surprised at the clarity of his speech. "JJ, you don't seem the type to be living in a tent on the side of the highway." JJ crossed his arms in a relaxed stance. "I get that quite a bit, I guess I am a little new to this, but people fall on hard times and I just haven't figured out how to get back on my feet yet." James was studying JJ closely. "You weren't out here Friday when the fire occurred, at least we didn't see you here during the initial investigation." JJ looked around at the burnt areas assessing the scene as if he hadn't noticed. "No, I wasn't here then, I mean my tent was here, but I wasn't." James had taken out a notepad and started jotting down information. "Where were you?" JJ had returned his gaze to James, still with his arms across his chest, feet shoulder width apart in a very relaxed stance. "Well, I had come out and set up my tent fully intending to stay here when a friend of mine who knows where I'm staying, because you should always let someone know where you are, came out and said I could stay with him for a short time while his girlfriend was out of town. So, I stayed with him until Saturday afternoon. Then I came back here and saw the burn marks, but I don't know what happened out here." James turned and pointed toward the other tents in the area. "You haven't talked with any of your neighbors?" JJ shook his head. "No, I haven't gotten to know them yet." James had a smirk on his face. "Not a great time to be homeless out here. The people in that tent were murdered." JJ took a couple of steps back in surprise. "Whoa, really? Oh man I didn't know that. I thought maybe a campfire got out of control or something." James's face had returned to a stern look. "You should really be careful, there's been some bad stuff going on in the homeless community. Aside from that, I came over here to ask you about this area. You wouldn't know who came out here and disturbed it would you? Someone has done some cleaning." JJ was nodding his head a little, "Yeah, it was really weird, a guy showed up last night. Middle of the night, pitch black out here, drove in with a little pickup truck and just started loading up trash." James had a confused expression, but he was listening intently. "In the middle of the night?" JJ uncrossed his arms and pointed down the tire tracks. "Yep, he drove right down through here, I was trying to sleep but I heard his truck pull in and he parked right behind that burnt spot." JJ pointed where Caveman's tent had been, and the biggest round burnt spot was on the ground. "He got out and started loading stuff into the back of his truck, all the bags of stuff, which honestly is just trash to anyone else. He also was picking stuff out of the bushes and anything that was just laying on the ground, all of it. Anyway, I could hear stuff going on, so I finally got out of my tent to look around, it was so dark all I could see were shadows of the guy." JJ was rather animated in his telling of the story, pointing at the places where there used to be piles of trash. James was following the hand gestures trying to envision the scene. "Did you get a good look at him?" JJ stopped moving so much and put his hands in his pockets. "No, not really, like I said it was really dark. I tried to talk to the guy, but he was mostly just mumbling, he didn't make much sense. I heard a couple of words, one was 'Disgusting' and the other was 'Help'. So, I helped him." James was taken back a little by that. "You what? You helped him?" JJ shrugged and nodded. "Yeah, he said help and I thought he meant help him load stuff up, so I helped him load stuff into his truck.

It was just trash so I didn't think it was hurting anything." James nodded some, then took another look around the site. "You're mostly right, it wasn't hurting anything. It is still a crime scene, but I think we had pulled all the evidence we were going to get out of it anyway. You didn't happen to get a plate number on the truck? Or a description, color, anything?" JJ grimaced. "I didn't get a plate, I didn't even think about it because I didn't think it was a big deal, kind of weird, but he was just picking up trash." James shifted his stance. "How about a description of the vehicle?" "It was dark out, but it was a compact truck, you know one of the small ones. Dark in color, couldn't tell you if it was black, blue or green, just dark. I don't know well enough to tell you what brand." James made some notes next to JJ's name. "Okay, it's better than nothing." JJ held up a hand as if to ask James to wait a minute. "Do you think he had anything to do with the murders?" James looked at JJ very seriously. "He might have, he might be our guy. Maybe he came back to clean up evidence. Pretty bold move, but it could be him." JJ hung his head, and just stood still for a moment. "Maybe I should relocate." James reached out to shake JJ's hand. "Whatever you do, be careful, watch your back. Thank you for your time." James walked to his car, took one last look at the area before he got in and drove away. JJ got a blanket from the tent, sat down in his lawn chair and took a nap.

John stopped at Ted's Grocery on his way home from work. Gathering lunch supplies, some snacks and water bottles. Hoping he had enough room in his backpack. Outside the store he was putting his items into his backpack, they didn't all fit, most of the heavy items fit inside so he carried the snacks and chips in a plastic bag. John took the trail that cuts through the rodent camp, in the back of his mind he was curious if anyone would recognize him from the night before. Far to his right, deep off the trail there were three tents that he had seen before but never paid attention to the comings and goings of the occupants. Today there were two men standing between the tents on the left. One man was bearded and heavy set, he had a beer belly. The other, shorter than the first, was thin and wore a dirty blue baseball cap with long hair sticking out all around, he was not clean shaven but the scruff on his face wouldn't be called a beard. They were talking, Beer Belly was waving his arms about, seeming to be in the middle of a story. John watched them until they looked his way, neither of the men seemed to care that John was there. They went back to the story with the arms making all sorts of gestures. Blue Cap stepped back so not to be hit with the gestures of Beer Belly. John kept walking, *'They didn't seem to care, probably didn't see me last night.'* There was another tent John hadn't noticed before farther down on the same side, but no one could be seen. The trail veered toward Trendy's tent; John could just see the top of it over the bushes before coming to the tire tracks left by Jesse. When he got closer, he could see that Trendy was sitting in his inherited lawn chair watching traffic go by on the highway. Trendy looked his way and gave a friendly wave. "Hello, nice day for a walk." John paused, "Yes it is, just on my way home." John surprised himself offering more information than he needed to. Trendy took a sip of water from a bottle he had in his chair. "I've seen you come by on the road a few times. Do you walk this way every day?" John recognized the bottle, *'Could be just coincidence, but those are the same ones I have.'* He was slightly distracted now. "Uh, yeah, pretty much every day." He paused looking around for show, "It looks a little cleaner out here." Trendy stood up, wearing blue pants today and a green cardigan, his long hair tied into a ponytail below his shoulders. "It is a little bit. Had someone come by and clean up some of the trash the other day." John gave a head nod, "Good, good. Looks like there could be some more of that done, but at least it's better." Trendy started to walk toward John then stopped a few feet away. "Oh yeah, it could use a little more picking up. Maybe that guy will come back." Trendy was looking straight into John's eyes. He had a very mellow easy going look on his face, giving John a chance to own up to it. "Say, you wouldn't know of any jobs open in the area, would you? I'm not looking to stay homeless forever, I'd rather get back to work." John was caught off guard by Trendy looking into his eyes. *'Does he know it was me? Maybe it doesn't matter, he doesn't seem to care.'* "Not off the top of my head, the best bet would be to walk down Main Street, sometimes there are help wanted signs posted in shop windows." Trendy held up his water bottle as in a toast. "Sure, thanks, I haven't ventured over there yet, I'll check it out. My name is Jake by the way, I go by JJ." JJ reached over to shake hands. John hesitated, he really didn't see this coming, he slowly reached out, took a step and shook his hand. "I'm John." Then he stepped back again. "Good luck with the job search." John gave a half wave and started walking toward the road, he turned back as JJ was heading back to his chair. "Good luck." JJ waved a thanks and John kept going. *'That guy doesn't seem to be the rodent type, he's way too put together.'* He stepped up to the road from the ditch and followed the white line the rest of the way to Fir Street.

23

Wednesday

Scruffy woke early Wednesday, his stomach wasn't feeling well. He was pretty sure it was something he had eaten the day before. Not that it was rotten, just too rich for him, he doesn't get to eat well on a regular basis so when someone offers him food, even though it's good food, it can have consequences. Scruffy had been on the streets going on ten years, his body reminded him of that every day now. The aches and pains of getting older combined with sleeping on the ground in the cold weather was taking its toll. Scruffy, formerly known as William Hart, was a military veteran, and had seen some action in multiple overseas conflicts. He suffers from PTSD but that's not the reason he's on the streets. He had a job when he returned from active duty and tried to make a go of civilian life. His parents passed away in a car accident several years after his return and that put a strain on him. He couldn't keep up with the house that they left him. His jobs were the dead end variety, they weren't good enough to keep the lights on, let alone pay the mortgage and taxes. He eventually lost the house and since he was never one with close friends he ended up on the streets. His military background helped him cope with living on the streets, he was able to fend for himself quite easily. After a short stint living in the city, sleeping in doorways, Scruffy moved far out into the wilderness, living off of the land and what he could build with his hands, surviving by capturing his own food. It worked for several years, he was actually the happiest living in the wilderness. He could go months without ever seeing another person, longer if he didn't make the trek to civilization on occasion. That trek would take a week round trip if he only spent one day in town gathering whatever supplies he could find and carry. Eventually the cold winters were more than he could endure, he wasn't able to stockpile enough food to get through the winter. He moved closer to town so the trek to civilization wasn't as far. He ventured into town more often to try and scavenge what he could from dumpsters and possibly get some handouts when he could. At one point he decided to travel to different parts of the country, walking mostly, hitchhiking some, though his body odor was prohibitive. There were times that he would get picked up by a truck driver at a fuel stop and told to get out of the truck less than ten miles down the road because the driver couldn't take the smell. Other times he was able to gather enough change to clean up at a pay shower, then he would be able to get rides without offending the driver. Scruffy traveled much of the west coast and across the south. Eventually he made his way back across the central U.S. by traveling back roads and lesser known highways. He settled in the Northwest, Portland area to be specific, due to the generally mild winters as well as mild summers. Much of the U.S. has extreme weather in one way or the other. While the Northwest is pretty wet in the winter, it isn't that cold. There are dryer climates but the summer months are just too hot in those areas. Scruffy had given up living in the wilderness, he was in his fifties and couldn't do what he needed to in order to survive that. He had found that he could survive closer to town, there were a large number of people that were generous with handouts and many of the local shelters would provide clothes and tent supplies when he needed them. Scruffy now lives in a tent off Highway 18 near other homeless people, some of them have been homeless for years like he has, others are new to the game and are prone to making mistakes that could end tragically. He's not that social with them, but he does talk to some of the others on occasion. They tell each other of food opportunities, where good shelter areas might be, as well as warn each other of possible dangers. He is fully aware of the killings that have spread across the area, the news travels quickly amidst the homeless. They have their own network of communication. For William, like it or not, they are a community. He watched as the police and investigators combed over every inch of the lot across the highway where Caveman and Cave Woman were killed. He wasn't close to them but had met them a few times. They had some substance abuse problems that Scruffy didn't care for. Scruffy had tried illicit drugs, tried to dull the pain of life at times, but didn't like the after effect it had on his ability to survive, yes it dulled the pain but it dulled everything else as well. He had noticed the new arrival of other homeless people across the highway, the clean and trendy man with his new camping gear. He wondered how long he would last, Trendy didn't seem built for it. Once the winter came he suspected that Trendy would find better accommodations. He had seen Beer

Belly and his friend Blue Cap, they had been around for a few years in different locations, Scruffy had talked with them many times and shared information with them. They were drinkers to help numb their senses but they were survivors. The third tent next to Beer Belly's was a mystery, the man that came and went from there seemed shady, he was a scary looking individual, even to someone that has been on the streets for years. He was one to steer clear of, even Scruffy made sure he crossed to the other side of the street when he saw him coming. There were a few homeless people living on the same side of the highway as Scruffy, he talked with them some, keeping the community close, they had to look out for each other. Scruffy had an interaction with John that made him stop and think about where he was and how he lived. John had caught him digging through the trash bins outside of his apartment, while John was kind to him he asked him to leave and not dig through his trash, then handed him a bottle of water before he left. *'It's discarded rubbish, why would he care if I dig through it looking for something useful?'* That was a mystery to Scruffy, *'It's just trash.'* Then Scruffy took a look around his camp one day, realizing that some of the 'trash' was gone. He wasn't sure where it went but it looked better. The homeless have nowhere to put the trash that they themselves make, or things that they want to discard, sure they could take it to a dumpster and throw it in, but most won't, it was too much effort. Scruffy talked with Trendy across the highway, JJ, he told him that someone had come to his camp and cleaned up as well and that he helped him put trash into the back of the little truck. It occurred to Scruffy that it was likely the same person that cleaned up around his area. Just another strange occurrence in the life of a homeless person.

24

Thursday

Jesse and Clint had gone out for dinner on Thursday evening while Katy was at work, it was around 7 PM. Jesse picked Clint up and when they were done they went back to Jesse's apartment, Jesse had bought some new fishing gear he was anxious to show Clint. The conversation eventually came around to John. "I tried to talk to John the other day about him going out to rodent camps at night. He didn't want to hear it." Jesse had gotten up to grab a couple of beers from the fridge. "Oh yeah? Did he shut you down?" Clint reached out to take one of the beers. "Well, kind of. He told me that he went out to the river site where those rodents had been killed. He wanted to see if the site had been cleaned up." Jesse was smiling, almost laughing at that. "Yeah right, he wanted to see how good of a job he did in the middle of the night." Clint downed half his beer in one long guzzle. "Well maybe, but what struck me when I asked him why he went out there was how much it meant to him that the sites get cleaned up.

He was very passionate about the fact that our nature is being ruined by the rodents." Jesse was sitting with his elbows on his knees looking at Clint while he spoke. "That doesn't let him off the hook as far as being the killer now does it? Seems like he's pretty worked up about the rodents making the messes. Besides, how else do you stop the messes but get rid of the rodents?" Clint nodded then hung his head down thinking about it. He looked back at Jesse. "It doesn't mean he is doing it, but it doesn't mean he's innocent either." At 9:30 Katy got home from work, "Hello boys. Clint, nice to see you, it's been a couple minutes hasn't it?" Clint stood up to greet Katy. "It has been a bit, good to see you. You're here already? What time is it?" Clint pulled out his phone to check. "9:30, should probably get going soon, I have to work tomorrow." Jesse gave Katy a hug. "Clint rode over here with me, so I will have to take him home in a bit." Katy sat on the sofa next to Jesse. "Okay, no rush. What's the topic tonight? I could use some good conversation." Clint sat back down as well. "We were just talking about your neighbor John, what kind of weird stuff he's been up to, going out and cleaning out homeless camps." Katy shrugged a little and tilted her head to the side. "It is weird, I've been thinking about it some off and on while I was at work. Jesse said he was in a trance or something, acting like a zombie when he was dumping stuff in the bin outside. What if he doesn't know what he's doing? What if he really is in a trance, like he's hypnotized and someone is controlling him?" Jesse and Clint were both looking at Katy almost squinting their eyes at her trying to decide if what she was saying was plausible. Clint scratched his head and ran his hand down his face. "That seems so far out there that I can't grasp that as a possibility. But... The trance thing, like he's asleep. Maybe that's it? Maybe he's sleepwalking?" Katy pointed at Clint excitedly. "Yes! Maybe that's it! I just wonder what in his subconscious would make him go out and clean up homeless camps." Clint looked at the carpet for a moment then back at Jesse, then at Katy. "Do you think that John has something to do with the murders?" Katy hesitated. "I don't know. Going out in the middle of the night to 'clean up' homeless sites is pretty weird. I wouldn't say that he is off the suspect list, that's for sure." Jesse had just been listening to them go back and forth before he spoke up. "He could be the guy. I have seen him dumping stuff that he picked up at rodent camps twice and I saw him at one of them out there picking stuff up. I wonder if he is going to hit that one next?" Clint looked at Jesse, "It doesn't fit." Katy watched Jesse's reaction, he stiffened. "Why not? What doesn't fit?" Clint straightened up ready to give his explanation. "Up to this point as far as we know, he has only gone and picked up trash at the site after there has been a murder. So why did he go to that one and there hasn't been anyone killed there?" Jesse laughed, "There goes my theory. I don't know what's up with that guy. The whole, 'being in a trance' or 'sleepwalking' part is kind of freaky to me. Does he even know what he's been doing?" Clint chugged the rest of his beer. "I tried to talk to him about it, but I didn't get around to asking him if he knows that he has been going out at night. I need to figure out a way to bring it up that isn't suspicious." Katy took Jesse's beer and took a drink. "That might be tough. At this point he doesn't know that anyone knows he has been out at night does he?" Clint looked at Katy then back at Jesse. "No, I don't think so. I just found out Sunday when Jesse told me about the late night dumpster episode." Katy shrugged at both of them. "What does it even matter? We shouldn't be involved, just report the weirdness to the police and let them handle it." Clint stood up thinking he would get ready to leave. "Yeah but I don't want to turn a guy in that isn't guilty of something. I like the guy, I work with the guy. I would rather confront him first and see what's going on. He told me on Monday that he went out to the river site where those other three were killed, just to see if it had been cleaned up and when I asked him why, he got kind of defensive about it, well, maybe defensive is the wrong word, he was very passionate that 'nature should be restored,' or something like that. He just really wanted the area to be cleaned up." Katy shrugged and nodded. "So you think that maybe that's really all he is doing? He really just wants all the trash cleaned up?" Clint raised his hands and shrugged. "Yeah maybe." Katy got an enthusiastic look on her face. "Oh! I went and talked with Berta on Monday. That whole mess with the firetrucks and police cars over by Ted's Grocery! That was a murder. It was the same as the other ones! The people in that tent, there were two of them, a man and a woman, they were tied up and then the tent was burned." Clint was shocked. "Oh crap! It wasn't just an accident? Man, I thought it was a campfire that got out of control." Katy gestured at Clint, "Yes! That's what I thought too. Berta's nephew is a policeman and he tells her all about the crime scenes. He told her it looks like the same guy that had done the other ones around town." Clint shook his head and looked at Jesse for his reaction. Jesse didn't have much expression on his face. "The news said that two people died. I guess they didn't specify that they were murdered." Katy was shaking her head. "No they didn't, nor did they say that it was the same type of murder or that it's probably the same person that did it." Clint motioned to the door. "I think it's time to go, it's going to be tough to get up in the morning." Jesse got up and started for the door, giving Katy a kiss on the way past. "I'll be back in a little bit." Katy gave Clint a hug. "See you later Clint, don't be a stranger." Katy walked them both to the door. "Jesse, I'll probably be in bed when you get back."

Jesse and Clint left in Jesse's truck. As they were leaving the lot John pulled out in front of them. "Hey, speaking of, isn't that John?" Clint shook his head, "Would you look at that. Where do you suppose he's going?" Jesse was shaking his head as well. "I guess we are about to find out. What are the odds that he's going to a rodent camp?" Clint could hardly believe his eyes. "Well it's almost 10:45, it's either a rodent camp or a booty call. My guess with his recent history is rodent camp." Jesse followed, giving John plenty of distance. As they approached the rodent camp John started to slow down. "He's slowing down, looks like he's going into the brush." Jesse looked over at Clint. "Those tracks where he turned, that was me." He had a big smile on his face but Clint could barely see him in the dark. Clint looked at him with a furrowed brow. "What? Across the rodent camp? That was you?" Jesse was nodding. "Yeah I dropped my soda in my lap on the way home from work one day after I stopped and talked to you at the GasNGo. I reached down to grab it and it went everywhere, then I lost control, went into the ditch, flying through the bushes, almost ran down one of the tents. I hit a shopping cart and sent it flying. It was a mess." Jesse was laughing at the whole incident thinking it was pretty funny. Clint's eyes were wide with astonishment. "Why didn't you tell me about that?" Jesse was still chuckling. "I was embarrassed a little, it was pretty stupid." Clint pointed at the Ted's Grocery parking lot. "Pull in here, we can go back through the trail and see what John is up to." Jesse pulled in and parked his truck near the building. They both got out and closed the doors quietly with just a click. With only one street light in the parking lot there was just a gray light casting shadows across the lot to where the bushes started at the edge of the pavement. The air was cool and clear, a light breeze rustled distant leaves. They walked to the edge of the lot with their arms spread out, reaching for the first bush they would come to. Jesse pointed to their right, whispering to Clint. "I think there's a trail over here, if we go down there a little we should be able to see what he's doing." They found the trail and walked, crouching below the shadows of the bushes from the light in the parking lot, feeling their way carefully with each step. Jesse was in the lead, he stopped after several minutes. "Look, just up there, to the left of those three tents." Clint raised up a little to try and see over the bushes, he could make out the shadowy domes of the tents in front of them. John was moving in the dark, bending down, standing back up, moving over to his truck, then coming back. "Is he picking stuff up?" Jesse moved farther down the trail, trying to get a better vantage point. "It looks like it. I can't really tell. He's really close to those tents." Clint passed Jesse on the trail and moved closer to where John was working. They could see John's dark shadow moving back and forth, he was 20 yards away. "Looks like he's picking up that pile of bags by those tents." Jesse raised up to get a better look. "Looks like it, should we go talk to him?" Clint got a little closer. "No, I've heard it's not good to wake someone up if they're sleepwalking. Besides, if he is up to no good, I don't want him knowing I was here." Jesse started to turn back toward the truck. "Yeah, that's probably a good call." Clint started moving toward the truck as well. "I've seen enough for now, let's see what happens tomorrow." They made their way back to the truck as carefully as they came in. Jesse fired up the engine and put the truck in gear. "That was pretty interesting, I didn't think we would get to see that." Clint was looking out the window toward the bushes where John was. "No kidding, and it seems like he is just picking up trash. That's really strange, I guess he is pretty set on cleaning up these camps." Jesse chucked at that. "I'll stop back by to see what he's doing when I come back through."

JJ heard the truck pull in, this time it went farther past his tent and backed up into the bushes by his three neighbors. He was tired and really didn't want to get out of his sleeping bag, but eventually the curiosity got to him. He pulled himself out of the bag and put on some warmer clothes. He unzipped his tent quietly, not wanting to alarm whomever might be outside. He crawled out of the flap and got to his feet, looking around in the dim light, seeing mostly shadows and no movement at first. JJ walked around to the other side of his tent, still trying to make out where the vehicle he had heard went. A car passed on the road casting a quick flash of light and long shadows across the lot of bushes and vines. He caught a slight reflection of something off to his right. He stopped and watched that direction, trying to get his eyes to focus in the dark. He heard something, some tromping and rustling in the bushes, then caught a shadow moving in front of the street light in the distance. JJ was feeling a little skittish after speaking with the detective about the recent murders. He moved cautiously toward the shadow and the rustling sounds until he could make out the shadow of the same little truck he had seen previously.

He stopped to watch, seeing the shadow of the human moving from the pile of trash to the truck and back again. He was picking things up as if he could see clearly in the light of day. He wasn't feeling the urge to help this time, he just watched for a bit, the shadow moved quietly back and forth. He could hear a rustle now and then, or a bush dragging on something as it was moved to the truck but nothing else. JJ was satisfied that the cleaner was harmless and went back to his tent; back to his sleeping bag and blankets to try to get warm and sleep the rest of the night.

Jesse pulled back into the grocery parking lot and parked in the same spot he had parked when Clint was with him. He looked around the lot just before disappearing into the brush, just to make sure no one else was around. He crouched low as he moved down the path toward John, he spotted him as he was tying the load into his truck. Jesse stayed low, watching John work the ropes back and forth across the bed of the truck. John moved from one side to the other, securing the rope and the pile of trash as he worked to make sure it wouldn't fly out as he drove back to the apartments. Soon enough, Jesse saw John get into the truck and watched as he drove away, seeing his taillights bounce and swerve through the bushes on his way out of the field, up the ditch and onto the road heading back to the Fir Street apartments to pile the trash into the dumpster.

25

Friday

Friday morning John woke up on time, it was like that movie *Groundhog Day*, *'It just keeps happening'*. He knew he had been out again the night before, his arms were sore and he had some scratches on his hands and forearms. His hands were dirty and the skin on his hands was incredibly dry. He ignored it for the most part after inspecting his hands. *'This is my life now,'* and started moving through his morning routine, getting ready for work. Nothing was too far out of place from the previous times he had been out at night. His clothes were dropped at the door along with his shoes. Nothing was too dirty, it had been dry the last several days. He was tired though, he had purple rings under his eyes, the late nights were wearing him down. He sipped his coffee generously before leaving the apartment and refilled his go mug. Once in the parking lot he checked his truck, *'At least I am still emptying the back, I don't want to have to do that in the morning.'* It was now the second week in October, the weather had been off and on stormy but mostly holding out nicely for the fall. There were many more leaves on the ground and soon there wouldn't be any more in the trees. John walked along the edge of the road, watching the white line, listening for cars coming from behind and letting them whoosh past without flinching. He glanced over toward Scruffy's camp, no movement, some new bags of trash had been strewn about. John couldn't tell if they came from Scruffy or one of his neighbors. *'I was hoping Scruffy would take better care of his camp.'* He looked across the highway where JJ's camp was, it didn't look any different. He couldn't see the other tents from the road, where Beer Belly and Blue Cap were staying. When John got closer to the GasNGo he could see that Clint was at work already, checking the readings on the pumps, handling the shift change. He arrived a few minutes late but Steve didn't mention it. John got a refill on his coffee and took one out to Clint. "Good morning Clint." Clint looked up from his paperwork. "Good morning. Damn! You look beat." Clint then realized why but didn't say anything just yet. John felt a little shocked about Clint's reaction. "I didn't think it was that obvious. I haven't been sleeping very well, I think it's catching up to me." Clint raised his brows at John. "Yeah, I would say it's catching up to you. Those are some dark circles under your eyes." John gave him a shrug and went off to help a customer. Most of the morning was routine until about 10 AM.

Blue Cap had been out of his tent for a few hours, he had gone around the back of Ted's Grocery and looked through the dumpsters for potential throw away food items. Then he went down the street to the local coffee shop where, on occasion, he would be treated to a coffee by one of the morning patrons. He had struck out this morning and returned to the camp to see if Beer Belly had gotten out of bed yet. Blue Cap was rather oblivious to his surroundings, he hadn't noticed that the large pile of trash near his camp was no longer there or that he didn't have to step over trash that was strewn on the path in front of the three tents all in a row. He hadn't noticed that there was a large slit in the side of Beer Belly's tent when he left, the slit was on the opposite side of his tent, so he didn't see it when he walked past. Beer Belly's tent was at the end of a row of three other tents, buried deeper in the bushes than the tent of Trendy JJ. Blue Cap noticed the slit when he returned. *'What happened there? I guess he got careless with his pocket knife.'* When he walked up to the tent and peeked through the slit, it was not what he expected to see. He jumped back so quickly he nearly tripped over his own feet. *'Oh no!'* In a panic he rushed to the zipper that was already open and took another look. He reached in and grabbed Beer Belly's leg and shook it, *'Hey! Hey wake up!'* There was no response. Blue Cap didn't bother to take the bag off his friend's head. He jumped up after Beer Belly didn't respond and started jogging toward Ted's Grocery. Blue Cap was looking particularly ratty, his black pants looked dark gray and were torn up one leg, his jacket was two sizes too big and frayed all the way around the bottom. His high top sneakers were untied and flapped loosely on his feet. Everything he had on flapped in the breeze with every jogging motion he made. Once inside the store he started shouting, "Hey, my friend needs help! Can someone help my friend?!" Blue Cap was a regular at Ted's Grocery and not appreciated as a loyal customer, he had been run out of the store on many occasions for trying to shoplift. "NO! You need to go." The first clerk at the counter, Brian Sweeney, was pointing his finger toward the doors. "Just turn it around and go right back outside!" Blue Cap was pointing outside where his friend was laying in his tent. "I need help, my friend needs help!" Brian wasn't having it, he had been yanked around by Blue Cap too many times. They would often come in the store in teams, one of them would try to distract the employees while the other one would pocket as much food as possible. Brian was sure this was another attempt at such a rouse. "No, you just need to leave, I'm not in the mood for your crap!" Blue Cap looked panicked. "I know we've tried to fool you before, but really, he needs help. He's not moving." Brian rolled his eyes at Blue Cap. The store manager, Darin Rogers, heard the commotion and came to the front of the store. "What's happening now?" Brian looked his way and gave a thumb over his shoulder at Blue Cap, "He says his friend needs help, says he's not moving or something. I just don't trust them." Darin rolled his head and his eyes in a circle at the same time. "Oh, I know! I don't trust it either." Blue Cap was making motions toward the door panicking. "Please come help, Please!" Darin drew a deep breath. "Okay, I'll go take a look. Brian, you watch here, make sure another one doesn't sneak in after him." Darin started walking toward Blue Cap and pointed to the door. "Okay, show me where he's at." Blue Cap turned so quickly his clothes spun outward from his body like a ballerina, and rushed to the door. He was jogging out in front of Darin who was not about to hurry on this goose chase. Blue Cap kept looking back at him. "Come on! Hurry up, he needs help!" Darin was getting exasperated with the situation, looking around for someone that needs help. "Well, where is he?" Blue Cap pointed out into the lot of bushes. "He's out here, in his tent." Darin slowed down. "I don't want to go out there. What kind of trick is this? I really don't trust what's happening right now." Blue Cap was excited, almost jumping up and down. "He NEEDS help! I don't know what to do!" Darin gave in and quickened his step again. "Okay, show me where." Blue Cap led him to the trail through the bushes, hurrying in front, looking over his shoulder every few steps to make sure Darin was still behind him. "It's right up here, see those tents? It's the one on the end." Blue Cap rushed to the tent on the end and pulled the flap back before Darin could get there. Darin walked up to the tent and bent at the waist to look in. "Whoa! What the hell?" Darin took three steps back. He was shocked, he lost all the blood in his face, he went completely pale white, his mouth was hanging open. He started to wretch, unable to control his gag reflex. Blue Cap stared at him with his jaw hanging down. "What do I do? Can you help? What do I do?" Darin was trying to catch his breath, bent over staring at the ground. "Did you check for a pulse?" Blue Cap stuck his head into the tent. "I don't know how." Darin had caught his breath and moved closer to the tent. "Move over." Blue Cap moved to the side to let Darin get closer. Darin reached into the tent, trying hard not to get his head inside in case there might be a smell. He found Beer Belly's hand and grasped at his wrist. There was nothing, he tried again thinking he didn't have the right spot. Darin realized the wrist was cold and pulled his hand back quickly. "I think we're too late. I would say pull the bag off of his head but he's already dead." Blue Cap fell backwards onto his behind and scooted backwards away from the tent with a look of horror on his face. Darin moved away from the opening of the tent as well. "I'm going to go call the police. I think you shouldn't touch anything in there." Blue Cap sat there with a ghostly look on his face with his arms wrapped around his knees, rocking slightly front to back. He had lost the color and expression from his face. Darin stood up, still feeling the slight gag reflex in his throat. He started walking toward the store, then turned around and looked at Blue Cap. "Do you want to come with me?" Blue Cap didn't respond, he was staring blankly at the tent. Darin shouted. "Hey!" Blue Cap looked at him this time. "Do you want to come with me?" Blue Cap looked back at the tent then slowly got to his feet and started to walk toward Darin. They walked single file down the worn dirt path in silence. When they got back to the store Darin approached Brian and spoke in a low quiet voice. "Will you please get him a cup of coffee and find him a place to sit down for a few minutes?" Brian had a concerned look on his face. "What happened?" Darin shook his head, looking into Brian's eyes. "He wasn't joking, his friend is dead out there in his tent." Brian's jaw dropped. "Holy crap! Okay I'll take care of him. Are you calling the police?" Darin turned toward his office. "Yeah, going to do that now."

Clint was on break when he heard a siren going by on the highway, he stepped out of the break room with coffee and a powdered sugar donut in his hand to watch them go past the station. John had just finished with a customer and was standing at the end of one of the pump islands. They both watched as the police cruiser pulled into the Ted's Grocery parking lot. The officer got out and went into the front of the store at about the same time as a second cruiser with lights and sirens went blaring past the station. Clint looked at John. "Shoplifter?" John looked back at him and shrugged. "Seems excessive for that." They both looked back at the second cruiser parking near the first one. The second officer disappeared into the store. Clint walked over to where John was standing. "Well, this should be interesting." Moments later both officers came out of the store with Blue Cap and Darin and started walking toward the vacant lot. One of the officers stopped and appeared to be talking into the radio on his shoulder before he disappeared into the bushes. Clint looked over at John thinking about what he and Jesse had seen the night before. He didn't say anything, but was wondering what had happened out there that would cause police activity. "What do you think is happening?" John looked at him, "I'm afraid to think of what it might be." There were several more customers in the next 10 minutes, by the time they had finished with them there were three more police cruisers in Ted's Grocery lot that had pulled close to the trail that led into the bushes. John and Clint watched as one of the officers surrounded the area with crime scene tape. John withdrew a little, he was worried that it might be something that he had done. Clint was watching him for signs that he might be involved. John didn't let it show on the outside, but on the inside he wasn't sure. Over the next hour, several more police and detective units arrived at the scene. There were police combing the area for evidence. James Milkey had been called out, he was leading the investigation of the other homeless murders and was onsite at the last murder in the same vacant lot. James walked the area around the three tents, taking notes and looking at the scene, trying to recreate what had happened in his mind. This scene was much more telling than the last one due to the fire that had destroyed most of the evidence. This scene looked more like the riverfront crime scene, except the bodies weren't in tents at that one. *'There are so many similarities, but each one is just slightly different.'* Blue Cap was out at the edge of the lot, they had given him a chair to sit in and he was being questioned by officer Roak, Blue Cap was clearly in shock. "Did you hear anything unusual last night?" Blue Cap was staring up at Officer Roak with a blank look on his face. "No, we had scored some malt liquor last night so we had tied one on pretty good before we went to sleep. I didn't hear anything." Roak was taking notes to give to Detective Milkey. "What time did you get up this morning?" Blue Cap looked down and shrugged. "I don't know for sure, I don't have a watch. It wasn't too much after sunrise cause I had to pee really bad." Roak nodded. "Sure, Okay, what did you do after that?" Blue Cap started rubbing his head trying to remember how his morning went. "I uh.. I went over to the back of Ted's Grocery to check the dumpsters, then I went down to the coffee shop to try and get a cup of coffee." Roak made a few notes. "Is that common? For you to be out before your buddy?" Blue Cap still had his hands on top of his head, rubbing them back and forth. "Yeah, yeah, it is... Uh... was. He always sleeps late so I didn't even look at his tent when I went past it. I noticed it when I came back after the coffee shop." More notes: "Okay, how long do you think you were gone?" Blue Cap groaned a little, "Oh man, I don't know, maybe it was two or three hours, that's when I found him, I was going to wake him up. He wouldn't move and I didn't know what to do so I ran over to the store and tried to get them to help." Roak took a few minutes to make more notations. "Did the manager 'Darin' come out right away?" Blue Cap was shaking his head and looking at the ground, he had his elbows on his knees looking like he might throw up at any minute. "No, it took some convincing for them to come help." Roak was watching Blue Cap, he had no reason not to believe what he was saying, it all seemed to be true. He made a few more notes on his pad to give to Detective Milkey.

"What about that other tent next to yours on the end? Who stays in that one?" Blue cap looked over toward the bushes like he would see what officer Roak was talking about. "That guy comes and goes, he disappears for a few days, then he'll come back and stay a night or two, then he's gone again. I haven't seen him in about three days." Roak noted 'Tent three missing three days' "Do you know his name?" Blue Cap shrugged. "Not his real name, goes by 'Lightning' or 'Thunder' or something stupid like that. He's not too social." Roak chuckled. "Please wait here, I'll see if the detective wants to speak with you." Blue Cap looked up at him. "I don't have anywhere else to go." Officer Roak returned a few minutes later and handed Blue Cap a bottle of water, then went down the trail to find Detective Milkey. Officer Halloway had finished closing off the area with crime tape and was watching the perimeter for people that just want to gawk at the scene. "Excuse me Detective, I have some notes from the homeless man, Kent Riley, that found the body." Detective Milkey was walking the area between JJ's tent and the three tents in a row looking at tire tracks and some drag marks in the dirt. "Sure, did he have anything interesting to tell you?" Roak started reading off his notes. "He stated that he didn't hear anything last night, he and the deceased tied one on with some malt liquor so he slept pretty hard, but he was up before the deceased, out looking for food. This was a common occurrence so he wasn't worried that his friend wasn't out of the sac yet. The third tent has been vacant for the last three days, he says that the fella that occupies it isn't very social and he comes and goes. I'll have this written up for you in more detail by tomorrow." Milkey had stopped looking at the tracks and was looking at Roak. "Thank you officer Roak, I appreciate the help. Any reason to think he isn't telling you the truth?" Roak shook his head, "Nah, he seems pretty shook up about it. I think the two of them were pretty good friends." Milkey nodded, "Yeah I don't doubt it. Would you mind going over to the station across the way and asking if any of them saw anything unusual out here, any vehicles in the area that aren't usually here?" Officer Roak looked behind him where the station would be but couldn't see it through all the brush. "Sure, I'd be happy to. I'll let you know what I come up with." Jamie was smiling inside, he was getting to do a little detective work, *'Nice change of pace. Better than guarding the perimeter.'*

John and Clint had been watching off and on between customers, they couldn't really see anything from their vantage point except officers coming and going, medical transport had arrived and was still on site. John looked over after hanging up a pump and saw that an officer was walking their way. "Hey Clint." John gave a sideways nod toward the officer. "Someone coming to ask questions." Clint looked over. "Oh wow, okay. This should be interesting." Just about that time another car pulled in. Clint went to help knowing that John would have to talk to the officer first. John was standing in front of the fuel island watching Officer Roak walk toward him. "Hello Officer, what can we do for you?" Officer Roak approached with a slight smile on his face. "Good afternoon, I recognize you from the last incident we had out in that lot." John reached his hand out to greet Officer Roak. "Yes sir, Officer Roak isn't it? I'm John Dell, that is Clint Jacobs, he should be done there in a minute." Roak retrieved his notebook from his pocket and flipped to a clean page. "That's right. If I remember right, you walk past that lot every day on your way to and from work here, correct?" John leaned against one of the fuel pumps with his hands in his pockets. "Yes, that's correct." Clint finished with his customer and walked up next to John. Roak turned to him. "I'm Officer Roak, do you mind answering a few questions?" Clint shrugged, "Sure, no problem." Roak looked at his notes. "John tells me your name is Clint Jacobs?" "Yes it is." "What time do you two start work here in the morning?" Clint spoke first. "We start at 6 AM." Roak was looking around the station, checking to see if anyone else was around. "Did you happen to see anyone down toward Ted's Grocery this morning? Any vehicles that you don't normally see?" John was shaking his head. "I don't recall seeing any down that way." Roak looked at John. "Even when you passed it this morning on your way in?" John shook his head again, "No, nothing." Roak looked at Clint. "How about you? See anything out of the ordinary?" Clint shook his head as well. "No, sorry I haven't seen anything." Roak was disappointed but not surprised. "Thank you gentlemen. Enjoy your day." Roak made a couple of notes below the names he had written down then walked back to the vacant lot.

Detective Milkey was walking the area in larger and larger circles looking at the ground trying to figure out if the tire tracks tied together with the murder. He had noticed that JJ was sitting in his lawn chair from the time that he had arrived on the scene. He didn't start with JJ, somehow he knew that JJ wasn't going to go anywhere. Eventually his circle got large enough that JJ was his next order of business. "Good afternoon JJ. I was hoping we wouldn't have to see each other again. No offense intended." JJ stood and shook the Detectives hand. "I completely understand and agree. I haven't been briefed on the situation but since you're here, I am guessing it isn't good." Milkey smiled. "You would be right. It isn't good. So I'll jump right in. What did you see?" JJ pointed at the tracks in the dirt that James was looking at. "Those tracks that you were looking at, I saw that truck last night. It was the same one that was here the other night cleaning up trash." Milkey turned and looked at the tracks again. "He went to a little bit different of an area, did you help him last night?" JJ shook his head and crossed his arms. "No, I was too tired. I got up and looked around real careful like, you have me spooked with all this murder stuff. I saw the guy picking up trash in the shadows, it was the same truck, he was backed up over there near those tents. He was just loading up bags. I didn't think he was going to do anything like that, so after a couple of minutes I went back to my tent and went to sleep." Milkey made a few notes on his notepad. "You didn't see him drive out?" JJ shifted uncomfortably. "No, but I did hear him drive out. I hadn't fallen to sleep yet." Milkey was watching JJ's body language. "What time do you think that was?" JJ instinctively looked at his watch. "It was about 11:30, maybe a little later, I looked at my watch when I got up and it was about quarter to 11." "I am guessing you didn't get a plate number again did you?" JJ looked at the ground. "No, sorry, he was just picking up trash like last time. I had no idea this would happen." Roak nodded. "Yeah I figured as much. So you didn't hear anything else? There must have been at least a little bit of a struggle, that guy was pretty big." JJ shook his head again looking right at Detective Milkey. "No, I didn't hear a thing." Milkey closed his notebook and put it away. "Please be careful out here, I don't really think it's safe." He reached out and shook JJ's hand. "Thank you for your time." Detective Milkey turned and walked out the trail toward Ted's Grocery as JJ watched.

"John, what the heck is going on?" Clint was standing in front of him with a concerned look on his face. "I saw you drive out into those bushes last night and start picking up trash or something near those tents." John's eyes widened and his neck started to turn flush red. "You saw me?" Clint looked over his shoulder to make sure the officer was far enough away. "Yeah I did! What the heck were you doing out there?" John looked down and rubbed his forehead with his fingers. "Oh man, I'm not sure. I mean I thought I knew what was happening but now I don't know for sure. I kind of remember a dream that I was putting garbage bags in my truck, but it's really spotty. I can't even tell you for sure that it wasn't a dream." Clint was standing rigid with his feet far apart and arms across his chest. "Do you need some help? Tell me what's happening." John was still looking down. "I don't know, I didn't think I needed help but maybe I do." Clint bent down and looked up at John's face trying to look into his eyes. "Did you do that?" Then pointed behind him to the rodent camp. John looked up at where Clint was pointing. "I don't know." Clint straightened up again. "I think you need to tell me what you do know." John stiffened and rammed his hands in his pockets like a toddler that doesn't want to follow directions. "Okay, I'll tell what has been going on, but not here at work. After work." A car pulled in behind him to the forward pump. Clint squeezed his lips together. "Okay fine, I get that. Today though, after work." John nodded his agreement and went to help their customer. There were only a few hours left in their - shift, with a steady flow of cars to keep them occupied it felt like it went quickly. Clint went and clocked out first. "Hey John." Getting his attention as the second shift was showing up for duty. "How about we go over to the Burger Joint and get food, we can talk there?" John went into the break room to clock out. Clint wanted to make sure he wouldn't say no. "I'll buy, shakes and all." John hadn't eaten out in quite some time and it actually sounded good. "Yeah, that sounds great. I'll meet you over there?" Clint shook his head. "Nah, you can ride with me." They went to Clint's truck, John got in after Clint cleared the passenger seat off from his extra clothes and jacket, just in case the weather turned bad. The Burger Joint was just down the street, they were there in minutes. The Burger Joint is a cute little locally owned shop, one of those retro 50's diners with black and white checkerboard floors and red and white curtains, each booth has red bouncy vinyl seats and a red formica table top with a metal band around the edge. They specialize in burgers of all sorts and have a big ice cream shake machine that makes 8 different flavors of shakes. Clint and John stood at the counter for a minute, gazing at the menu, trying to decide which of the 15 burgers to indulge in. Clint placed his order. 'A Colossus, no onion, fries and chocolate shake.' John went a little more reserved, 'A Western Bacon, no grilled onions, no tomato, strawberry shake and fries.' "Easy peasy," said the lady at the counter. Clint paid the bill and they went and sat at a booth on the end of the window row. There wasn't anyone in the shop except them, privacy wouldn't be an issue right now. "John, I'll tell ya man, last night was a shocker. Me and Jesse left his place about 10:45 and we had already been talking about you." John pulled his head back in surprise. "What? Why?" Clint raised his brows and folded his arms across one another on the table. "Jesse had seen you at one of the rodent camps, as you call them, picking up trash. Then you woke him up at 4 AM dumping trash into the dumpster outside his apartment." John gritted his teeth some.

"Oh, I hadn't even considered that someone I know might see me. I know I have been going out at night, it took awhile for me to figure out what was going on, but then I pieced it together." Clint motioned with his hand for John to stop a moment. "Wait, you know you have been going out and doing this? How long have you known? How long have you been doing it? I have so many questions." John pulled his head back straightening up his spine, he looked at the ceiling for a moment then back at Clint. "Okay, well, the first couple of times I didn't know what was happening. I got up in the morning and my clothes were dirty and I was super tired, then I found that my truck was full of trash." The server brought out the milkshakes and set some condiments on the table. "The first time weird things started happening was about the time when those people were killed in the car at my apartment complex. Do you remember when Jesse came to work and told you about them?" Clint was sucking on the straw to his extremely thick milkshake, his cheeks caved into the sides of his mouth. "Oh yeah, I remember that." John was drawing circles with his finger on the table like he was connecting the dots of everything that had happened. "That was around the time that Steve said he saw me out in my truck in the middle of the night. I had no idea and still don't know where I went that night." Clint's face brightened. "Yes! Booty call night." John chuckled. "Yes booty call, I wish that's what it was." John unwrapped his straw and plunged it into his milkshake, stabbing it up and down as if it would help mix it together more. "I didn't know where I went and those people were murdered in front of the apartments. I wasn't so sure that I didn't do it." Clint held up a finger. "Are you sure now that you didn't do it?" John stopped drawing circles for a moment and stared at the tabletop. "No, not entirely, but I'm pretty sure it wasn't me." Clint pushed his milkshake aside and bounced on the seat trying to get more comfortable. "Can we back up for a minute? What is happening when you're out? Are you in a trance?" John took a deep breath and looked out the window for a moment. "When I was a kid, I used to sleepwalk. I haven't done it in years to my knowledge. It seems that is what's happening to a pretty extreme level. It would happen when I was under some kind of stress, some situation that I couldn't control. I don't know if you've noticed but I get hung up on things and it works on me in the back of my mind, in my subconscious. I think that is where this is coming from." Clint had a thoughtful expression on his face, just looking at John. "Now that you mention it, no, not really, I take people at face value and I hadn't really noticed that. I notice that you do things pretty orderly and keep things pretty neat and tidy but other than that you don't really let on what you're thinking about too much." John nodded and looked back at the table and started drawing the circles again with his finger. "I suppose that's true, I don't let out what bothers me much. Anyway, the next thing that happened for me that I can remember was when I went out to the lake for a hike on my day off. I came across a rodent camp and it really set me off. It was such a mess and I can't stand to see that mess out in nature, what should be a beautiful setting is ruined by some careless homeless person." Clint's eyes got bigger, he stopped fidgeting with his milkshake. "Is that what this all boils down to? It's the giant messes? You keep working on this in your subconscious." John stopped drawing on the table again and looked Clint in the eyes. "I think so, I won't let it go until there is a solution." Clint cocked his head to the side. He lowered his voice. "You still don't know if you're killing those people?" John lowered his voice as well.

224

"I really don't know for sure, I had an episode just before that guy at the lake was killed. I really have no idea if I did that or not. I do know that I went out to that camp later and cleaned it up in the middle of the night." Clint breathed out, not realizing he was holding his breath. "When did you start to figure out that you were going out in the middle of the night and cleaning up camps?" The server brought out the baskets of fries and burgers setting them in front of John and Clint. "I think it was just after that murder, I found my truck wasn't parked in the right spot and then one morning it was full of trash, I had to empty out my truck and I didn't know what I had done." John was shaking his head, "The timeline gets a little fuzzy for me, it's hard to keep straight especially since I wasn't really awake for it." Clint was munching fries. "HA! Yeah that would make it hard to remember I guess." John was unwrapping his burger. "I don't remember any of the times I have been out, only little dream like bits of it, and most times not even that. I just get up in the morning and find my dirty clothes and I know that I did something." Clint was eating his burger and thinking about the timeline, considering what he would ask next. "This whole thing explains to me why you were so happy when you told me about going out to the river and seeing that the rodent camp had been cleaned up. Did you clean that up?" John nodded his head while he finished a bite of his burger. "Yeah, I had been out there and cleaned up some of it. I don't think I could have gotten all of it cleaned up, because there was a sofa out there, I don't remember seeing a sofa stuffed into the dumpsters." Clint rolled his eyes. "Wow this is a lot to take in, So when you went out there the second time when you went for a drive, it was all clean? Who do you think cleaned the rest of it?" John shrugged. "I don't know, I guess the county would come out and clean up after a crime scene." Clint was still trying to piece together a timeline in his head. "You don't know for sure if you killed those people... 'Rodents', but you do know that you went and cleaned up their camps. Moving forward, what about the one we could see from the GasNGo? The burnt one? Jesse said he saw you that night cleaning up the camp across the street. Do you think you killed that guy?" John stopped eating and looked at the table for a moment. "I saw that the next morning, I knew I had been out the night before because my clothes were dirty. There were two people in that tent, Caveman and Cave Woman." Clint held his hand up again. "Wait. Caveman and Cave Woman?" John looked at him across the table. "Yes, I give them all names. Those two looked like cavemen. He was a pretty rough looking guy with deep set eye sockets. He looked like a caveman." Clint smirked at giving them all names, "Okay, continue." John took another breath, getting ready to dive back into his story. "Well, I saw that their tent was burned up in the morning and I talked to the police. But what doesn't add up to me is that I only cleaned up on the other side of the road. I don't think I went over to that side. Also that was the first time I cleaned an area before there was a murder." John took another bite of his burger and his mood seemed to lighten up a little. "Don't take this wrong, I really despise the messes the rodents make, but I don't think I would kill them. I have met a couple of them, they aren't so bad." Clint stopped with fries in his hand, just before dipping them in ketchup. "Who did you meet?" John pushed his basket away from him with just a few fries left in the bottom. "There is one of the guys, where I cleaned up the night that Caveman was murdered, I call him Scruffy. I have had a couple of run ins with him. He was prowling around the neighborhoods where I live and I ran him off. I have seen him a bunch of times, he seems to move around more than most of them. Then there is the new guy that moved in where Caveman used to be, I call him Trendy but I guess his name is JJ." Clint interrupted, "You know his name? His actual name?" John nodded. "Yeah, after I realized that I had gone in and cleaned out Caveman's campsite at night I thought that I might have been seen and I wanted to know if anyone in there would recognize me. I think he did recognize me but he didn't say anything about it directly. He introduced himself then." Clint finished off his milkshake with a loud slurping sound as the straw sucked air at the bottom of the cup. "So you actually interacted with that guy?" John shrugged and nodded. "I did, he doesn't seem the type to be homeless. He's very well spoken and he's clean shaven, has clean clothes. I'm really not sure why he's out there." Clint frowned a bit. "That's odd, but okay, we can't change that. Did he say anything about you being out there picking up trash?" John shook his head, "No, I mentioned that it looked better, like someone had done some cleaning and he was looking me dead in the eyes and agreed and that maybe that person would come back and clean up some more." Clint threw his head back and laughed. "Then you did! Just yesterday. Are those all the times you have been out sleep cleaning?" John smirked at him with a sideways grin. "I think so, you get the idea, there are details lost in the story somewhere but that's the basics of it. What did you and Jesse see?" Clint leaned forward against the table. "You were pulling out of the lot at the same time we were, and since we were just talking about you dumping trash in the middle of the night we decided to follow you. We were going the same direction anyway so it wasn't like we went out of the way or anything. So, you slowed down at the vacant lot, 'rodent camp,' and turned in where those tire tracks went down through the ditch. We didn't know that you were sleepwalking so we kept our distance. Anyway we went and parked at Ted's and walked into the bushes from there. All we could see was you in the shadows, going back and forth, picking up garbage and putting it in your truck. We didn't stay too long, we just watched a few minutes then left." John seemed to be processing that for a few moments, "Thanks for not telling that to the officer. I feel like that would have raised some suspicion." Clint raised his eyebrows. "Yeah, I think you would be a prime suspect for sure. Honestly, I'm not convinced you didn't do it." John looked down at the table again. "I'm not convinced either. I have gone back and forth a couple times not being sure if I had anything to do with the murders. I was pretty sure that I didn't again until today, now I don't know." John paused for a while letting that soak in. "Thanks for the burger." Clint reached out to shake hands. "You're welcome. I'm not going to say anything, but you have to promise me that you will keep me informed if you go out again." John took his handshake. "Not sure what good that will do, but I will do it." They both got up and went outside. "Do you want a ride home?" John looked at the sky, there were no clouds and it was warm. "No, I'll walk. Thanks again." Clint gave him a wave as he got in his truck. "See you tomorrow." John raised a hand, then turned and walked down the street toward 18. He followed the white line, not cutting through the rodent camp, there were still a few investigation units on site, crime scene tape still flapping loosely from its hanging points. John spotted Scruffy sitting on the ground outside his tent rummaging through a trash bag, looking at whatever treasures he had picked up recently. John didn't see JJ near his camp, *'Maybe he's out looking for a job.'*

John felt a little relieved to have told someone what he has been going through, and a little anxious about it at the same time, *'What if I am responsible for the murders, now someone knows.'* He enjoyed the sun on his face as he walked home, but it was hard not to think about all the things he just went over with Clint. He was feeling run down and needed to get home and rest. He hoped that he would stay home and sleep.

26

Saturday

Katy and Jesse sat at their kitchen table in the morning, drinking coffee and catching up from the week, wearing baggy sweatpants and sweatshirts. They don't get to see each other much when Katy works the late shifts. Jesse had filled her in about seeing John Thursday night while taking Clint home. "I saw some more detective vehicles next to Ted's last night on my way to work. Do you know what they were there for?" Jesse got up to get more coffee. "Yeah, they found another dead rodent Friday morning. Clint told me the police came to ask him and John questions about it." Katy had an astonished expression on her face. "Did Clint tell them that you guys saw John in there the night before?" Jesse smiled a sheepish grin. "No. He said he left that out because the officers questions didn't really point to the night before and he was covering for John." Katy threw her head back "Oh my gosh! Why? He's doing all kinds of weird stuff and now it looks even more like he killed someone. Why is he covering for him?! You guys saw him there! He had to have killed them!" Katy was getting worked up. Jesse filled her mug after his. "I don't know for sure why he's covering for him, it does look like he did it. Clint doesn't think that he killed them though." Katy was shaking her head in disgust. "Why does he think that? Did you ask him?" Jesse sat back down across from her. "Yeah, we talked last night, he said he took John out for a burger and made John tell him everything." Katy leaned in with her mug in both hands on the table. "And now he thinks John didn't do it?" Jesse leaned onto the table as well. "Sort of, he isn't too sure really, but he did say John has a sleepwalking issue. When he sleepwalks he doesn't remember any of it, then he pieces it together the next day." Katy's mouth fell open. "So he *is* in a trance! Wow, that's so weird." Jesse leaned back again, "It is weird, he talked to him about cleaning up the various camps and stuff, things that we kind of knew already but he wasn't able to come up with anything that doesn't make him look like he isn't guilty." Katy thought about it for a while with her face over her mug of coffee, breathing it in. "I can't believe he was there last night and Clint didn't tell the police that he saw him. It has to be him, right?" Jesse shrugged as he got up from the table, "It sure looks like it. I am sure the police would think it looks like it too. Do you want breakfast?" Katy leaned back from the table and sipped her coffee. "No, I'm going to go have breakfast with Berta, I want to tell her about John and his sleepwalking, trance-like escapades." Jesse laughed at her description of John's outings. "Okay, I don't have plans today so I will be here."

Berta opened the door and the smell of bacon hit Katy at once. "Oh, I love bacon. Good morning Berta." Katy stepped in and hugged Berta tight. "It's good to see you Miss Katy. Come on in, I'll let you pour your own coffee this morning while I work on this French toast. Have some bacon too, I cooked the whole package so we may as well enjoy it." Katy came in and picked a mug from the cupboard and filled it up, topping it off with creamer. "Berta I'm just going to jump right into this craziness. Have you heard anything about the latest homeless camp killing?" Berta shot her a sideways look. "Oh goodness no, another one? I haven't had the news on the TV this morning which is weird for me, but I slept in a little this morning, then just got right to making breakfast." Katy went around to the outside of the kitchen and sat at the counter. "I don't know if there would have been anything on the news about it yet. It just happened yesterday, over by Ted's Grocery in that vacant lot where the homeless camps are." Berta turned to face Katy. "Wasn't there a murder there last week? Oh goodness." Katy nodded, her eyes wide with astonishment. "Yes there was! I can't believe there was another one already. There's something a little more creepy about it though." Berta cocked her head sideways at Katy then looked back and forth between the stove and Katy. "What is more creepy than having a murder every week?" Katy motioned with her thumb over her shoulder. "We might know who did it, and he lives close by." Berta gasped and stopped what she was doing. "Tell me from the beginning." Katy took a sip of coffee first. "Do you remember that guy I told you about that was dumping the trash in the middle of the night?" Berta nodded. "Okay, Jesse and his friend, Clint, followed him out of the lot the other night, he drove down to the vacant lot by Ted's and drove right into the bushes. Jesse and Clint went around to the side of the lot and walked the trail that goes into the bushes from the side to spy on him and see what he was doing. Jesse said it was really hard to see him because it is really dark out there but they watched him picking up trash and putting it in his truck for a while. We knew he was doing that already, Jesse had seen him at another spot one night picking up garbage and then he saw him throwing it into the dumpsters here at the apartments. Anyway, they watched him do that for a while, then they left, figuring that he was just out there picking up trash again." Berta was looking between Katy and the stove where she had finished the bacon and started the French toast. "I remember you telling me about that guy, pretty strange to be doing that in the middle of the night but I commend him for picking up the mess." Katy held up a hand as if to say wait a minute. "Sure, I think I would commend him for picking up the trash too, even though the middle of the night seems like a really strange time to do it. The problem is, the next day there was a dead guy in a tent right next to where he was at!" Berta had to move a pan off the stove so she could focus on what Katy was saying and not burn breakfast. "Are you kidding? You don't think it would be coincidence, do you?" Katy was shaking her head as far from side to side as she could. "It just seems too far out there for it to be coincidence. Jesse and Clint were there watching him but they didn't see him actually do anything to the guy in the tent." Berta looked down at the pan in her hand. "They actually saw him there? Have they turned him in?" Katy was shaking her head more regularly now, but slower. "For some reason Clint doesn't think that John is guilty, so they haven't said anything to the police. I was wondering if you could casually tell your nephew about John and that he may have been at the last murder site?" Berta dropped her shoulders and turned back to the stove to put the pan back on. "Well, I think that I will tell him about it. They should at least be able to investigate him and find out for themselves what this John guy was doing out there. Why does your friend Clint think that he isn't guilty?" Katy slumped down a little, feeling the weight of the situation. "He works with John and found out that John sleepwalks, that's what he has been doing when he goes out and picks up trash at the homeless camps. So Clint thinks all that John is doing is cleaning up the camps and the killings are unrelated." Berta shook her head. "They might be unrelated but when he's there and they find a dead body, that looks pretty guilty to me." Berta handed Katy a plate with French toast on it. "Here you go, you can get started with that. Jamie is coming over tonight for dinner again, I plan on bringing this up." Katy was getting her plate ready, then moved to the table and waited for Berta to serve herself. "I know Jesse and Clint won't be too happy about it, but I think the police need to have a conversation with John." Berta served herself a plate and moved over to the table and sat across from Katy. "Where exactly does John live again?" Katy pointed across the room. "He lives over in building B, I'm not sure which apartment." Berta lifted a fork as an exclamation. "That will be good enough to get them close."

Katy returned to her apartment an hour later, Jesse was lounging on the couch playing a video game. "Hey love, how was your visit with Berta?" Katy came in and sat next to him. "It was good, she made French toast and bacon." Jesse had paused his game. "That sounds good, I had coffee. Did she have any new information?" Katy lounged back on the sofa and looked up at the ceiling. "No, she didn't know about the latest incident. I told her that you and Clint saw John out there that night." Jesse gave her a thoughtful look, "Yeah I figured you would. She will undoubtedly tell her nephew about him."

Katy nodded. "Yeah, she's going to see him tonight. Is that okay?" Jesse shrugged and looked at Katy. "Yes. I think it is. I know Clint thinks he might be innocent but I think he needs to be looked at." Katy looked back at him. "Good, I was worried you might be upset. I wasn't sure if you thought he might be innocent too." Jesse smiled. "Nope. I think he did it. Everything points at him, at least this time for sure, and possibly the other ones too. So I guess we will see what the police come up with. I would guess they will want to talk to me and Clint since we saw him at the vacant lot." Katy leaned in and gave him a hug. "Yeah they might, sorry to get you involved." Jesse held on to the hug for a while. "It's okay, it will all work itself out."

John slept better Friday night, the dark circles under his eyes were lighter. He was ready for his next day off, all he could think of was napping on the couch all day. He had spotted Scruffy on his way to work Saturday morning before it was fully light out, it looked like he was getting ready for a day out exploring, he had a heavy jacket on and was loading some things into his backpack. *'I wonder where he is headed.'* John tried to watch for him once he got to work but was too distracted with morning commuters to pay attention when Scruffy went past the station. Scruffy was going the opposite direction from Johns apartment and the local neighborhoods. He was heading toward the industrial side of town, there were several warehouses where they transfer materials from rail cars to semi trucks, some of them were short term storage facilities for the transfer companies. There wouldn't be very much in the way of materials that a homeless person would want or care about. Scruffy had been out to that side of town before, he knew that the area wasn't good for digging through dumpsters or for getting handouts from strangers. Most of the truck drivers that frequented that area weren't very kind to the homeless people. Scruffy was on the lookout for better shelter. He had heard from some of the others in nearby camps that there were areas out behind the warehouses that were undisturbed by local traffic and could be semi secluded, out of the public eye. That was attractive to Scruffy, it was farther out of town which would require a longer walk for supplies and dumpster diving but he felt it wasn't safe where he was anymore. Scruffy felt it would be worth an hours walk out of town if he could feel safe at night. He found a few good spots once he got out past the railroad tracks and the warehouses. He discounted a few spots based on their proximity to the traffic of the big trucks and a few others based on the train tracks, even though they had potential to keep him dry in the wet season. He would keep those in the back of his mind in case it got really wet out. There was a stand of trees a quarter mile north of where the tracks cross Route 18 and run into the warehouses to unload that Scruffy could see from the intersection, *'Not too far, I'll check that out.'* Along the road, the tall grasses of the farmers' fields were lying flat from being beaten down by the rain, some scrubby bushes in the ditch had loose paper stuck in their limbs. As Scruffy approached the stand of trees, he walked through piles of leaves that got stuck in the grass and limbs that had fallen from a strong gust of wind. There were no fences around the trees, the closest buildings were the warehouses back a quarter mile from where he stood and to the north of him he couldn't see any buildings. This looked promising. The grouping of trees, mostly cottonwood, was about eighty yards in length down the road and stretched over one hundred yards deep. Scruffy found the remains of what looked like a trail in the middle of the tree stand and followed it, disappearing from sight only moments after entering. The trail hadn't been used in years, it was overgrown with blackberry vines and the limbs of younger trees hung low across it, making it difficult to navigate. Scruffy pushed through until he felt he was nearly in the center. He had found what he was looking for, a secluded area just big enough for him to make a camp, even once the leaves were gone from the limbs, he was far enough off the main road that he wouldn't be seen. This fit, it was out of town, but close enough that he could resupply often. He stood still in the small opening in the trees for a few minutes, listening to the surroundings. A slight breeze blew through the tops of the trees rustling the leaves together, limbs rubbed against one another creaking lightly high above. He found a tree that had toppled over near the opening where he stood. It was the perfect height to sit. He went and rested his legs and listened to the peaceful sounds all around him, a vehicle passed out on the road, it was a dull sound from where he sat, much better than his current camp location. Scruffy was feeling relief that he had found a good place to camp, he would start making plans to move himself out here. Within a week he should be able to relocate himself and be settled. He sat and listened, making plans in his head to relocate for half an hour, then got up and made his way to the edge of the tree stand. He looked up and down the road for signs of anyone coming before leaving the cover of the trees and heading south toward the warehouses, then west on Route 18 back to town. Scruffy was feeling happy about finding this new location and somewhat excited to make this next move.

It was midday in John's shift when he spotted Scruffy walking west on Route 18. *'Huh, I missed him when he went past the other way. I wonder what kind of trouble he was getting into.'* John wasn't busy at the time and stood at the edge of the station watching Scruffy walk slowly down the white line, eventually crossing the road and disappearing behind Ted's Grocery. Clint watched John stand there for a moment watching Scruffy. "What's going on?" John turned to face Clint. "Just watching Scruffy, wondering what he's up to." Clint glanced back toward Ted's where Scruffy disappeared. "Looks like he's going to dumpster dive." That's exactly what Scruffy was doing. The long walk out to the warehouse district used a lot of energy, Scruffy was hoping to find some nourishment, maybe some baked goods or produce that had past its prime had been sent out to the dumpsters. He was in luck, there was a box of apples that had some bruising on them, *'Unfit for sale,'* that had been set out on the edge of the loading dock. He helped himself to several, putting them into his backpack for later as well as eating one on his way back to the front of the building as he went back to his current camp.

Saturday night when Jamie knocked on Berta's door for dinner, she wasn't in the happiest mood. "Hello handsome, please come in, I was just working on dinner." Jamie came in and closed the door behind himself. He took his coat off and laid it over one of the counter stools. He was really enjoying the company, the food was pretty amazing as well. "You don't sound like your chipper self. What's happening?" Berta stopped and looked at Jamie with one hand on the counter and the other on her hip, standing in the kitchen. "I have been thinking about this latest homeless murder, and I heard something about it and I just don't know how to tell you."

Jamie got a serious, stern look on his face. He put both hands on the counter and leaned in. "What have you heard?" Berta paused, still standing with her hand on her hip. "One of my neighbors might have something to do with it." Jamie's expression didn't change, he was on the verge of switching to work mode. "What exactly do you mean?" Berta picked up a dish towel and flipped it over her shoulder, then shuffled the pans on the stove for no reason. "I was talking with one of the neighbor ladies and the subject came up about the latest incident. She said that her boyfriend saw someone from the complex in that lot Thursday night." Jamie was fishing in his coat pocket for a notepad and a pen. "Can you tell me what his name is?" Berta stopped fidgeting and looked at him. "Who? The guy they saw? Or the guy that saw him?" Jamie got a confused look then smiled as he sat down at the counter. "Fair question, how about the guy they saw, he's the one that lives here in the complex right?" Berta nodded. "Yes he does. His name is John, I don't have his last name but I think he lives over in building B. I could ask what his last name is though if that would help." Jamie scribbled down his notes. "Well yeah, if you get a chance let me know what his last name is. I will check back on my notes but I am pretty sure there was a guy named John that we talked to. Also, what is the name of the guy that saw him? Just in case." Berta leaned onto the counter with both hands as if this whole thing were getting a little too heavy for her. "His name is Jesse Kohl, now he isn't going to be in trouble is he?" Jamie cocked his head and pursed his lips. "No, not if he hasn't done anything wrong. I don't believe we have tried to talk with a Jesse yet, so it's not like he was withholding from us." Berta nodded as she watched Jamie scribble some more notes. "Well that's good, that's why I hesitated. I wouldn't want him to get in trouble." Jamie folded his notebook and looked up at Berta. "Any other tidbits you want to drop on me?" Berta smiled big. "Oh, I don't think I have anything too interesting. Well, maybe." She hesitated again. "Katy did tell me that John fella was dumping trash into the dumpsters in the middle of the night. I guess they saw him out by the side of the road picking up trash and he was dumping it here at 4 in the morning." Jamie pulled open the notebook again. "Okay, that is something else interesting. Picking up trash in the middle of the night? That's unusual behavior for sure. Do you know what day that was?" Berta watched him scribble some more. "I didn't think much of it the first time they said something about it, thought maybe he was just doing good deeds, but the timing is a little peculiar. He was out there the night that other place was lit on fire." Jamie gave her a 'DUH' look. "Yeah, I'll say it's peculiar. I'm going to have to take this to the detective and see what he thinks. I would think he will follow up on it. That's a little too much for coincidence to be in both of those places." Jamie closed the notebook again, not wanting to put too much interest into it, thinking it might lead to nothing. "So, what's for dinner tonight?" Berta went about gathering dinner supplies while they chatted. "We're going to act like it's still summer time and have some homemade burgers and macaroni salad." Jamie rubbed his hands together in anticipation. "That sounds great. Have you seen this John guy?" Berta glanced over at him as she pulled the salad from the fridge. "No, at least I don't know his look by name. Maybe I've seen him around but don't know who he is." Jamie nodded. "Sure, sure I get that. I was just wondering because this latest victim was a big guy. It would take some muscle to wrestle that guy down and tie his hands behind his back." Berta got a thoughtful expression. "Oh really? So are you part of the team yet? Investigating?" Jamie laughed. "No, I did get another chance to ask some of the potential witnesses some questions but nothing came of it. I still just watch from the side and make my own deductions from what I see. I just noticed the size of the guy and figured whoever did it would have to be pretty big. Looked like he went through the side of his tent too. Maybe trying to catch him off guard." Berta kept cooking, looking up every so often as Jamie was telling the story. "He went through the side? Like how?" Jamie made a slashing motion. "Like he cut through it with a knife, then attacked." Berta changed the subject and it never came back up that night. She was feeling like she only talked about the recent murders with Jamie and didn't want him to think she was too hung up on it. Jamie stayed a few hours like normal. "After we look into this John guy, I'll let you know how it went." Berta gave him a hug at the door and handed him his coat. "That sounds fine, maybe over dinner next weekend?" Jamie chuckled. "I would like that very much. You be careful, I'll talk to you later." Jamie walked out to the lot and stood still for a moment, looking over at building B wondering if John was home, *'Perhaps he's out picking up trash? Or is it not late enough?'*

27

Sunday

John woke up confused Sunday morning, his head hurt and he didn't want to open his eyes. He drug himself slowly out of bed and went into the bathroom for some Tylenol, then to get into the shower. *'Maybe a hot shower will help.'* After dressing for the day in sweats and a hoodie, he went to the kitchen to get the blood flowing with some coffee and breakfast. He didn't have muddy shoes on the floor by the door or a heap of clothes. A good sign that he stayed in the night before. His mind kept racing over watching Scruffy walking down the highway, *'He went out to the industrial end of town. There's nothing out there but warehouses and train tracks. What could he be doing out there?'* He kept trying to visualize what was at that end of town that Scruffy could be interested in. His head was fuzzy inside with the pain, he wasn't sure what was causing it, too many thoughts running through his mind or lack of sleep. He sat down in front of the TV with breakfast to watch the news. Nothing new, not even a blip about the last killing next to

Ted's Grocery. *'The news has lost interest.'* John turned the channel to the old timey TV shows, he liked them because they were simpler, they felt more wholesome, reminding him of his childhood. He watched TV for a couple of hours, then got up to straighten the apartment. After some cleaning chores he got curious again about Scruffy, *'I wonder if I could tell what he was doing if I drove out to the edge of town.'* It was an overcast day but looked like it would stay dry, the clouds were high and moving quite fast with the wind. John drove east out past the GasNGo, where the railroad tracks cross the highway and go into the warehouses. He couldn't see anywhere that rodent camps had been, there was no trash or sign of tents. There didn't seem to be enough to support their lifestyle out that far. *'Maybe he was just exploring, wondering if there were any trash bins worth going through in this area.'* John turned around at the intersections just past the railroad tracks and headed back toward town. It was about a fifteen minute drive back to the GasNGo where he spotted Scruffy walking the other way. John sat at a stop light watching Scruffy turn north to walk through town. Sunday would be a good day to find food, the restaurants were busier on the weekends and had more to throw away. Scruffy walked the alleys behind the shops where the dumpsters were, checking under each lid casually as he passed by. He found a full pizza in a box, it wasn't warm anymore, it must not have been picked up by a customer. Scruffy just found lunch and dinner. He tucked it under his arm like books from a library after taking a piece out of the box and sampling it. He continued to walk down the alley, still looking under lids just in case there were other treasures to be found.

Katy worked the mid-day shift Sunday and got home around

5 to have dinner with Jesse. "I got my new work schedule today. It's not great. I'm on late nights again." Jesse was standing in the kitchen stirring a pot of chili. "Dang, again? why are they giving you that shift so often?" Katy's shoulders slumped. "I don't know for sure, we are a little short handed so our rotations for night shift aren't coming out even. At least I make good tips on the first half of the shift." Jesse replaced the lid on the pot and turned it down some. "That's a plus, but we don't get much time together when you have to work that shift." Katy came over and wrapped her arms around Jesse. "No, we don't. But it's not forever, I'll find something better soon and we will buy a house, then things will hopefully be more normal." Jesse gave her a squeeze and a kiss. "That's true, that will be worth it. Are you okay to drive yourself to and from work late at night?" Katy stepped back and made a little pouty face. "No? I really don't like it. Would you please take me to work and pick me up? Please, please?" Jesse rolled his eyes. "Only because you said 'Please, please.'" Katy smiled and gave him another big hug and a kiss. "Thank you, that means a lot to me. I am just freaked out with everything that's happening. I know it seems like whoever is killing those people is only targeting the homeless, but I'm still scared that at some point it will be someone other than a homeless person." Jesse pulled away to tend to dinner. "I know it scares you. It's okay, I'll take care of you."

28

Monday

When Jamie Roak arrived at the station to check in Monday morning he was earlier than usual, he wanted to go over his notes from the interviews he had done Friday after the murder next to Ted's Grocery. He sat at his desk with the file folder that he'd kept after filling out his paperwork about his case. He had already given his report to detective Milkey with the details of his conversations with Clint Jacobs and John Dell. As he read over the file it was coming back to him that he had talked with John before, it was at the same site when the camp had burned. Jamie was struck by an instinct, he went to his file cabinet and pulled out the manila folder he had tucked away about the first murder victims they had found, at least the ones that seemed to be the same type of killing. The people in the little red car. He laid it open on his desk and started paging through his notes until he came across the statements he had taken from people in the area. *John Dell: "Walking to his apartment." stated: "I saw the car this morning with the windows fogged up. Tried to see if people were in the car."* Jamie sat back in his chair with a loud squeak and almost tipped too far, having to lunge his arms forward so not to fall over backwards. Dumbfounded he stared at the folder laying open on his desk. *'He was at three of the crime scenes.'* He sat forward again and double checked the notes from the burnt tent killing, *"John Dell: questioned as he walked by on his way to work at the GasNGo."* *'Either this guy is really unlucky being seen at the scene of three murders, or he's our guy.'* Jamie closed all the files and stacked them on his desk, then looked around the office to see who was in. Detective Milkey had not arrived, Jamie sat back in his chair again, slower this time, and stared at the ceiling, putting the connections together again in his head. *'Three of the murder sites, not the others. Could we find a link?'* He heard a shuffle from across the room, it was Detective Milkey coming in through the back office entrance. Jamie stood, gathering his files and walked out into the open offices. "Detective Milkey. Good morning." Milkey looked up and smiled. "Good morning Officer Roak, you're in early this morning." Jamie held up the files. "I had something I wanted to look into this morning before shift. I'd like to go over it with you if you have time." Milkey was hanging his tan sport coat over the back of his chair. "Sure, what's it about?" Jamie went to the other side of Milkey's desk and sat in the chair, setting the files on the desk in front of him. "I got a tip that a person in the complex where my aunt lives was spotted at the crime scene on the night prior to the murder on Friday." Milkey had sat down but the tip had caught his interest. "What does the fact that your aunt lives there have to do with it?" Jamie let out a smile from the side of his mouth. "It was my aunt that gave me the tip. But it came from one of the other residents that has seen this guy up to some strange

246

activities." Milkey smirked at James and the connection to his aunt. "Is this some kind of gossip ring?" Jamie blushed a little, he didn't want to look foolish to Detective Milkey. "Well, yeah probably, but after looking into it, I think there might be something here." Milkey stopped smiling. "What kind of activity is he up to? What makes you think this guy is worth looking at?" Jamie pulled his files off the desk and opened the latest file. "What I was told is that this guy, John, has been seen late at night in the homeless camps. They said he has been picking up trash, then bringing it back to the apartments and dumping it into the dumpsters there." Milkey had a, 'Yeah so?' look on his face. "Okay, yes, late at night cleaning up trash is strange behavior but that doesn't get us anywhere." Jamie cocked his head sideways. "No. No it doesn't, not by itself. He was seen in that lot Friday night just before the murder though, and he was seen the night those other people were lit on fire." Milkey tilted his head up with an enlightened face. "Really? Do you have a name?" Jamie nodded. "I had a first name, but when I checked on him, he was one of the people I had questioned on Friday, then it occurred to me from where he lives to check on an older case. The one with the two people in the little red hatchback. I spoke with him there as well. That one didn't seem to be interesting at the time because he lives in the complex but now that he's been seen at three of the scenes I feel like he is more interesting." Milkey's face lit up. "I'll say! That is *way* more interesting. What's his name? Are those the files?" Jamie picked up the files and handed them across the desk to the Detective. "These are just the notes that I kept on the cases where I talked to people. His name is John Dell, lives in the Fir Street apartments, works at the GasNGo on the morning shift." Milkey thumbed through the notes that Jamie had handed him. "Is he at work this morning?" Jamie was sitting very upright like a kid in front of the Principal at school. "I believe he is." Milkey handed the files back to Jamie. "I think we should pay him a visit, maybe see if he is willing to come back to the station for some questions." Jamie didn't flinch. "Do you want me to come with you?" Milkey was getting up from his chair. "Yes I do. I'll clear it with Captain, it's always good to have some backup when you go see a suspect."

Detective Milkey and Officer Roak arrived at the GasNGo at 7:05 AM. John had been at work for about an hour. They pulled into a spot near the building in Officer Roak's cruiser, not wanting to arouse any interest in their being on site. John was filling a truck with his back to them when they got out of the car. "I'm going to go inside and see if there is a manager onsite." Milkey walked away from the car toward the front of the building. He stopped at the break room door, it wasn't latched so he peeked inside with a slight knock. "Anyone inside?" He pushed the door open slightly and spotted Steve. "Hello, I'm looking for a manager." Steve got up from the table where he was doing his morning paperwork and reached out his hand. "I'm the manager, my name's Steve, what can I do for you?" Milkey shook his hand. "I'm Detective James Milkey, I need to speak with one of your employees. I just wanted to give you a heads up that we will likely be taking him for a ride to the station to have a chat." Steve's brows went up in a question mark. "Okay, anything I need to be aware of?" Detective Milkey shook his head. "Nothing I can share with you at this time. I am doing an investigation and he might have some information that we could use." Steve shook his head and sat back down. "Okay, who is it? And how long do you think it will take? I need to plan for more help if it takes too long." Milkey paused to reflect on Steve's non caring of the situation. "I'll be speaking with John Dell. It could take an hour or it could take 4 hours. You do what you need to do." Milkey walked out of the break room, looking across the fuel pump islands, spotting Clint and John standing at the far island. He looked over at Jamie and gave him a nod to come this way. He waited for Jamie to catch up before calling over to John. "John Dell? Excuse me, we would like to talk with you." John and Clint turned around to see the men approaching. "Good morning, Officer Roak, right?" John reached out to shake his hand. "That's right, and this is Detective Milkey. Could we talk a bit?" John shrugged and looked at Clint. "It's slow, you got this for a bit?" Clint gave a nod with his hands in his pockets, trying to keep them warm on the chilly fall morning. "Sure you go ahead." They walked toward the break room but Detective Milkey stopped them outside the door. "John do you mind coming down to the station with us, we want to talk to you about a few things. It would be better if we didn't talk here in a public place." John stiffened a little, that sounded a bit intimidating. "Hmm, well I am at work. I need to stay here. It's not easy to make ends meet as it is. I can't afford extra time off." Milkey was standing with his feet shoulder width apart and his hands in his sport coat pockets trying to look as relaxed about it as possible. "I know it's not easy but this is very important. I already cleared it with your manager, Steve." John looked down at the fancy shoes Detective Milkey was wearing, they matched his gray wool suit but the tan jacket was a bit out of place. "Okay, I guess I don't have much choice. Let me check out." John stepped into the break room and looked at Steve with an apprehensive expression on his face. Steve nodded at him as John clocked out but didn't say a word. John returned to the men standing outside and they walked him to the car. Officer Roak opened the back door for John and closed him into the car with no handles on the inside. John felt a sinking feeling in his chest that sat in the pit of his stomach. He felt sick but was trying not to show it as they backed out of the lot and proceeded toward the police station.

The local police building is a normal looking office building, brick outer walls, flag poles out front with manicured lawns and clean pressure washed sidewalks. It became more cold and sanitary once inside. It had a very down to business, stark, feeling of security. Everything was in its place and nothing left out that could be used as a weapon. John was escorted through the rear entrance with Milkey walking in front of him, Jamie Roak following behind to make sure he wouldn't try and make a run for it, *'no handcuffs so far'*, John had agreed to come along and speak with them, so really no need for that. John was in disbelief that this was even happening, *'Why am I here? I don't think I have done anything wrong. Who am I kidding? I don't even believe I didn't do anything, I just don't know if I did anything.'* Milkey opened the inner door of the back entrance with his key card and let John pass him on the way in. The detective motioned to some chairs in a lobby area at the back of the inner offices, "Please have a seat here for just a minute, I'll make sure we have a room to talk in." Detective Milkey unlocked another door to the inner offices with a wave of his card and a beep was followed by a click as the door unlocked. He walked in, saying hello to some of his fellow detectives. The sound of him speaking to them faded to a low mumble as the door closed behind him with a solid thunk. Jamie stood facing the inner office windows watching the detective as he passed from area to area, then finally toward a wall of doors that led to the interrogation rooms. Detective Milkey checked in on the first room he came to, turning the lights on and making sure it would suffice for what they needed. He came back to the waiting area and invited Officer Roak and John to follow him back to the room that he had secured for questioning. "Please have a seat there at the table." Milkey had picked up a folder from his desk and brought it into the room. "Officer Roak, would you mind standing here at the door while I ask John some questions?" John sat across from an empty chair that the Detective seemed to be holding down with his hands. Detective Milkey set the folder on the metal table that was bolted to the floor in front of John. John glanced around the ugly tan room with its gray concrete floor, *'Just like the movies, empty room, camera, one way glass. Huh, I was never sure that was a real thing.'* Milkey watched John as he looked around. "Is it what you expected?" John looked back at him, he was smirking a little. "No, not really. I wasn't sure these rooms actually existed." Milkey gave a single big nod. "That they do, but only for special customers." John got an even more concerned look on his face. "I think I would prefer not to be a special customer." Milkey pulled his chair out and made himself comfortable. "That's pretty understandable, but this is a very serious situation that you find yourself in." John looked down at the table, his hands folded in his lap. He was nervous but not scared. "Well, I can see why you would want to talk to me, but I don't think I had anything to do with the killings." The detective started paging through his notes in the folder then looked at John realizing John had deduced why he was in for questioning. "Well, that is exactly why we're here isn't it? We need to figure out what happened and if you were involved." Milkey pulled a sheet of his notes from the middle of the stack and laid it on top. "We have a witness that puts you at the scene of the last murder at the time it happened. That doesn't look good for you. What were you doing out there?" John fidgeted in his seat. "Shouldn't I have a lawyer or something?" Milkey raised his eyebrows with an eye roll. "Yeah, if you're guilty, you most definitely should. Are you guilty?" John's back stiffened, he sat a little more straight up. "No, I didn't do anything to that guy." Milkey leaned against the back of his chair. "Well, then let's talk about some stuff. I don't want to make you uncomfortable, I just want to get some details. Can we get you something to drink?" John was sitting very still, he didn't believe that he had anything to do with the murders but he had questioned that about himself. He couldn't explain some of the nights he had been out, he didn't know for sure where he had been. *'Maybe they won't ask about those days.'* "Yes please, some water would be nice." Detective Milkey looked at Jamie. "Would you please get some water for Mr. Dell?" Jamie obliged and disappeared out the door. "John, we have gotten some information that paints you in a pretty dark picture. I just want you to be able to clear that up for us." Jamie came back into the room, handing John a chilled bottle of water. "Thank you." John opened it right away and took a long drink. "Okay, I'll answer your questions." Milkey took out a large notepad and laid a pen on it. "Let's start with why you're out in the middle of the night at homeless camps." John looked between Detective Milkey and Officer Roak then took a deep breath. "Okay." He hesitated for a long time, "I was cleaning up after them." Milkey's expression didn't change, he had a serious look that bored into John's eyes. "Why are you doing that in the middle of the night?" John stared at the table, his hands gripped the chair at his legs as if he would fall off of it if he didn't hold on. "This is where it gets a little weird." Milkey nodded. "As if cleaning up after the homeless in the middle of the night isn't weird enough?" John furrowed his brow. "I sleepwalk." Milkey still without changing his expression. "So? What does that have to do with it?" John glanced at Roak who was watching between John and Milkey taking in the exchange in more of a fascination of what was happening than in a police capacity. "That's when I go out and clean up the camps. I'm sleepwalking." Milkey looked over his shoulder at Officer Roak to make sure he heard what John just said. "You sleepwalk and clean up homeless camps? Can you tell me how this all came about? Without me having to drag it all out of you?" John slumped a little in his chair, feeling the reaction at least wasn't a rejection as he had expected. "When I was young I used to sleepwalk when I would get upset or hung up on something. My brain doesn't let go of it, it just keeps working and working until my subconscious takes over and I end up doing something about it." John took another drink of the water, his mouth was getting unusually dry. "I have been watching the rodent camps get worse and worse, all the messes they make have me pretty upset. I can't stand to see our community being dumped on by these people. Eventually I started noticing that I had been going out in the middle of the night, I would wake up in the morning with my truck filled with trash and I would have to empty it out into the dumpsters at my apartment, sometimes really early in the morning. Then at some point I was emptying the trash when I got back to the apartment at night but I was still sleepwalking." Milkey had started to take some notes, he underlined the word rodents and paused for a few moments before moving on. "When was it that you first noticed you had gone out sleepwalking?" John paused for a while looking at the ceiling trying to recall the timeline. "I think the first time I recall something like that happening was after the guy out at the lake was killed." Milkey gave him a sideways squinting look. "Why would you put your timeline together with that murder?" John turned a dull shade of red forgetting that he didn't want them to know he was anywhere near the other murders. He could feel beads of sweat forming at his hairline. *'Damn, now I have to go down that road.'* He continued slowly. "I remember at that time I was getting pretty worked up about all the messes where the rodents were camping. I decided to go for a hike out at the lake and I saw that guys camp out there. Turned out that he was killed a couple days later and I ended up sleepwalking out to his camp and cleaning it up after he was killed." Milkey was still squinting at John, only straight on now, like he was trying to see through John's skull. "How do you know it was the camp at the lake that you cleaned up?" John looked down at his lap, *'this is why I didn't want to let them find out I was at other sites.'* John took a deep breath and continued. "I recognized the junk in the back of my truck when I had to unload it the next day, I was pretty sure that was where it came from." Detective Milkey eased up on his squint into John's soul. "You've called them rodents a couple of times now. What's that about?" John was still red from the last question. "I don't remember when it occurred to me that they are a lot like rodents, the way they bring trash into their living space then just step over it all the time instead of cleaning up after themselves, or the way that when one of them dies the others scavenge everything the dead one had and take it for themselves. I started referring to them as rodents and it just stuck with me." Milkey looked at John with a disgusted look but moved on. "Are you sure you went to that camp by the lake *after*, the murder?" John nodded positively. "Yes for sure, because my truck was full of the trash the next morning when I came out to go to work, I remember there was crime scene tape all wrapped up in the bags of trash." Milkey made some notes about the camp site by the lake and the crime tape, and noted that John spoke more excitedly when he talked about how *'they remind him of rodents.'* "What about the incident in front of your apartment complex? Do you recall cleaning up anything there?" John looked at Milkey confused. "No, I don't recall there being anything there to clean up. That car just showed up one night and then I saw it the next day with the windows all fogged up. When I came home from work it was surrounded by police cars. I remember speaking with Officer Roak when I got there." Milkey made notes about John seeing the car that morning, with an asterisk, *'*Check if his story matches.'* "Alright, tell me about dumping trash early in the morning, we have a witness that said you were dumping trash at the apartments about 4 AM." John tucked his hands under his legs, his palms were sweaty as well as under his arms, the pits of his shirt were uncomfortably wet, *'Do they make it so hot in here on purpose?'* "That was one of the times that I was dumping the trash after I got back from cleaning up a camp, I had started doing that I guess so I wouldn't have to do it in the morning before I left for work. I told you my subconscious works on problems for me, then it just takes over." Milkey didn't move much when he was asking questions, his gaze stayed much the same the entire time, there were a few moments that he reacted to what John was saying, but mostly it was a flat, stern look on his face. Jamie noticed that Milkey's look rarely changed as well and would watch him when John was talking to see if he would react. "Do you know where you went that night?" John was starting to feel comfortable until that question, he knew that there had been a murder discovered the next day and he couldn't be sure that he didn't do it. He sat still looking at the table, his palms soaking into his pants and his underarms dripping down his sides inside his sweatshirt. He finally spoke quietly, not wanting to give it up. "I think so." Milkey waited for John to go ahead and tell him where he had been, but after several minutes he couldn't let it hang out there in the nothingness any longer. "Where was that John?" John could feel sweat starting to run down his hairline onto his neck and his brow was wet. "When I was walking to work the next morning I could see on the south side of the road that the area next to Scruffy's camp had been cleaned up, I'm pretty sure that's where I went." Milkey was feeling pretty satisfied that all of this was going to plan, he was going to get a confession out of John. He had made him feel comfortable and John seemed to be answering his questions without hesitation. "Who is Scruffy?" Jamie noticed Milkey relax some, he could see his confidence, like he was getting exactly what he wanted. John looked down at the table, then farther down at the floor next to the table. "He's one of the rodents that lives in a tent next to the highway. I have seen him in the neighborhood a bunch of times going through people's trash. He's just a really scruffy looking guy and I call him Scruffy." Milkey made a note of 'Scruffy, Hwy 18, *Check on Scruffy' Jamie remembered that Scruffy had been talked to the day he was at the burnt tent scene and that Scruffy had pointed out John as someone that went by there every day. Milkey turned his attention away from his notes back to John. "You're aware that there was a murder there that night, correct?" John was feeling the heat, he thought he was sweating before, now it seemed like a faucet had been turned on over the top of his head. "Yes, I figured that out when I spoke with Officer Roak at the scene on my way to work that morning." Milkey had not moved, no nod of acknowledgment, no blink of an eye or twitch of a finger. "You can see how this looks pretty bad for you can't you?" John blinked sweat out of his eyes, still sitting on his hands, he looked at Officer Roak then back at Detective Milkey, he finally spoke in a very quiet voice "I can see what you're getting at, but I didn't do it." Jamie was watching both of them back and forth, from Milkey to John. He could see the sweat running off of John, and Milkey hadn't moved in what seemed like ten minutes. Milkey was quiet for a minute, he sat perfectly still staring at John even though John wasn't looking at him, he knew John could feel his stare. "How do you know? How do we know? What proof do you have that you didn't do it?" John blinked away more sweat, it was burning his eyes. He reached for the bottle of water and drank all that was left, then wiped his brow with the back of his sleeve. "I was on the other side of the road, that's where I cleaned up the camp." John's voice was shaky and low, he was starting to smell the sweat from his pits. Milkey broke his gaze at John and looked at his notes. He made a few more under the Scruffy notes. "Let's talk about last week. You went back to the same area, only this time on the other side of the highway." John felt for a moment like his fever just broke and he shivered, his voice was still low, he was shaken but still felt that, *maybe* he hadn't done anything wrong. "I did, I figured that out the day after it happened too, when I walked past in the morning. Actually I had gone to that side of the highway twice." Jamie noticed a look of surprise in Milkey's eyes when John said that. Milkey made a note, '*North side of highway, two visits.'* Then he remembered talking with JJ after the investigation of the burnt out camp. "When was the first time you went?" John tried to take a breath and calm his nerves but it came out uneasy. "It was a couple of days after that camp was burned, I walked back through there after I realized that I had cleaned up that area. I figure I might have been seen by some of the rodents that live there." Milkey's eyes squinted down, looking at John, trying to see if he was telling the truth, John couldn't, or wouldn't, look at him. "And were you? Seen?" John did look up at Milkey and froze his eyes on Milkey's. "Yeah, I think so. There was a guy there that I hadn't seen before, his name is JJ, he didn't say directly that he saw me but he hinted at it." Milkey knew this part of the story from talking with JJ, but let John continue. "We talked a little bit about the area looking better, JJ mentioned that someone came by and cleaned up the area, but he didn't directly say that he saw *me* do it." Milkey made a note about JJ, confirming he saw someone clean up the camp. "So that was the first time you went there. Why go back?" John shrugged and could feel the pit sweat all over again. "It wasn't done. I remember JJ saying something about that. We talked about it needing more clean up and he said maybe that guy would come back. That might have triggered it for me, I'm not sure how the subconscious works with that." Milkey shook his head. "No, I'm not either. But I do know that there was a murder that night and we have a witness that puts you at the scene, one that can identify you, even if JJ can't." That made the water works start all over again, John could feel his hands get instantly clammy and beads of sweat form on his forehead. Milkey watched him as sweat started to run down his face. "Officer Roak, would you step out of the room with me for a moment?" Milkey got up as Jamie opened the door and they stepped into the hall. "What do you think about all this sleepwalking stuff? Do you think that's even possible?" Jamie looked through the door glass at John. "I'm obviously not a professional on the subject, but I have heard of things like this happening with people that sleepwalk, I don't think it's out of the realm of possibilities." Milkey was stretching his back out from sitting in the chair so perfectly still. "Yeah, as crazy as it sounds, I've heard of it too. He seems to be pretty straight forward with his answers. That stuff he was talking about with JJ checks out, I talked to JJ and he said the same thing. It feels like he really doesn't know when it's happening. As far as the murders, he could still be our guy, he may just not know it. I want to talk to the witness before we lock him up though, right now this is circumstantial until that witness is willing to testify." Jamie watched John wipe his face off with his sweatshirt. "Poor guy is really sweating it out in there. Are you done with him? I can take him back to work." Milkey chuckled. "He really is, I was starting to smell it come off of him. Yeah we're done for now." Milkey opened the door and stepped into the room. "John, we're done for now. We need to verify some of what you said and then we will be back in touch. Not to worry, you did great, but please stay in the area, no leaving town. Officer Roak will take you back to work." John got up from the table, noticing that his legs were a little wobbly and that the chair was wet from sweat. "Could I get another water bottle?" Officer Roak handed him one as John came to the door. "One step ahead of you, I thought you might need it."

Jamie dropped John off at the GasNGo with just a few hours left in his shift. John went inside to check back in. *'There's half a day I don't get paid for.'* He was feeling stressed about it. *'What am I going to do if they decide I'm the guy?'* He was reviewing the whole thing in his mind but it became a jumble, his nerves were blocking a lot of what was said. He knew he hadn't told them about every time he had gone out at night. *'There were some that I have no idea where I was. No point in bringing those up, they didn't seem to know about those times anyway.'* Steve was in the break room when he walked in. "Hey John, you okay? How did that go?" John felt beat down, he was still damp with sweat. "It was rough, I don't think I did anything wrong but I don't exactly have an alibi." Clint had walked in while John was talking. "They let you go though, so that seems good." Steve had a confused look on his face. "Why wouldn't they let him go?" Clint looked at Steve and gave him a *'don't ask'* look. "John if it's okay, I'll fill Steve in on that later?" John looked back and forth at both of them. "That's fine, but Steve the short of it is, I sleepwalk and I have been seen at some of the crime scenes here lately so I am a suspect in the rodent murders." Steve jolted back slightly. "Really!? You sleepwalk?" John looked down at Steve for a moment without saying anything. "That's what you take from this conversation? Yes, I sleepwalk and apparently I pick up trash in the middle of the night while I'm doing it." Steve's face lit up. "Wow! That's amazing! I mean too bad about being seen at crime scenes, but damn! That's crazy! I need to go, but you guys take care, I will check in with you both tomorrow morning." Steve got up and left the room, both John and Clint looked at each other and shrugged. "I don't get that guy. I guess at least he doesn't seem to care so I still have a job." Clint nodded. "That's a positive I guess." The rest of the shift was uneventful. When John checked out he left a note for Steve asking if there was another shift he could pick up to make up the hours he lost.

John stopped at Ted's Grocery before making his way home. He was thinking about JJ, wondering what he had told the detective. *'Why not walk past his tent and see if he's there.'* The crime tape was still up at the trail by the parking lot, he would have to walk in from the roadside. John left the white line where the tire tracks went into the ditch and followed the new trail to JJ's tent. He could see the top of JJ's tent over some of the bushes before he got to it, the area around his tent was fairly well kept, no piles of garbage or unused junk discarded carelessly in his close proximity. JJ didn't seem to be around. "Hello? Anyone here?" There was some rustling. "Yeah. Are you talking to me?" John stopped about ten feet away from the tent, standing next to a shopping cart with a bicycle leaning against it. "Is that JJ?" The zipper of the tent wound its way from side to side. "Sure is, who's asking?" JJ popped his head out of the tent, he slipped on his shoes as he exited. "Oh, it's you. Nice to see you. What was your name? Not sure I got it last time we spoke." John hadn't expected this type of interaction. It was friendlier than he thought it would be. "I'm John." JJ stood up and straightened his shirt out. "Good to meet you John, What can I do for you?" John's train of thought had derailed a little with the friendly exchange. "Well, I guess I just wanted to know what you talked about with the detective that was out here last week and if he talked to you again after Friday?" JJ crossed his arms and looked around at the sky with the dark broken up clouds moving slowly across the blue background and trees with golden leaves rustling gently in the fall breeze, as if John had asked about the weather. "He asked if I had seen anyone, I told him that someone had come out and cleaned up last week and then again on Friday night.

I told him both times that I didn't see who it was, it was too dark." John shuffled his feet a little and looked around as JJ had, wondering what exactly he was looking at. "Did you know that it was me?" This time JJ looked at John and hesitated. "I only had a suspicion it was you, but I didn't know for sure. Was it you both times?" John nodded his head. JJ backed away, looking beside the tent then pulled his lawn chair out and sat down. "What was wrong with you? I tried talking to you but you wouldn't respond. You just mumbled. Then I helped you load trash into your truck." John pulled his head back and looked to the side where he had picked up trash. "I sleepwalk. I was in sort of a trance. I didn't know you tried to talk to me." JJ folded his arms across his chest and put one leg across his knee. "So, I have to ask a very straight forward question. Friday when you were cleaning up, over by those other tents. I didn't go help you, I was feeling too tired. Did you kill that guy?" John was a little shocked that JJ came right out with that question, he looked at JJ who was looking right back at him. "No, I don't think so. I don't really know for sure to be honest, but it doesn't feel right." JJ looked away across the lot at other tents he could see from where he sat. "Okay, I hope not." His voice trailed off a bit, then there was a long pause as he considered what to say next. "If I see you again, should I wake you up?" John froze at that, he hadn't considered what would happen if someone were to wake him up while he was in a trance. "I don't know for sure." John looked around the site, it was a mess still, out at the edges near the other tents, even with all the trash he had already picked up. He could see himself coming out here again, there were shopping carts near some of the other tents full of who knows what and next to them were piles of junk, that, from a distance, he couldn't tell if it was usable or just discarded junk. He looked back at JJ. "I think so. I think you should try, I don't want to be responsible for anyone dying. This has all become pretty troubling, I don't know if I'll sleepwalk any more. I can't say how my subconscious will handle this." John pulled his backpack off his shoulders and opened it. He pulled out a bottle of water and tossed it to JJ. "Thank you for talking to me. I really hope you don't have to wake me up but would appreciate it if you do." JJ raised a hand to John. "No worries, thank you for the water." John put his pack back on and walked past the tent, back toward the road, following the tire track trail. He walked the white line to Fir Street thinking about his interaction with JJ, *'Why is he homeless?'* John had said that this situation was troubling but he wasn't feeling very concerned by it. The stress of the questioning was real, but now that it was over, he wasn't worried about it. He didn't think that he had anything to worry about, he had told the detective everything he knew, answering all the questions as honestly as he could. *'I really don't think that I killed those people.'*

29

Tuesday

Tuesday morning John was still in the routine of checking his clothes for signs that he may have gone out on an adventure the night before. When he swung his legs over the edge of bed in the morning he wasn't overly tired and his clothes were in the basket that gave him a good feeling knowing those were some of the signs. He showered and got ready for the day, then made his way out to the kitchen to make coffee and breakfast. He noticed with a glance that his shoes were in the right place, his jacket was hung up and the keys were on the table. *'I think I was good last night.'* He threw a lunch together, poured coffee in his to-go mug, then headed out the door. When he got to the bottom of the stairs he looked over to his truck. *'Right where it should be, next to the dumpsters. Maybe things are getting better. There's still an obscene amount of garbage in two of those camps next to the highway that has been bothering me, but maybe I can go about it a different way.'* John felt upbeat and like a weight had been lifted from his shoulders. He walked the white line on the south side of the highway, it had rained at some point in the night, the road was wet and the spray was cold when cars would pass as he walked the edge of the roadway. Clouds hung low in the cold morning air, they were dark and threatening, the sky looked like it could open up and pour rain at any minute. John would glance away from the white line to look up at the sky as he walked, checking for rain ahead by looking for the dark streaks of water dripping from the sky that indicate a shower was coming; so far it looked like he would make it to work before it started raining. When John passed Scruffy's camp he saw the three other tents near the tree line, the amount of trash was disturbing to John. Shopping carts had appeared with heaps of items piled on them, black plastic trash bags two and three at a time piled not so neatly next to each tent. Some of the bags were broken open, contents showing from inside, some of them spilling out onto the ground. Bicycles and pop up tents in disrepair scattered here and there without organization, piles of items that John couldn't tell what they used to be, strewn between tents and the trees. The sight disgusted John right into his gut, it was actually a pain that he felt when he saw such disrespect. He tried to keep his eyes on the white line, but at times he caught himself looking, unable to keep his eyes away. He was nearing work and would have to cross the highway as soon as he got to Ted's Grocery, then he would be far enough away from the camps that he wouldn't have to look at it for the rest of the day. After crossing the highway John's mind turned to the day ahead and the thoughts he had about a different way to handle the rodent camps.

"Good morning Clint." Clint raised his coffee in a toast to John. "Good morning, how are you after yesterday's ordeal?" John raised his coffee back at Clint. "I feel surprisingly good. I feel like a weight has come off my shoulders. It must be because whatever has been weighing me down and overworking my subconscious has come out into the open and I have talked to people about it." Clint nodded and smiled. "That's great, I hope that continues for you. Is there anything I can do to help you out? Do you need to talk more or anything?" John raised his head up a little bit and took a deep breath. "Maybe there is, I was thinking on the walk this morning that there might be a better way to go about getting these sites cleaned up and then my brain won't overwork it and I can sleep through the night." Clint laughed a little. "That would probably be the best for you." John shrugged. "Yeah probably. I need to start a volunteer clean up committee. You know, to clean up those places in the daylight." Clint raised his hands in a Hallelujah. "Yes! That's a great idea, that's exactly what you should do." John was surprised at the response but happy that Clint was on his side and supporting his idea. "Thanks, for the support. You wouldn't have any idea how to go about that, would you?" Clint smiled and shook his head. "Sorry buddy, I haven't got a clue. I would bet that you could start by asking the fine people at the police station that you were just at." John tilted his head and looked toward the sky. "As intimidating as it was to be in there with them asking all kinds of questions, I'll bet your right. That would be a good place to start."

About thirty minutes after Jesse arrived home from work, Jesse and Katy's conversation was interrupted by a knock on their door. Jesse peeked out the window and saw a police officer and a man in a suite standing in front of the door waiting. "Oh man, I wonder what they want." Katy looked expectantly at Jesse. "Who is it?" Jesse was moving slowly toward the door.

"Police?" Katy stood up from the kitchen table as Jesse opened the door. "Hello Officer, what can I do for you?" Jamie Roak was standing behind Detective Milkey. "Good afternoon Mr. Kohl. I'm Detective James Milkey. This is Officer Roak. I was wondering if we could come in and talk to you about a report that you may have seen a suspect near the murder site last Friday night next to Ted's Grocery store." Jesse stepped back from the entryway allowing them to come in. "Yeah, sure. That would be fine. Come into the kitchen, we can sit at the table." Jesse led them in and offered them seats, then introduced Katy. "This is my fiancé Katy." After shaking hands with everyone, Detective Milkey sat across from Jesse and pulled out his notepad, setting his pen on top of it. "Thank you for agreeing to talk with us, we appreciate your cooperation. We got a tip that you spotted someone in that area the night of the murders. Can you tell us about that?" Jesse sat with his hands folded on the table. "Yeah I did, we were leaving the apartment. I think about 10:30 or 11 and one of our neighbors pulled out in front of us. We were going the same direction so it was natural to follow him." Detective cut him off. "Who was with you? Was it Katy?" Jesse shook his head. "Oh no, it was a friend of mine, Clint Jacobs. He was over for a couple of hours that night and I had to take him home." Detective Milkey wrote down Clint's name and a few other notes as Jesse was talking. "This neighbor that pulled out in front of you, did you recognize him? Do you know his name?" Jesse was nodding before the question was finished. "Yeah, I've talked to him a couple of times. His name is John Dell. He works over at the GasNGo with Clint. He seems to be a pretty strange guy." Milkey glanced at Officer Roak when Jesse said they work together. Officer Roak caught the look and remembered talking with both of them

267

the morning after the murder. "Okay, go on." Jesse adjusted himself in his chair. "Well, we were following him and when he turned into the ditch before coming to Ted's Grocery, we thought it was pretty weird so I slowed down and pulled into the parking lot next to the vacant lot. We were super curious so we stopped and watched him go into the bushes there by the tents." Detective Milkey stopped him again. "How well could you see him from that lot? It seems pretty closed off by all the bushes from there." Jesse leaned into the table, stretching his arms out in front of him, drawing imaginary lines on the table, outlining the vacant lot and the parking area of the store. "Well, from the edge where we parked, here," Pointing to an invisible line that he had drawn on the table, "we walked this trail that is toward the back of the lot, far enough that we could see where he was by those tents that were back there." He drew another line representing the trail and where the tents were located. "We stood there for a while and watched him. Looked like he was picking up garbage and stuff like that. It made sense at the time because we had figured out that he was picking up trash and bringing the trash back to the apartments and putting it in our dumpsters. I didn't know he was going to kill that guy though. We might have tried to stop him if we would have known that." Detective Milkey was making notes as Jesse told his story. "How did you figure out he was picking up trash at night?" Jesse shrugged a little. "I had seen him out at night before and then I saw him at the dumpsters early in the morning emptying his truck out. After that last guy was found I started putting together that he is probably the killer, I saw him out at the homeless camp across the street the day before that other tent got burned up." Milkey sat up, leaning against the back of the chair. "Why didn't you come forward with that information?" Jesse grimaced. "I'm sorry that I didn't, but when me and Katy talked about it, it didn't seem real and that maybe I was just over thinking what I saw." Detective Milkey relaxed his shoulders a bit, he was still looking at Jesse with a stern expression, shaking his head. "Might have saved someone's life if you had." Jesse looked down at the table, his hands in his lap. "Yeah, it might have, I knew that guy was up to something." Milkey closed his notebook and looked around the table. Katy had sat there quietly the entire time, watching the exchange. Officer Roak had done the same, however he was studying the detective, watching him work. "We should have enough with this information to make an arrest. When it comes to convicting though, we will need you to testify that you saw him, not just at the last murder site but at the previous one. Are you willing to do that?" Jesse perked up a little in his chair. "Yes. Yes I will do that." Detective Milky was starting to stand up. "It can take a very long time to get to that point but it's very important that you continue to be willing to help." Jesse stood up and reached out his hand, shaking with Detective Milkey. "I will do that, just let me know what I can do to help." The detective and Officer Roak made their way to the door. "Thank you again for your time and cooperation. We will be in touch." Jesse closed the door behind them, then looked at Katy with wide eyes. "That was wild! I didn't expect that to happen today." Katy was still sitting at the table looking toward the door and Jesse. "I didn't expect it today. I did tell Berta that you and Clint saw him out there. Oh and I think the officer was Berta's nephew. I am glad that they are doing something about it though. I wonder when they will arrest him." Jesse had come back into the kitchen. "Yeah, that would be interesting to know." Katy got up from the table. "I still want you to take me to work, he's still out there as far as we know." Jesse pulled her in for a hug. "Okay, I'll do that, it's almost over." Katy let him hug her for a long time before pulling away to start making dinner before she needed to go to work.

Dark clouds, heavy with rain had moved in late in the day, by 6 PM the rain was falling so hard that it was darker than usual. The headlights on Jesse's truck were barely enough to light the way as the light bounced off the wet roads, making it seem like the headlights weren't working as he delivered Katy to work.

John had finished dinner around that same time that Jesse took Katy to work and settled in to watch some TV before going to bed for the night. His evening was uneventful to this point but within a few hours he would be outside making his way to the rodent camps, quieting his subconscious as he cleaned up the messes left by the rodents. At nearly 10 PM, only 2 hours after John had gone to sleep, he was sitting up at the edge of his bed pulling on the jeans that he had worn that day. He put on a sweatshirt and a jacket as he went out the door with his keys in his hand. The rain had stopped a few hours ago but everything was very wet and heavy from the dark storms that had gone through. The clouds that hung overhead blackened out all the light that could have been reflected from nearby neighborhood street lights. If John weren't in a trance he wouldn't pick this night to clean out a rodent camp, it was too cold and dark, but his subconscious had taken note of the camps on his way to work. Now he was on his way in his Ranger pickup to relieve his subconscious stress.

Jesse parked his truck behind Ted's Grocery, it was a couple hundred yards from the homeless camps, but out of sight from anyone driving past. The opportunity was too good to pass up. He had spotted John leaving his apartment and followed him to the rodent camp. John had pulled his truck into the bushes just at the east end of the rodent camps, it was wet and swampy getting his truck through the bushes next to the trash piles. It might be difficult to get it out. *'That's even better. Maybe they catch him while he's here, with a dead rodent just steps away.'* Jesse had found someone to take the fall for him, the police suspected John as the killer and he was sure John would get arrested for the murders in the next day or so. But now there would be no questioning, another murder with John at the scene would leave no doubt about who had committed the crimes.

Jesse had always been into hunting and fishing, he played sports as a teenager but he found hunting to be more thrilling. Wild game always had a season, so he had to wait for each season to come before he could get his kill thrill. Jesse wasn't good at waiting; he recently had found a new prey to hunt. There was no official season for it, but the thrill was ten times better than game hunting. The thrill was like nothing he had ever experienced before, hunting rodents was Jesse's extreme sport. There were so many precautions he had to take and so much preparation that went into each hunt that it made it more challenging than anything he had ever done. He was on a thrill seeking mission. He knew exactly what he wanted to do, he had calculated it, planned and measured out every move. With all the preparations, above all he had to be out of sight, hidden in the shadows. It wouldn't take long to execute his plans. The hunt he was embarking on now was bold, being so close to the road, it was almost as bold as the first one in the little red car. That hunt was risky, not just attacking the person sleeping in the car but leaving the scene and bringing another body back from another camp in the back of his truck. Slipping it into the passenger seat without being seen, making it look like they were both attacked in the car. That was a huge thrill! The next day when the bodies were found he could almost not contain himself, he wanted to tell someone what he had done and that he did it completely undetected. He enjoyed leaving something different at each site, posing the bodies in different ways was entertaining, even now when he thought about the three bodies in the trees by the river it made him smile. Jesse had experimented with different ways of killing. The first time was with a shotgun in an abandoned trailer in the woods that some homeless people were squatting in, but that wasn't personal enough, it was over too quick. BANG! BANG! Watching their bodies explode into vapors was interesting and the way they squirmed and twitched on the floor afterward was really something to behold. But that was it, pull a trigger and it was over. The thrill wore off too quickly. The way he preferred to do it was up close and personal. He wanted to wrestle the life out of someone, feel them go limp when they died. He would do it by hand every time if he could, but the kill wasn't smooth like that every time. He made mistakes as he learned to kill. Even with all the planning he had put into hunting his first few victims, he didn't plan on people fighting back, some did and some didn't. He wanted to kill with his hands but if the opportunity went sideways he would do whatever it took. Burning the bodies added a twist and he hoped it would help cover his tracks. That too, was almost an accident the first time it happened, but the results were more then he could have hoped for.

Jesse checked his surroundings, he looked up and down the

road making sure not only that there were no cars but also no signs of people moving about. It was 10:40 PM so there was still a chance that any random person could happen across his path, though he felt it unlikely in this area of town where the homeless camps were. It was dark and dreary with low black clouds overhead, the drizzly rain had started coming down again. He moved quickly and as quietly as possible, avoiding the one streetlight in the middle of the parking lot. John was farther to his left, moving back and forth from his truck to the piles of trash he was picking up, sloshing through mud, pushing through the bushes between tents and piles of trash. Jesse moved off the road as soon as he could after crossing highway 18, pushing into the brush just past the ditch, coming close to several of the rodent's tents. He took extra care not to make noise even with his footsteps. He was a trying to be a shadow, wearing all dark clothing, slipping behind each bush, staying low, out of sight. Several cars passed by, giving him the opportunity to push past more heavy brush as the cars sent up spray from the wet roads and made more noise than he did scratching through the stiff bushes. Jesse moved down the tree line slowly, staying in a low crouch as if he were a sniper stalking the enemy. He snuck up to the scruffy man's tent, the last one in a line of several with generous spacing between them, it was very dark, with only the distant streetlight casting long gray shadows through the wet night air and between the bushes. Jesse had the tools he would need for the job, plastic bags, a rope, and a rag. He planned to slice open the tent like he did with Beer Belly's tent and jump Scruffy who was sleeping unaware of his presence, putting his knees on him and tying his hands, just like he had with his other victims. Then he would stuff the rag in his mouth and slip the bag over his head and tie it there, leaving the scruffy man there to suffocate as he watched, with his knees on Scruffy's back. It should only take seconds to subdue Scruffy, Jesse was much stronger than any homeless rodent that he had seen. He would like to burn the tent as well, like the one at the lake, and the other one across the road, but he wasn't sure it would burn well enough in the rain. Jesse had forgotten to fill his gas can that was in the back of his truck after he torched Caveman's tent. He's had practice and learned how to be efficient but sometimes he has to improvise. He was very quiet as he moved toward the tent, the slight pitter patter of raindrops covered the sloshy mud sounds of his gentle foot falls. Jesse was poised just outside the tent, crouched down, knees bent, standing just on his toes, as he pulled his knife from his pocket and opened it with a slight click. Inside the tent, Scruffy wasn't sleeping very well and heard the click. At first, he didn't think much of the sound but he was awake, aware that there may be something or someone outside. This wasn't unusual, many of his fellow homeless campers moved around at night but he was aware that the sound was close by. Outside the tent, Jesse's adrenaline was rushing through his veins. With an arcing swing Jesse made a plunge at the tent with his knife to slice the thin nylon fabric. The knife sliced in just fine but caught and stopped cutting with only about a ten-inch slit cut through. He jabbed it in again and tried to cut it more but now there was too much slack in the fabric and the knife wouldn't grab. Jesse's heart raced with excitement, he was desperate to complete his mission, so he dropped the knife and ripped the tent open with his hands, then lunged in. He pushed hard with his legs causing his feet to loose traction, he slipped, stumbling to his knees in the mud. Jesse struggled to enter the tent, clawing with his hands and pushing with his feet in the mud to crawl inside. Scruffy was startled and jumped when Jesse made the first cut, he scrambled half out of his sleeping bag and grabbed a club he had by his side for protection. It was difficult to see but Scruffy didn't need much more than shadows to swing at. He hurriedly swung hard, landing a blow to Jesse's ribs just as Jesse tackled him. Scruffy took another swing, but he couldn't connect very well with Jesse on top of him and his hands around his neck, the club struck Jesse's back. Jesse grunted with the blow, it hurt but it wasn't enough to break Jesse from his attack. Scruffy was able to pull his legs up in between them, curling into a fetal position. He used his legs to kick Jesse back hard enough to break free. Scruffy swung his club again wildly, as hard as he could. He swung blindly at a shadow, hoping he would stop the attacker, he felt it connect with Jesse, clunking him on the side of the head with a gruesome hollow thud. Jesse fell to the side with a yell in pain, dazed, his head ringing so badly he thought he heard sirens. He reached for the side of his head in an instinctive reaction, he rolled up and propped himself on his knees and elbows in a pile of sleeping bag and who knows what else. As Jesse was starting to gather himself he could hear Scruffy scrambling to get to his knees. Scruffy had time to get up and struggle to find the zipper of the tent, trying to escape. Jesse's consciousness was quickly fading in and out, he felt dizzy but was still trying to focus on his mission. Scruffy was in a panic and couldn't find the zipper. Jesse's senses came to him and he tried to move but his head was throbbing, he pushed his hands to the ground and lifted his head off the sleeping bag. Scruffy's military training came to him in an instant and he stopped panicking, he turned and picked his club back up then put his body weight behind his next swing. Jesse was about to turn and try to grab Scruffy again when he heard the whoosh of the club as Scruffy swung with all his might and landed a deadly blow to the back of Jesse's head, smashing into his skull, splattering blood and bone across the insides of the tent. The ringing in his ears stopped, the flashing lights in his head went out, Jesse collapsed in a heap, not moving, not breathing. He wouldn't attack another rodent ever again. Scruffy sat back on his heels, out of breath, watching the shadow of Jesse for any signs of movement. A minute passed as Scruffy's ragged breathing returned to a normal pace, his heartbeat coming back to normal range. He searched with his hands for his clothes, feeling his way to find pants, then a sweatshirt, and finally his coat, then he slipped on his shoes. Jesse's body was blocking the hole he had cut in the side of the tent. Scruffy finally found the zipper and unzipped the flap he was next to and crawled out on his hands and knees. He slowly stood, looking around to see if anyone had heard the struggle. He didn't see anyone around, no movement from neighboring tents, no cars on the roadway, just light rain pattering the ground. Scruffy knelt back down, crawling part way into the front of the tent. He grabbed his backpack, started gathering his most personal belongings and what clothes he had. He grabbed at his sleeping bag but got a hand full of hot, sticky blood, it would have to stay here. He wiped his hand off on Jesse's pant leg. Scruffy stood back up, outside the tent, hoisted his pack onto both shoulders and took a couple of steps back, away from the mess. He stood there facing the tent, not able to see inside of it in the dark, but the terror that he had just experienced made him gasp now that it was over. He bent over with his hands on his knees and took a couple of deep breaths to try and calm his nerves again. Once he stood up, he turned his face up into the rain, feeling the rain wash down his face he was thankful to be alive, he put his hands on his face, rubbing them up and down, washing the blood spatter off in the cool drops. Scruffy walked away from the tent, feeling dazed but thankful. He would look for a new place to sleep for the night, then start gathering new supplies to take to his new camp in the morning. He walked away, headed toward Ted's Grocery, planning to spend the night on the loading dock behind the store even though it was frowned upon by the owners. He had wished he would have moved a few days sooner and avoided this whole mess, but now at least it seemed that the terror the homeless were feeling might be over. He walked east on the road, staying on the white line. There was something moving in the tents off to his right in the bushes. Scruffy stopped to follow the sounds. He needed to see if it was one of his fellow homeless campers, wondering if they had seen what had happened. He was looking into the darkness but was unable to see anything moving. The sounds continued to come from the bushes, over the sounds of the rain, pattering the pavement behind him and the wet ground in front. Scruffy stepped off the edge of the road into the ditch pushing past some overgrown Scotch broom, getting even more wet in the process. He followed the sounds until he came to where John had parked his truck, he had driven it into the camp from the far east end, following the trail that the homeless used to enter and exit their camps. Scruffy watched as John was bending over, scooping trash into his arms, dripping wet piles of old clothes and blankets, then bringing the piles of slop to his truck and dumping it in. In Scruffy's low, raspy voice he tried to get John's attention. "Hey, what are you doing?" John didn't stop, he turned around from the truck and went back to another pile

277

of junk, picking it up and half dragging it back to the truck. Again, Scruffy watched him work. He recognized him this time when he came back to the truck, the light inside the cab was on with the door standing open. "Hey, what are you doing? I've seen you before." John stopped and looked at Scruffy with no expression. "Mpmphh. Leetph dreeet." Scruffy was confused, his eyebrows went up and his eyes got wide. "You need to get out of here. There is a dead guy over that way, he just tried to kill me. You don't want to get blamed for it, you need to go." Again John turned to go pick up more trash. Scruffy shook his head, watching him slosh through the mud, finding another pile to pick up, then returning to the truck and dropping it in. Scruffy went to the other side of the truck to get a closer look at John. "What are you doing, why aren't you listening to me?" Scruffy stepped in front of John, making him stop. Scruffy was trying to look at John's face but it was so dark he couldn't make out his features. John started to move past but Scruffy stepped to the side to get in front of him again, edging him closer to the truck. John hesitated and tried again, again Scruffy stepped in front of him, pushing him yet closer to the truck. Scruffy was now next to the open door of the Ranger, John was looking into the cab of the truck. Scruffy could see the blank look on John's face, it wasn't registering what was happening at the moment. Scruffy put a hand out and pointed into the truck. "Get in. You should get in and go." John stood still for a few more moments with his head down and his eyes toward the cab of his truck. "Go on! Get in!" Scruffy was more demanding that time. John seemed to respond, he shuffled his feet toward the truck then put one foot in and sat on the edge of the seat. He looked at Scruffy with a blank stare, "Thus mmph hope, phsst." Scruffy hadn't a clue what that meant. "Okay, sure. You need to go." He waved his hands in a shooing motion, trying to get John to get into his truck. Finally, John slid farther into his seat and put his other foot into the cab. Scruffy closed the door, having to push John's shoulder slightly to get it shut all the way. "Now go. Back it up the way you came in." Scruffy waved his hands at John sitting in the truck. John started it up and turned on the lights. He was cut short of his clean up duties but somehow now his timeline seemed to be reset. He started backing out of the rodent camp, spinning his tires on the sloppy, muddy terrain, but making progress. Scruffy followed John as he backed his truck out the trail he had come in on, scraping brush along the sides of the truck as he went. The headlights blinded Scruffy as they bounced through holes and puddles along the trail. John had enough speed when he got to the gravel of the ditch that he popped right out onto the road. Scruffy watched as John went west toward Fir street, his taillights glowing red in the rain, reflecting off of the wet pavement. Once John was out of sight, Scruffy crossed the road, moving toward Ted's Grocery in search of a dry place to sleep for the night. With the events that just happened swirling in his head, he walked slowly across the giant empty lot of the grocery store, staring at the pavement as he took each slow step, disappearing behind the building in the shadows. Scruffy found his way to the loading dock and made himself comfortable under the cover of the dock against the wall. His adrenaline had worn off, leaving him exhausted. His mind kept running over that man bursting into his tent, attacking him, it made him jumpy, but somehow he also felt relieved knowing he would move on to his new camp the next day. Scruffy pulled his jacket off and leaned his head back on his backpack, pulling the jacket over himself like a blanket. Not sure he would be able to sleep, he closed his eyes and tried to think warm thoughts until he dosed off.

30

Wednesday

Katy was waiting inside the diner at 12:15 wondering how late Jesse was going to be. She tried calling but he didn't pick up. Thirty minutes later one of the cooks offered her a ride home that she accepted. Jesse's truck wasn't at the apartment, when she got inside it was dark, as if Jesse had left the apartment to pick her up, but he wasn't home. She was worried, it wasn't like him to let her down. She called Clint but he didn't answer either, '*It's close to 1 AM, he's probably sleeping.*' She tried Jesse's phone again, it was ringing in silent mode in his blood soaked pocket. She left a message that was cut short by Clint returning her call. "Hey Clint, sorry to wake you." Clint was groggy but had a worried tone. "Hey, it's okay. Is something wrong? You don't usually call in the middle of the night." Katy's voice had started to waver. "Jesse didn't pick me up from work and he's not home. Have you seen him tonight?" Clint was awake now, that had made his heart jump and hit hard. "No, I didn't see him tonight. When was he supposed to pick you up?" Katy gulped at the air, she was hopeful that Jesse was with Clint and they just lost track of time. "He was supposed to be there at 12. I got a ride home from a co-worker." Clint was sitting on the edge of his bed, his mind had started to race, thinking of what might have happened to Jesse. "What can I do? Should I come over?" Katy was standing in the center of the living room, her legs gave out and she collapsed, luckily landing on the sofa. "Clint, I'm worried, he doesn't do this stuff. He doesn't just disappear." Clint stood up and went to get some clothes while he was still on the phone. "I'm coming over, I'll keep an eye out on my way." Katy's hands were shaking. "Okay, I have a bad feeling. Please be careful." Clint disconnected after telling her he would be careful. He dressed quickly and left right away. Clint was scanning the sides of the roads on his way, trying to see if he could spot Jesse's truck, either crashed along the road or parked somewhere. He rushed up to Katy's apartment when he arrived and let himself in without knocking. "Have you heard anything?" Katy had been crying, sitting on the sofa. "No, nothing. I thought about calling his parents but if they haven't seen him I don't want to worry them." Clint was pacing nervously in the little room. "Have you called the police?" Katy looked at him blankly. "No, every time I see that on TV they say it has to be 24 hours." Clint stopped pacing and waited a moment, then hung his head and started pacing again. "Yeah, I guess that's true. I think we should go look for him." Katy stood up quickly, then hesitated. "What if he comes home?" Clint stopped pacing. "Well, maybe we will see him if he's headed this way. Leave him a note, tell him to call you if he gets home." Katy went to the kitchen and scribbled on a scrap of paper, leaving it on the edge of the kitchen table. "Okay, I'm going to call his cell again to see if he picks up." Katy dialed as they left the apartment. It was starting to rain harder as they walked to the truck, big drenching drops, it was nearly 2 AM and it was cold. "Nothing, just voicemail. I really hope his battery has died and that's why I can't get through." Clint started his truck and was already driving out of the lot before Katy had buckled her seat belt. "That would at least explain why you can't reach him. But it doesn't tell us where he's at." Clint drove fairly slow down the highway toward Ted's Grocery and the GasNGo, looking out the side windows for signs that he might have veered off the road. Katy was watching out the opposite side. "It's so dark, I can't see much out there." Clint reached over to the glove box and pulled out a large flashlight. "Here, roll your window down some and use this. It might help." Katy was using the flashlight as a spot, trying to look into the bushes as they drove slowly past. Clint rolled his window down as well, then he turned the heat up, trying to keep some warmth in the cab of the truck. Katy shined the light through the rodent camps on the south side of the road, across from Ted's Grocery, as they went past, seeing only the tops of a few tents. "Can you see on your side?" Clint glanced over at her. "Yeah, a little bit. I haven't spotted anything yet." They turned north at the GasNGo, the same way that Clint had come to get to Katy's place. "We should go through town and look around to see if we can see him anywhere." Katy kept looking out the side window, using the flashlight to look down side streets. "Maybe we should go out to his work and see if he's there for some reason. He won't answer his phone when he's at work." Clint looked over at her. "That's a great idea! That's got to be it, I'll bet he got called into work for something." Clint drove to the next light and turned around. He didn't drive as slow going back the other way since they had already looked past that area. He turned left at the GasNGo, heading east toward the warehouses and the railroad crossing. It took about ten minutes to get to the warehouses, Clint pulled into the employee parking area and drove a circle around the lot. "I don't see his truck, is there anyplace else he would park at work?" Katy was looking out her window. "No, I think this is the only parking area." Clint exited the lot, heading west back toward town, driving slow with the windows down, windshield wipers flapping back and forth, the rain beating on the top of the truck, drowning out the sound of the engine. Clint stopped for the red light near the GasNGo, he was squinting through the rain splattered windshield across the dark streets, deep into the black shadows. "What's that over there? Near the back of Ted's." Katy leaned forward trying to get a better look out the front window. "Oh gosh, maybe we should go see what's happening." They both spotted a police car with flashing lights behind Ted's Grocery. When Clint drove into the parking lot, the headlights of his truck flashed across Jesse's truck, it looked darker in the rain, "Is that his truck?" Katy gasped. "I don't know, it looks darker than his." There were shadows cast across it from the police car's headlights. Red and blue lights flashed, reflecting off the raindrops in the air. The flashing was mesmerizing against the back of the building, flashing against the side of the truck, then the light disappeared into blackness behind the building in the shadows. Clint pulled in close to the police car, they sat there looking out the front of the truck for any signs of movement. "It's his truck alright, I don't see the police officer?" Katy looked out her side window, then used the flashlight to look into the darkness. "I don't see anyone." Clint opened his door and stepped out into the rain, Katy opened her door but hesitated getting out. Then she heard Clint's voice. "Hi Officer, have you seen the driver of this truck?" Officer Halloway was walking from the front of the building, flashlight in hand. He shined it into Clint's face then flashed it across at Katy just getting out of the truck. "I haven't seen anyone yet, I stopped to check on the vehicle. I don't usually see any vehicles in this lot at night. Can I see some I.D. please?" Clint fished his wallet out of his pocket and produced his I.D. for the officer to examine. "Here you go, that truck belongs to a friend of mine. He didn't show up to pick up his girlfriend from work. We're looking for him." Officer Halloway handed back Clint's I.D. Halloway motioned toward Katy. "Is that his girlfriend?" Clint looked over at Katy and waved for her to come over. "Yeah that's her, she's a little worked up." Officer Halloway was careful not to blind Katy with his light but gave her a look up and down with the light. "Do you have some I.D. on you?" Katy reached into her front pocket and pulled out her driver's license, wrapped in a few bills from tips, and handed it to Halloway. He looked it over with his light. "What's your boyfriend's name?" Katy started to speak but her voice cracked and she had to start again. "It's Jesse Kohl." Halloway handed back her license. "Miss Robinson, when was he supposed to pick you up tonight?" Katy tucked her license back in her pocket with the bills. "Midnight, he was supposed to be there at 12 and I waited until after 12:30 before I left and went home. He hasn't picked up his phone at all." Halloway had taken out a notepad and written down Jesse's name. "Seems that the vehicle has been here for quite a while, the hood is cold. It's also possible it never got very warm. Where would he have been coming from to pick you up?" Katy motioned down the highway to the west. "Fir Street

hands on his pants. "I hit him." He paused looking at his hands still stained with blood and grime. " With a club. That's how I got away." Halloway was watching Scruffy closely. "Did you hurt him?" Scruffy squinted up at him again. "Yeah, I think so, he wasn't moving when I left." Halloway took another step back, reaching for the radio strapped to his shoulder he called for backup. "Mr. Hart, I need you to get to your feet." Scruffy looked at him like he couldn't believe what he was hearing, then realized it wasn't a joke. Scruffy struggled a little, but got up slowly and picked up his backpack. Halloway led him to the stairs. "I'm going to put you in my car while I check out your tent across the road. It's warm in there and you can take a nap if you feel like it." Scruffy walked slowly and cautiously down the stairs, letting Halloway lead him by the arm, following the stream of light from the flashlight. Clint and Katy saw some flashes of light coming around the corner from the back of the building. They couldn't see that Halloway was leading someone with him until he got to the police car. They watched him put Scruffy into the back of the cruiser, then lean down and say something to the man. The man responded and made some pointing motions. Halloway closed the door of the cruiser then came around to approach the passenger side of Clint's truck. Katy rolled her window down to greet him. "Who is that?" Halloway kept his voice low. "He was sleeping at the back of the store on the loading dock, said that he had a run in with someone at his tent earlier tonight. He said he was attacked and that the other person might be injured. I need to go check that out. I have called for backup, there are going to be other cruisers arriving soon. Do you mind waiting here?" Katy hung her head then looked over at Clint. Clint looked at the officer. "Yes, we'll wait. Thank you." Halloway walked back to his cruiser and turned the red and blue flasher off, then walked toward the front of the store heading to the road. They sat in the truck and watched him walk away. Katy rolled her window up. "Do you think it could have been Jesse that jumped that guy?" Clint looked at her with a worried expression. "It doesn't look good. Why is his truck here and he isn't? I don't understand what's happening." They could no longer see Officer Halloway so Clint put the truck in reverse and backed up a few yards so they could see to the roadway in front of the store.

Another police cruiser with lights flashing had pulled up to Officer Halloway, they were talking at the edge of the road, Halloway was pointing back to the store and then across the roadway to the homeless camps. The second officer got out of his cruiser, joining Halloway as he walked across the road, disappearing into the bushes. Officer Roak had joined Halloway, tromping into the brush to find out what had happened when Scruffy was attacked. There were several tents in the camp but according to Scruffy, his tent was the one farthest to the west. They moved carefully through the brush, stepping cautiously past piles of trash and over puddles. They had entered the camp near the center, shining their lights across the area. They could see there were a couple of tents to the west. Making their way west past each tent and pile of trash, they looked closely at each one to see if anything looked strangely out of place. This was a tough call since they all lived very disheveled existences. When they got near what they assumed to be the last tent in the camp, they knew they had reached the right one when they saw the rip in the side of the fabric. From a distance they could see that something had happened here that wasn't normal, even for the homeless camp. They paused ten yards back from the tent, shining their lights at the tent and surrounding area. Outside the tent looked like every other homeless camp, piles of trash and discarded items laying haphazardly here and there. When their lights were on the side of the tent directly, they could see the open gash where Jesse had torn through the fabric in his attempt to kill Scruffy. Halloway took the first step toward the tent and motioned for Roak to move around to the south side where the opening flap should be. They walked carefully over the sloppy wet ground, keeping their flashlights directly on the tent. There was no movement as they approached. Halloway, standing two feet back from the torn open fabric, peered inside, his light shining across Jesse's body and the blood soaked sleeping bag. The back of Jesse's head was mashed in, caked with blood and matted hair. Halloway motioned to Roak to check from the front of the tent. Roak couldn't see as much from there, the flap was hanging down in his line of sight. He moved to the side where Halloway was crouched, still surveying the scene. Roak looked in to see the body slumped in a heap, he realized this was likely the killer they had been looking for. "Wow, I'll bet this is our guy." Halloway looked at Roak confused. "What do you mean this is our guy." Roak looked into the tent then back at Halloway. "This is the guy that's been murdering the homeless people." Halloway stood up from his crouched position. "Well, it might be. I'm going to check for I.D." He carefully patted Jesse's pockets until he found his wallet and pulled it out. "Jesse Kohl." He read off of his license. "This is the guy those two in the parking lot are looking for. That's going to be a shock." Halloway was looking at Roak. "I'm going to call this in, would you mind getting supplies to secure the area?" Roak nodded. "Sure, I'll head that way." Roak picked his way through the bushes, not knowing if there was a trail close by that would make it easier or not, finally slopping his way through the mud to the road and back to his cruiser. Katy and Clint saw Officer Roak appear and go to his car. "Let's go ask what they found." Clint turned the wheel and put the truck in gear, driving toward the officer. Roak popped the trunk of his cruiser and was rummaging for supplies as Clint pulled in next to him. Roak stopped what he was doing. He knew what they were waiting to hear but didn't want to have to deliver the news. He looked over at them, trying not to show what he knew on his face. Katy could already see it in his eyes, she was shaking and started to break down before Clint could even roll down his window to ask the question. Clint got out of the truck instead to have a conversation with Roak, one that Katy didn't want to hear, even though he was sure she knew what Roak was going to say. As Clint approached Officer Roak the two of them looked into each other's faces with a grave expression. "Officer Halloway said you were looking for your friend. What's his name?" Roak asked Clint in such a low tone that it was almost inaudible over the rain. Clint took a breath slowly before speaking, afraid that he wouldn't be able to get the words out. "Jesse Kohl." It came out as a croak, like something was caught in his throat. Officer Roak's eyes squinted at Clint. "We found him, I'm sorry, he's not alive." Clint's shoulders slumped, he heard Katy wail from inside the truck, her heart just broke, so did Clint's. Officer Roak put his hand on Clint's shoulder, "You should get into your truck and warm up. I have to secure the area. Don't go anywhere, we will want to get some statements from you both. I'm sorry for your loss."

Officer Roak gathered some supplies to cordon off the crime

scene and walked back across the road. As he walked down through the ditch he could hear the distant sirens of police cruisers coming. It would be another long cold night, keeping the scene secure.